The Ultima Variant

Also by Ray Green
Buyout – A Roy Groves Thriller (1)

For five ordinary guys and one rather extraordinary woman, the only escape from the corporate rat-race is to buy the company they're working for: take it all to a new level, save hundreds of jobs and make some serious money.

But it quickly becomes clear that nothing is as easy as it seems. The bid is quickly undercut as twisted corporate politics and personal vendettas take over.

When the buyout becomes all or nothing for the management buyout team, it all spins out of control: marriages fall apart, lurid secrets are discovered; life savings are spent on the stock market; illegal insider dealing becomes a matter of fact; and blackmail, theft, betrayal and manipulation are the new rules of the game.

A once-in-a-life-time opportunity turns into a lurid nightmare.

BUYOUT is a gripping and compulsive page-turner about the power of money to unveil the deepest in human nature. It's also a story about chasing one extraordinary dream. At an extraordinary price.

Also by Ray Green
Payback – A Roy Groves Thriller (2)

Roy Groves is Operations Director of a successful company manufacturing dashboard instruments for luxury cars.

A fatal motorway fire is traced back to a fault in the product supplied by Roy's company. Was it a tragic accident or something more sinister? As Roy and his colleagues battle to establish the cause of the fire, and save the company from bankruptcy, they discover that they have been the victims of sabotage.

Eventually, it emerges that an old enemy of Roy and the rest of the team has reappeared and is intent on destroying the company and every member of its management team. Once just a business adversary, their nemesis is now so consumed with hatred that he is on the edge of insanity; he resorts to blackmail and even murder in the pursuit of his goal.

PAYBACK is a chilling tale of how hatred can twist and corrupt the human soul.

Also by Ray Green
Chinese Whispers – A Roy Groves Thriller (3)

Chuck Kabel is on a business trip to China, visiting the factory to which his UK-based company subcontracts the manufacture of its products. He unexpectedly collapses and dies at the airport before he is able to report on his visit. When the Chinese authorities are evasive about the exact cause of death, the suspicions of his boss, Roy Groves, are raised.

Roy decides to investigate further; it soon becomes clear that there are serious financial irregularities within the Chinese company, and that dark forces are in play, intent on ensuring that these do not come to light. When Roy edges closer to uncovering the truth, he is warned off but refuses to back down, unaware that he is about to confront the Chinese Mafia, who will stop at nothing to achieve their objectives.

When his own family are targeted by his opponents, Roy embarks on a desperate battle to protect them, now well aware that if he should turn to the police, their lives will be in even greater danger.

CHINESE WHISPERS is a frightening tale of organised crime and the way in which it uses and abuses legitimate business for its own illegal purposes, relentlessly destroying the lives of anyone who stands in the way.

Also by Ray Green

Horizontal Living: A Tale of Expats Abroad - A Roy Groves Thriller (4)

Roy Groves has led a colourful career in business, during which he battled with corporate politics, deception, and even vicious criminals. But now Roy has retired, and he is looking forward to a quieter life. He and his wife, Donna, have bought an apartment in an exclusive development on Spain's Costa del Sol.

He soon learns, however, that there are financial problems: the community is, in effect, bankrupt. Roy is persuaded to take on the role of President of the community, confident that, with his extensive business experience, he should easily be able to sort things out. It soon becomes clear, however, that nothing is as simple as it seems. As he tries to come up with a rescue plan, Roy discovers that a poorly constructed retaining wall has begun to collapse, threatening the development with a landslide. And this is just the start ...

As the problems mount up, Roy becomes entangled with an astonishingly diverse cast of characters: the devious building developer; the vengeful former President; the Russian prostitute, and her mafia minders; the deranged Middle Eastern doctor; the devastatingly glamorous French girl next door; and many more ...

HORIZONTAL LIVING is an illuminating insight into the shenanigans which pervade an ex-pat community abroad: sometimes hilarious, sometimes hard to believe, but sometimes darkly disturbing.

Also by Ray Green
Lost Identity - The Identity Thrillers Series – Book 1

When research scientist, Stephen Lewis, wakes from a coma in a Miami hospital bed, he remembers nothing about his head injury, how he came to be in Florida, or even who he really is.

As fragments of his memory return, Stephen is shocked to find that even those closest to him seem not to know him. And when another man turns up, claiming to be the real Stephen Lewis, he begins to doubt his own sanity.

Desperate to learn the truth, Stephen is unwittingly drawn into a murky web of drug trafficking and murder. At its heart lies a terrifying conspiracy and a secret so appalling that, even if he survives, he knows his life can never be the same again.

Also by Ray Green
Identity Found - The Identity Thrillers Series – Book 2

Stephen Lewis and Carla Fernandez fled from Miami, Florida a year ago, to escape a terrifying battle with drug trafficking cartels and professional assassins. Now they are living a quiet life in Canada, under false identities.

But when a young female journalist is murdered in New York City, Stephen recognises that the killing has all the hallmarks of one of the world's most highly paid and notorious assassins. Why should this man, who can command a fee of millions of dollars for a single hit, be hired for such a seemingly insignificant contract? He concludes that the journalist must have been investigating something big – very big – and had been murdered to shut her up.

The police seem not to have made this link, and Stephen cannot approach them directly, as he is wanted in connection with the events in Miami. Fearful that there may be some terrible plot underway, possibly with many lives at stake, he decides to investigate. Carla insists on helping him.

Before long, Stephen and Carla find themselves battling for their lives once again.

Also by Ray Green
New Identity - The Identity Thrillers Series – Book 3

Jason Hardwick and Gabriela Suarez have been on the run for almost three years – pursued by a network of professional assassins. Now they are living under false identities in the market town of Chichester, in England.

Mark Bowman was the detective who helped the couple escape from a terrifying confrontation with their pursuers in New York City some fifteen months ago. Now he has been murdered. His killer is Jade Lacroix: a beautiful, highly intelligent, bisexual assassin. Jason and Gabriela are her next targets. When Jason and Gabriela learn of Mark's death, they realise that these people will never give up. What can they do to fight back?

Alexis Miller – also an NYPD detective – was Mark's girlfriend. She has vowed to bring his killer, and those she works for, to justice.

Will Alexis track down the assassin before she gets to Jason and Gabriela? Will she become a target herself? Who is the shadowy figure behind this murderous network?

'New Identity' is the thrilling, shocking conclusion to the 'Identity Thrillers' trilogy.

The Ultima Variant

By Ray Green

The Ultima Variant

Published in Great Britain by Mainsail Books in 2022
First Edition

ISBN 978-1-9999406-9-0

Published by Mainsail Books
www.mainsailbooks.co.uk

Cover design by Ana Grigoriu-Voicu
ana@books-design.com

Prologue

It was 2.20 p.m. and Ron Hancock was feeling exhausted. Ron was a London bus driver and had just finished his shift, which had started at 5 a.m. It should have been an eight-hour shift but had ended up being over nine and a half. The traffic – never easy at the best of times in central London – had been absolutely horrendous, exacerbated by a major pile-up which had completely blocked the multi-lane scrum which skirts around Trafalgar Square. It had taken well over an hour for the emergency services to clear the blockage and get things moving again, during which time the cacophony of blaring car horns had given him a splitting headache.

The situation hadn't been helped by several of the passengers constantly haranguing him with demands about how long they were going to be stuck there – a question which he could not answer, of course. And all the time he had had to keep his cool and remain courteous; if the travelling public started lodging complaints about him, it wouldn't be long before he was out of a job. Not that Ron intended to be a bus driver for ever; he had ambitions to become a design engineer in the automotive industry. For the moment though, this job was important to him.

As a child, Ron had never taken his education very seriously. His parents had never encouraged him to study, instead taking up his evenings with housework – which neither of them seemed to find time to do themselves – and sending him out at weekends to earn what little he could by doing a newspaper delivery round and washing cars. Even much of that money was taken from him to help fund his parents' heavy drinking habit. Now though, at age thirty-three he was married, with two lovely daughters – aged five and seven – and he was halfway through an Open University degree course in mechanical engineering. Money was always tight, but he and his family were happy.

Finally, the blockage was cleared, and the mayhem subsided. At last, he arrived back at the bus depot and prepared to make his weary way home. He slung his rucksack over his shoulder, said goodbye to the handful of fellow drivers who were there, and made his way to the bus stop just outside the depot. He only had to wait ten minutes before the driver emerged from the depot and approached the vehicle.

'Hi Ron ... how come you're so late knocking off today?'

He sighed. 'Major accident at Trafalgar Square ... took ages to clear.'

The driver gave a subdued chuckle. 'Hmm, well it happens to us all at some time or other. Say ... you OK? You're looking a bit pale.'

'Oh, just a bit of a headache ... I'll be fine. Looking forward to getting home, though.'

'I'll bet ...' chuckled the driver, stepping up into the cab. 'Well climb aboard ... there are a few more folks behind you waiting to get in.'

Ron took the nearest seat to the front of the bus, unslinging his rucksack and putting it on the floor by his feet, ready for the twenty-minute journey to the modest, two-bedroomed apartment that he and Sue called home. It was too small, really, for their growing family, but at the moment they couldn't afford anything bigger, even if they moved to a cheaper area – not that there was anywhere in London which could really be called 'cheap'. Sue had previously worked as a geography teacher but had had to give that up to raise the kids; now she worked from home, part time, as a telephone market researcher. Once the kids were older, she planned to return to teaching; if she did that and Ron was able to realise his career aspirations, then they'd be able to move up to something more suitable.

As they approached his stop, Ron checked his watch: almost 3.00 p.m. On this shift he'd normally be home by around 1.30 – 1.40 p.m. and he'd have time to have lunch with his wife before she went to collect the kids from school. Today though, she'd already have set off.

'Cheers Pete,' he called out to the driver as he stepped off the bus. 'See you Monday.'

The driver responded with a wave of his hand.

Ron made his way up to the second floor of the apartment block, where their apartment was located, and let himself in. As expected, Sue wasn't there, but there was a note on the dining table.

Lasagne in the kitchen — put it in the oven at 180C for around 40 minutes. I've already eaten. xxx

He smiled; Sue was always so thoughtful and understanding when his schedule got messed up for one reason or another, something which seemed to happen increasingly often of late.

He switched the oven on to warm up, before grabbing the newspaper which lay on the kitchen countertop and retiring to the couch in the living room. The headline on the front page was 'Train Drivers to go on Strike.' Why were the bloody train drivers always on strike? They were already paid far better than the bus drivers who just got on with the job without complaining. He couldn't be bothered to read the whole story.

That nagging headache wasn't going away; if anything, it was getting worse. *Thank God tomorrow's Saturday*, he thought; he had worked seven days straight, and the last thing he had needed today was the frustrating hold up at Trafalgar Square. Anyway, now he was looking forward to two days off and some quality time with his wife and kids.

After ten minutes, he put his lunch in the oven and settled back with his newspaper once more. As he flipped idly through the pages, he became aware of a faint tickling sensation in his throat. *Probably nothing,* he thought.

He had just finished his lunch and loaded his plate and cutlery into the dishwasher when the sound of the door chimes announced Sue's return with the kids. For some reason Chloe, his younger daughter, always liked to reach up, stretching for the doorbell, if she thought he was in, rather than let her mother open the door with the key.

'Dadeee!' cried Chloe, when he opened the door. She launched herself at him, wrapping her arms and legs around him as he swept her up in his arms. Charlotte was a little more restrained, waiting for her sister to be put down before coming forward for a kiss. Sue was third in line.

3

'Tough day?' she enquired, giving Ron a brief kiss.

'Uh huh … it was a really big accident … took forever to get it cleared. Never mind, we've got a proper weekend all together now.'

'Mummy,' called out Charlotte, 'can we do iPads now?'

'Just half an hour … then I want you to read a story for Chloe, Daddy and me.'

'O-kaay,' replied Charlotte, grudgingly.

As the girls settled down, iPads on laps and earphones on, Ron said to Sue, 'Fancy a glass of wine?'

They never drank when Ron was working but often treated themselves to a bottle of wine when he had a couple of days off.

'Mmm … yes please.'

Ron disappeared into the kitchen, returning a few minutes later with two glasses of Sauvignon Blanc; the girls were still happily engaged with their iPads. He handed Sue's wine to her, and the two of them clinked glasses.

'Here's to a nice quiet weekend,' he whispered, kissing her on the cheek.

'I'll drink to that!' she replied.

***

When the girls were finally in bed, asleep, Ron and Sue settled down on the couch.

'Want something to eat?' she said.

'Don't think so,' he replied, 'I had my lunch very late, and I'm not really hungry now. Lasagne was great, by the way.'

'Charmer,' she replied. 'Must admit though, I thought it was pretty good, myself. I ate much earlier than you but I'm not that hungry either … maybe I'll just have a few crackers and cheese or something, a bit later. Shall we watch that movie we recorded last night?'

'Uh, to be honest, I'm not feeling that great. Had a splitting headache all afternoon, and now I've got a bit of a sore throat. Think I might turn in early.'

She turned towards him, wrinkles of concern on her forehead. 'You think you might be coming down with something?'

'I don't know … maybe, but I definitely need a good night's sleep, anyway.'

'OK … well, I think I'll sit up for a while longer and watch the movie.'

'See you later then.'

He kissed her lightly on the lips and set off towards the bedroom.

But Ron was not destined to get 'a good night's sleep': although his headache had finally begun to subside, his sore throat was getting worse, and he just couldn't settle. He was still awake when Sue came to join him.

'What's up?' she said. 'Can't you get to sleep?'

He yawned, propping himself up on one elbow. 'Not so far … feeling a bit hot and sweaty. Anyway, how was the movie?'

'Oh not bad … actually I think I might have already seen it, years ago … didn't realise until it was almost finished. Never mind about that though … are you OK? Your voice sounds a bit sort of … croaky.'

'Throat's still really sore,' he said, massaging his neck. 'Hurts like hell when I swallow.'

Sue stretched over and placed her hand on his forehead. Her brow creased in a troubled frown. 'And you've got a temperature, too,' she said. 'I think you *are* coming down with some bug or other.'

'I guess you're right … maybe I should go and sleep on the couch. I don't want you catching it.'

'You stay where you are … I'll get you a couple of sleeping tablets. I can take the couch.'

He smiled, weakly. 'Thanks.' Although it didn't seem fair that his wife should be the one to rough it, in truth it seemed almost too much effort to haul himself out of bed and stagger through to the living room. He laid back and closed his eyes.

Sue returned a couple of minutes later with the sleeping tablets and a tumbler of water; he popped the tablets in his mouth and took a long swallow of the cool water, which gave some momentary relief to his raw throat.

'Now try to get some sleep,' she said. 'We'll see how you are in the morning.'

***

In spite of the sleeping tablets he had taken, he slept only fitfully, and the night seemed to stretch for an eternity. Each time he checked the glowing digits of the bedside clock, the time seemed only to have advanced by less than half of what he had expected. At last, though, the gentle glow of morning began to seep around the edges of the curtains. He rolled over to check the clock: 6.07 a.m. The kids would be up soon, and probably crawling all over him. He loved them to bits, but that morning it was the last thing he wanted. In any case, he didn't want them catching whatever bug he had contracted.

He sat up and took a sip from the glass of water on the bedside table. His throat was feeling considerably better, but he still had a raging temperature; his pyjamas and sheets were soaked with perspiration. He needed to get up.

He took a few more sips of water before swinging his legs over the edge of the bed and hauling himself unsteadily to his feet. For a moment he struggled to find his balance, gripping the edge of the bedside table for support for a few seconds until he found his equilibrium. Finally, he felt steady enough to make his way over to the chest of drawers where he found a fresh set of pyjamas. Raising one foot off the ground to strip off the soaked set, he nearly fell over, so he resorted to sitting on the edge of the bed to complete the manoeuvre.

Having changed into fresh pyjamas, he made his way through to the living room, where Sue was fast asleep on the couch. Mercifully, all was quiet in the girls' bedroom, so he went through to the bathroom. Splashing his face with cold water he gazed at his reflection in the mirror; he looked gaunt and pale, with dark circles under his eyes. *Christ you look like shit*, he thought … *you really aren't well.* When he went to pee, he expelled very little, and what did emerge was an unnaturally deep yellow colour. *Guess I must have sweated it all out during the night.*

Feeling a little better now, he made his way back towards the bedroom, creeping silently past Sue, not wanting to wake her. But he was suddenly beset by an unexpected fit of coughing. His wife woke with a start, sitting up and rubbing her eyes, looking momentarily disoriented.

As she found her bearings, she turned towards Ron. 'Oh, you're up … how're you feeling now?'

Ron was holding the edge of the sideboard for support, having been thrown off balance by the sudden coughing fit. 'Pretty rough to be honest ... the sore throat's improved, but I've got a hell of a temperature, and feeling a bit dizzy.'

'...and you've got a nasty cough,' she added. 'You need to get straight back to bed.'

'Yeah ... I just need to change the sheets. They're absolutely soaked.'

She jumped up from the couch. 'Sit down for a few minutes ... I'll do it.'

'OK, thanks,' he said, feeling too weak to protest.

Ten minutes later, Sue emerged from the bedroom. 'OK ... all ready for you now.'

At that moment, the door to the girls' bedroom opened and Charlotte emerged, hair all tousled and rubbing her eyes. 'Can Daddy play with us?'

'Daddy's not feeling very well this morning,' said Sue. 'Why don't you watch TV for a bit while I help Daddy and get some breakfast ready?'

'OK .... Chloe ...' she called to her sister, reaching for the remote control, 'want to watch some TV?'

Her sister came through and the two of them settled down, cross-legged on the floor, while Sue helped her husband back through to the bedroom.

***

Having spent the entire day in bed, Ron was still feeling no better. His appetite had completely evaporated, and when Sue brought him a cheese and ham sandwich around lunchtime, he only managed a few mouthfuls before apologetically turning the rest away. His cough had worsened, and he was beginning to feel short of breath. His efforts to catch a little sleep were fruitless, as every time he tried to drift off, a fit of coughing jerked him back to full wakefulness.

It was around 6.00 p.m. when Sue came to check on him again.

'How're you feeling now?' she enquired. 'Your cough sounds awful.'

'I've been better,' he admitted, forcing a small smile.

As she reached out and placed her hand on his forehead, her face creased in an expression of concern. 'God, you're absolutely burning up ... I think you need to see a doctor.'

Ron was not the sort of person to see a doctor unless absolutely necessary but, on this occasion, he had to admit she was right. 'OK, but it's probably too late to call today. Maybe if I take a couple more sleeping tablets, I'll be able to—'

His words were cut off as he was convulsed with a ferocious coughing fit. As he sat up in bed, lurching forward violently, a spray of blood burst from his lips painting the white sheet with a splatter of crimson spots. Sue's hand flew to her mouth, stifling a gasp.

As Ron slumped back down, panting heavily, Sue swiftly recovered her composure, 'Right, that's it … I'm calling an ambulance, right now.'

Ron was, by now, too weak to object. He closed his eyes, trying to stabilise his breathing as she made the call.

She returned just a couple of minutes later. 'OK, they're coming soon. Let's get you into some clean pyjamas.'

She retrieved another set of pyjamas set from the chest of drawers and laid them on bed. 'Here, let me help you.'

'It's OK, I can manage,' croaked Ron, not at all sure if he really could.

'Alright, I'll tell the girls … we're coming to the hospital with you.'

'Oh, that's not really necessary. I'm sure that—'

'We're coming,' she insisted. 'You just go ahead and get changed.'

***

When they arrived at the Accident and Emergency department, the paramedic attending Ron in the ambulance swiftly leapfrogged all the other patients waiting to be seen, hustling him through in a wheelchair. Sue could not make out the hushed conversation between the paramedic and the doctor on duty, but the concern on their faces was plain to see. Within a couple of minutes, a porter came and took the handles of the wheelchair pushing Ron down a corridor and out of sight. The doctor came over to Sue.

'Mrs Hancock? Hello I'm Doctor—'

'What's wrong with him?' she interrupted.

'We're not sure just yet, but as a precaution, we're going to admit him for observation and tests.'

'But you must have some idea … surely?'

'Well, it appears that your husband is probably suffering from some kind of respiratory infection, but until we carry out some tests, it's difficult to be specific.'

'What's wrong with Daddy?' came a small voice, as Charlotte piped up.

Sue reached out and squeezed her hand. 'They're not sure yet sweetheart, but don't worry ... they'll know soon.'

The doctor bent down so that he was on her eye level. 'What's your name?'

'Charlotte,' she said.

'And who is this?' he said, turning to the younger child.

'I'm Chloe,' replied her sister.

'OK, we're going to look after your Daddy tonight and give him some medicine to help him sleep. Then we're going to do some tests to work out what's wrong with him.'

The two girls looked at each other for a moment before Charlotte said, 'Can we stay with him?'

The doctor smiled. 'Yes, for a little while, but when he goes to sleep you should go home and get some sleep yourselves. OK?'

'OK,' replied Charlotte.

'Thank you, Doctor ... er sorry, I didn't catch your name,' said Sue.

'Doctor Myers,' he replied. 'Just wait here and I'll call you once he's settled in the ward.'

Forty-five minutes later, the three of them were sitting by Ron's bedside. As the doctor had explained before taking them through to see him, he was wearing an oxygen mask to ease his breathing and had been given a sedative to help him get some much-needed sleep.

The sedative he had been given was already taking effect, and he was barely conscious; his responses to attempts at conversation were limited to little more than the occasional smile or a weak squeeze of Sue's hand. Soon, he was fast asleep, his breathing regular, but shallow. Charlotte and Chloe were, by this time, both asleep in their chairs, too; it was way past their normal bedtimes.

A few minutes later, Doctor Myers returned. 'Why don't you go home and get some sleep now?' he suggested. 'He'll be asleep for some hours now, so there's really nothing you can do here. We'll be doing some tests, and by tomorrow morning we should have a better idea of what your husband is suffering from. Give us a call around mid-morning, and hopefully we'll have some news for you.'

***

Sue did not sleep well that night, and she was up and about early on Sunday morning. By the time the girls were up and dressed and they had all had breakfast it was still only just after 9 a.m. Probably still too early to call.

She let the girls go on their iPads while she waited for a suitable time to call the hospital. In truth they had probably already had too much screen time that weekend, but with the anxiety about Ron's condition she just couldn't face entertaining them herself. Instead, she sat in the kitchen, drinking coffee, and listening absently to the radio.

10.00 a.m. and she could contain herself no longer; she called the hospital.

'How is he?' asked Sue when she was finally put through to the ward sister.

'Well,' replied the sister – Sue thought she detected a note of concern in the woman's voice – 'I think it's best if you talk to the consultant who is treating your husband; he's here on the ward right now. Hold the line and I'll see if he can talk to you now.'

Sue's heart was thumping in her chest. Every instinct in her told her something was very wrong. The few minutes she waited felt like an eternity.

'Mrs Hancock?' came a deep male voice, eventually.

'Yes.'

'I'm Doctor Ramesh Patel – Senior Consultant treating your husband.'

'How is he?'

'The tests we conducted overnight indicate that your husband is suffering from a variant of the coronavirus which caused the pandemic which swept through the entire world some years ago.'

She couldn't quite take it in. 'But that's usually hardly any worse than a cold these days, isn't it? What my husband has got is far worse than that.'

'Well yes … with improved treatments, and a regular annual vaccination programme, most people who contract the disease suffer only mild symptoms now. It's not clear why your husband's symptoms are so much more severe. Has he been vaccinated recently?'

'Well, yes … just a few months ago. We both get the booster jab every year.'

'Hmm ...' murmured the doctor, the ensuing silence ominous.

'But anyway, how is he, doctor?'

'I'm afraid, Mrs Hancock, your husband's condition has rapidly deteriorated overnight. We have moved him into intensive care where he has now been put on a mechanical ventilator.'

A leaden boulder descended in her gut. 'What … what does that mean?'

'It is a machine to keep his lungs working – he has had to be heavily sedated to allow us to insert a breathing tube into his windpipe.'

'Oh my God, that sounds awful … is he going to be alright?'

'I'm afraid, Mrs Hancock, that's impossible to say at this stage.'

'What do you mean?'

'Look, I suggest you come to the hospital now where you can see your husband and I can explain the situation in more detail.'

Her head was spinning now. 'Y-yes, OK. Can I bring my two daughters?'

'You can, but it may be distressing for them to see their father in this condition.'

'OK … well, I … I'll see if my neighbour can look after them for a couple of hours.'

By the time she had deposited the girls with her neighbour, Alice, and got the car out of the underground car park, it was almost 11.00 a.m. The journey to the hospital took another forty minutes, though as she swung into the hospital car park, she realised she could not recall one single second of the journey, as though the car had simply taken over and driven itself there. She had no idea where the intensive care ward was, so she made her way directly to the ward where he had been the previous night.

Her voice was breathless as she rushed up to the nurse at the desk.

'Mrs Susan Hancock … here to see my husband, Ron.'

A shadow flitted across the young nurse's face. 'Oh, yes … Mrs Hancock … Doctor Patel would like to talk to you. If you could just—'

At that moment, a short, bespectacled man of Asian appearance emerged from the ward. 'Mrs Hancock?'

'Yes … what's happening? How is my husband?' she blurted.

'I'm Doctor Patel,' he said. 'I have been treating your husband.'

'How is he?' she repeated.

'It's OK Tammy, I'll take over now,' said the doctor, turning to the nurse. He turned back to Sue. 'Please … come with me.'

He ushered her into a small side room, inviting her to sit down.

'W-What's going on?' she stammered. 'I want to see him.'

The doctor's expression was grave. 'I'm very sorry to have to tell you, Mrs Hancock, that your husband passed away, just twenty minutes ago.'

Chapter 1

One year later

Ron Hancock had been one of the first recorded cases of the new coronavirus in the UK. It was never established where, or how, he had become infected. The nature of his job had put him in contact with numerous members of the public, many of them visitors from abroad, so perhaps he had caught it from one of his passengers. Whatever the source of the infection, within a few short weeks of Ron's death, thousands of cases were being detected every day across the UK. Analysis of the virus revealed that this was not, as first thought, a variant of the coronavirus which had swept across the globe some ten years earlier but was, in fact, a completely new virus within the coronavirus family. Of more significance was that the existing vaccines which had been instrumental in bringing the original pandemic under control were almost totally ineffective against this new virus.

Now, one year later, the virus was estimated to have infected around 10% of the UK population and had claimed almost two million lives. The National Health Service was in a state of near collapse, and the country was once again in strict lockdown. The picture was similar in almost every other country, too.

The world was back to square one.

Actually, not even square one; it was much, much worse than that. It was now apparent that the new virus was far more deadly than any of the variants of the previous one. Instead of targeting predominantly older people, this virus attacked people of all ages, including children. Furthermore, the death rate was much higher. In the UK, the original virus was estimated to be responsible for the deaths of approximately 1% of people who contracted the disease; the fatality rate for the new virus was around 30%. And to make matters worse, there was no existing vaccine or therapeutic drug with which to combat this disease.

Scientists throughout the world were now racing against time to try to develop vaccines and drugs which would be effective against the new virus.

***

Professor Felicity Maddocks was working late, but then she almost always worked late. For virtually a full year she and her team at Thomas Lewis College, University of London, had been working furiously to develop a vaccine which would be effective against the deadly new coronavirus which was ravaging the country, and indeed, the entire world.

Felicity had led the team which developed one of the first vaccines approved for use against the previous coronavirus pandemic, some ten years earlier. She had been widely applauded and praised for her ground-breaking work, but it had cost her her marriage. Her husband, Michael, just couldn't deal with the strain which her obsessive devotion to her work had placed on their relationship, and when she refused to ease up, he called time on their marriage. Once the vaccine, and a number of others developed elsewhere, had been rolled out and the disease brought under control, she was able to dial back the hours somewhat, but by then it was too late to save their relationship.

Since then, she had had a couple of brief relationships with other men, but nothing serious, and now that the race to develop a new vaccine was on, there was no time to think about anything but her work.

But the end was in sight. Third stage clinical trials were complete, and the results were better than she could possibly have hoped for: 96% efficacy provided by two doses of the new vaccine. She was now in the process of preparing the submissions for regulatory approval in all the major jurisdictions.

She was well aware that there were a number of other vaccine development programmes underway across the world, but none were as far advanced as hers. That meant that the entire world was depending on her and her team to provide a vaccine to be approved and put into mass production as soon as possible. The pressure was intense – but she was almost there.

However, her elation at the prospect of finally starting the long process of bringing this deadly disease under control had been completely shattered by the meeting she had had that day with her colleague, Doctor Sofía Méndez.

Sofía Méndez, daughter of Argentinian immigrants, but born and bred in the UK, was the vaccine project leader at Saturn Pharmaceuticals, the company, based in Scotland, which was working in conjunction with the Thomas Lewis team, and which would ultimately be the first company to produce the new vaccine in volume. The two scientists worked closely together, but due to lockdown restrictions, and the distance between the two of them, much of their communication was online. Today, though, Sofía had insisted that they needed a face-to-face meeting, offering to travel down to London and stay overnight.

Due to lockdown restrictions there were no hotels available, so the Thomas Lewis Vaccine Group kept a rented apartment available for visiting colleagues to use; that was where Sofía would stay. She hadn't really explained why they couldn't just meet online as usual, and even more intriguingly, she had suggested they meet in the apartment, rather than at the lab.

Felicity could not possibly have foreseen what was on her colleague's agenda. She had only known Sofía for a little over a year, but during that time they had forged a close working relationship and shared a similar drive to do whatever it would take to bring their joint project to fruition. Yet what she had suggested that day was utterly outrageous. She had argued her case logically and cogently, yet it went against every instinct and value in Felicity's being. Now she realised she really didn't know her colleague at all.

The question was, what to do about it? That was the question which had occupied her thoughts for the several hours since she had left Sofía in the apartment and returned to the lab. As she stared at her computer screen, she knew she would not be able to continue with her work until this issue had been resolved.

Her thoughts were interrupted by a light tap on her shoulder. 'Hey, Felicity … I'm off now. You should go home too … you look exhausted.'

She turned to see the bearded, bespectacled face of her number two, Doctor Peter Simmons. He was barely thirty-one years old yet seemed imbued with the wisdom and experience of someone years older. He had been at her side throughout the entire project, working with almost as much drive and determination as Felicity herself.

She looked around to see the lab was empty apart from just the two of them. She glanced at her watch: 9.05 p.m.

'I guess you're right,' she said, forcing a small smile. 'Can't seem to concentrate right now, anyway.'

'Anything you want to share?' he asked, having clearly picked up on her troubled mood.

She couldn't possibly reveal the real reason for her anxiety, so she stalled. 'Oh, just tired … it feels like the closer we get to finishing the submission for the regulators, the more we find little things that we haven't properly covered. We can't afford to slip up at the final hurdle.'

'We won't … the whole team will study and critique the submission before it goes in.' He placed a reassuring hand on her shoulder. 'Come on … go home. Another couple of days and it'll all be ready.'

'Thanks, Peter. OK, you go … I'll just clear up here and I'll be right behind you.'

***

In the event, it was over thirty minutes later by the time Felicity unplugged her laptop and slipped it into its carrying case. She picked up her mobile and put that in the front pocket of the case. Finally, she donned her coat and scarf, slinging the laptop over her shoulder before killing the lights and stepping out of the lab, checking that the keypad-operated door was secure.

As she made her way along the corridor, her mind was in turmoil: she was grappling with the shocking dilemma which now faced her. She knew she could never accept the proposal which her colleague had put to her, but if she confronted the issue head on, one or possibly both of them would most likely be taken off the project. That would inevitably delay the approval and rollout of the new vaccine, putting countless more lives at risk. The only way forward she could see was to try to persuade Sofía to abandon the course she was set on.

As she approached the door to the outside, she could see through the glass a steady snowfall, the large, fluffy flakes picked out by the yellow-tinted lighting outside the building as they drifted to earth. She stopped short of stepping outside; this couldn't wait.

She withdrew her mobile and dialled Sofía's number. Her colleague picked up after two rings.

'Sofía … it's me … Felicity. We need to talk.'

'Well, that's what we've been doing for most of the day … have you had a change of heart?'

'Well … not exactly, but … look, we have to work this out. We're almost ready to submit the final documents for regulatory approval. We absolutely cannot allow that to be delayed. None of the other vaccine projects are anywhere close to being ready; literally the whole world is depending on us.'

'I agree,' said her colleague, 'which is why your reluctance to accept my proposal risks everything.'

'Look, hearing your plan today was one hell of a shock, coming out of the blue like that. It's far too big a thing to resolve in a phone call. Can you stay for another day so we can meet again tomorrow and thrash it out?'

'Well, if that will give me the opportunity to allay your reservations, then yes, I can do that.'

That absolutely was not what Felicity had in mind, but she feared a point-blank refusal to engage in such a dialogue would result in her colleague heading back to Scotland in the morning. And then her only course of action would be to expose the rift between them with an inevitable delay in the approval and rollout of the vaccine.

She decided to duck the question. 'Look, let's just meet in the morning. Maybe we can work this out.'

'Hmm … does "work this out" mean you're going to try to talk me out of it?'

'Oh Sofía … I'm exhausted right now. I can't even think straight. Can we just meet tomorrow … say 10 a.m. in the apartment?'

An ominous silence ensued; somehow, Felicity could sense her colleague's scepticism in that silence. Was she going to refuse to even talk about it any further?

The reply, when it came, was delivered in a cautious tone. 'OK, 10 a.m. tomorrow.'

A wave of relief swept through her. 'Thank you,' she sighed. 'See you tomorrow.'

At least her colleague was prepared to continue talking. She knew it wouldn't be an easy meeting though.

She entered the appointment in her calendar on her phone, more out of habit than anything else – for she was hardly likely to forget such a crucial meeting – before slipping it back into the laptop case.

As she stepped out of the door, an icy blast of air shocked her out of her introspective musing. She pulled her scarf up around her neck and set off towards the temporary staff car park which had been set up for those scientists and technicians working on the vaccine project.

When she arrived at the dimly lit car park, there were just two cars parked there: her own Range Rover and a dark coloured BMW saloon.

She picked her way carefully across the tarmac; the snow in the car park had settled to a couple of inches depth now, and the last thing she needed at such a critical time would be to slip and injure herself. As she approached her vehicle, she blipped the remote control causing the indicator lights to flash and a loud click to be heard. Before she reached her car, though, a gruff male voice sounded from behind her.

'Professor Maddocks?'

She turned to see a man stepping out of the other car. He was tall, dressed in dark clothing, but she couldn't make out his face clearly in the dim lighting.

'Yes … that's me. Do I know you?'

'No,' he said, 'but I know you. I need you to hand over your laptop.'

'What?'

'Your laptop … give it to me.'

'No,' she replied, hugging her bag protectively. 'This contains important work. Who are you, anyway?'

'That really doesn't matter,' said the man raising his hand to reveal that he was holding a handgun, the muzzle elongated by the fitment of a silencer.

In an instant, her creeping discomfort crystallised into cold, hard fear, her heart hammering in her chest. 'Alright, alright … here it is,' she said, unslinging her bag from her shoulder.

'Lay it on the ground and step back.'

She did so. 'Look, that machine's worth about £1,000 but it contains data that's very important to me.' She held her left hand forward pointing to her wrist with the trembling index finger of her other hand. 'Take my watch instead … it's worth much more than that.'

'Uh-uh … it's the laptop I need, I'm afraid.'

Even as she registered the muzzle flash, she felt the pulverising impact to her chest, punching her backwards. As she fell to the ground, the carpet of snow cushioning the impact to the back of her head, the delayed hit of the pain to her chest kicked in, causing her to gasp in shock. She tried to get up but found herself unable to move. All she could do was lie still, gazing skyward.

As she lay there, she heard a loud click; her car, in the absence of anyone opening the door, had relocked itself. The next sound she heard was the crunch of several footsteps on fresh snow.

The man's face suddenly interposed itself between her and the blackness of the winter sky, the reflection of the yellow streetlights off the white carpet of snow finally allowing her to make out his features. It was an unremarkable face, thin cheeks, narrow nose, closely trimmed beard. Just an average looking guy.

That face was the last thing she was ever to see on this earth.

'Why?' she gasped.

'Nothing personal … just business,' he said, as he levelled the gun at her forehead and pulled the trigger.

Chapter 2

Ruby Collins, Lab Technician at the Thomas Lewis Vaccine Group, turned up for work at 7.00 a.m. She had been asked by Felicity to assemble some papers which were needed to complete the final submission for regulatory approval of the vaccine. Knowing how urgent it was to finalise the submission, she decided to come in early and get everything prepared before her boss arrived.

It was barely light as she swung into the staff car park, the last few flakes of snow fluttering lazily to earth picked out by the yellow glow of the still-illuminated street lights. In the silence of the early morning, the crunching of her tyres on the fresh carpet of snow sounded unnaturally loud.

She had expected to be first into the lab, but Felicity's car was already there. Although her boss regularly worked very late into the evening it was unusual for her to arrive so early in the morning. But then she noticed that the car was coated in perhaps three or four inches of snow over the bonnet, windscreen, and roof and, strangely, there were no fresh tyre tracks leading to the vehicle. Had Felicity actually been there all night? She was well known for being absolutely driven, but even *she* would need some sleep from time to time.

As she drove around the parked car, Ruby suddenly became aware of an unnatural-looking mound in the fresh snow. A drift? Surely not just there, right out in the open like that.

She parked and locked her car before investigating the unusual feature in the snow, an inexplicable uneasiness rippling through her. She found herself drawn forward by curiosity, yet at the same time repelled by apprehension; curiosity won. As she drew closer, she noticed that there was a strange pink colouration to the snow at one end and then she saw it: the pointed tip of a woman's shoe protruding from the snow at the other. Her creeping dread morphed into a chilling certainty as she bent down and began brushing away the snow with her hand. As she did so, the unmistakeable contours of a human body began to emerge. Terrified but fascinated in equal measure, she began brushing away the snow from the most deeply stained area. It was the nose which her trembling fingers found first, and then, as the rest of the face was revealed, her heart froze; she found herself staring into the lifeless eyes of Professor Felicity Maddocks.

She recoiled in shock and horror, falling backwards and scrabbling away on hands and backside in the powdery snow. In a panic, she glanced around for someone, anyone, who might help; there was no-one. Finally, she regained some of her composure and reached for her bag, which lay in the snow alongside her, withdrawing her phone and dialling 999.

Chapter 3

The whole world was waiting anxiously for the arrival of the vaccine being developed by the team at Thomas Lewis College. It was obvious, then, that the shocking murder of the leader of that team would attract widespread attention from the scientific community, the media, and the public alike. Naturally, there would be huge concern about whether Professor Maddocks's death would delay the development and approval of the vaccine, but the immediate spotlight fell squarely on the Metropolitan Police, who would be expected to swiftly find out who had perpetrated this heinous act, and why.

The task force assigned to investigate the murder of Professor Felicity Maddocks was headed by Detective Inspector David Prendergast. Forty-eight years old, David was at the height of his powers. He was not a flamboyant character, actually rather serious, quiet, and reserved, but he had a track record of getting results. Over the years that he had been with the Met he had accumulated a wealth of experience, solving the vast majority of the cases to which he had been assigned. He was the obvious choice for this high-profile investigation.

***

David wasted no time in gathering the task force together for an initial team meeting.

'OK everyone,' he began, 'this is what we have so far …

'The victim is Professor Felicity Maddocks – head of the project team at Thomas Lewis College developing the promising new vaccine for the coronavirus. She was shot once in the chest and once in the head. Time of death, according to the pathologist, sometime between 8 p.m. and midnight last night.

'Her body was discovered in the staff car park by a colleague, a lab technician named Ruby Collins, when she turned up for work at around 7.00 a.m. this morning. When Miss Collins arrived, the only car in the car park was that belonging to Professor Maddocks. It was locked and covered in a substantial layer of snow; this, and the lack of any visible tyre tracks leading directly to the car, suggest that it had been there all night. Our working assumption, therefore, is that the victim was killed last night before she reached her car.'

He paused for a moment, scanning his notes. 'That's about all we know right now ... questions?'

He scanned the faces of the four other detectives in the room; they were all looking at him expectantly, but no-one raised any questions.

'OK ... here's what we need to investigate: first, forensics.' He looked towards Detective Constable Priti Sharma. 'Priti, can you liaise with the forensics team working the scene. See if they're able to identify tyre tracks, footprints, or anything else which may be of interest ... and make sure the victim's car is checked for fingerprints. The killer may possibly have tried to get into her car. If we're lucky, he or she may have left some prints.'

'On it, sir.'

Next, he turned to Detective Constable Sam Lockyer. 'Sam, can you chase up Pathology ... ascertain which was the fatal shot and see if they can be any more precise about the time of death. Also, get the bullets to Forensics and see what they can tell us about the murder weapon.'

'Yes sir.'

Prendergast paused for a few moments, his bushy eyebrows knotted together. 'And then we come to the thorny question of motive. Kevin and Kate, I want you two to work together on this.' He was addressing Detective Sergeant Kevin Brown and Detective Constable Kate Evans.

'Find out if there was anyone who might have harboured a personal grudge against her. Ex-lover, husband, bitter colleague, and so on.

'It could also be connected with her work,' continued Prendergast. 'She was head of what I understand to be the world's leading vaccine development programme. Is there any possibility that someone from a rival programme would have had a reason to try to disrupt her project in favour of their own ... or force her to hand over vital data?'

'Got it,' said Kate, nodding. 'We'll follow up on all of those possibilities.'

'Good,' said Prendergast, pausing for a moment to check his notes. 'I think that's about all for now. Any questions?'

There was a general murmuring and shaking of heads.

'OK ... I'm going to talk to the other senior scientists who were working with her to find out what implications the death of Professor Maddocks has for the vaccine programme. Although our principal task is to bring her murderer to justice, bear in mind that any delay to the rollout of the vaccine could cost many more lives. The press will be all over this, and, while the main responses will have to come from the scientists and politicians, *we're* bound to be asked about it too. We need to be able to reassure the media, if possible, that the vaccine programme continues unabated.

'Let's meet back here, same time tomorrow, unless anyone comes up with a breakthrough before then ... in which case let me know at once. Let's get to it.'

***

'So,' began DI Prendergast, at the following day's task force meeting, 'let's see what we have so far. Priti ... what have Forensics come up with from the crime scene?'

She cleared her throat. 'Right ... well the snow covering has made the investigation difficult, but beneath the top layer they were able to discern plenty of tyre tracks which had frozen and then been covered with fresh snow. They can identify the make and model of each tyre from the tread pattern but it's impossible to say which, if any, might belong to a vehicle used by the killer. In any case,' she added, 'the barrier to the car park is protected by a keypad entry mechanism; only the laboratory staff know the code.'

'Hmm ...' muttered Prendergast, 'it's quite possible, though, that the killer might have somehow obtained the code.' He paused for a moment. 'OK, I want all the cars used by laboratory staff checked out. It's just possible that we may be able to eliminate many of their vehicles and identify a tread pattern that shouldn't be there.'

'OK, sir, I'll get right on it.'

'What else?'

'Well, much like the tyre tracks, there were plenty of footprints preserved below the fresh snow, but I think we may have a bit more luck there. The area close to where the body was found was relatively free of footprints; apart from those belonging to the victim herself, only two other distinct patterns could be discerned and, of those, one set in particular looked to be consistent with the estimated position of the shooter.'

'Sounds promising,' said Prendergast.

'Uh huh,' agreed the DC. 'The shoe is a man's Timberland brand boot – size ten.'

'Excellent … far from conclusive, but it sounds as though this boot may well belong to our killer. Anything else from the crime scene?'

'Well, the victim's car's been checked for prints, but all of them check out as being her own or belonging to friends or colleagues who have recently travelled with her.'

'OK … pretty much what we expected, but it was worth a try. Do you have anything else?'

She checked her notebook. 'That's it, sir … apart from two 9mm cartridge casings found at the scene.'

'Right, thanks, Priti.' He turned to Sam Lockyer. 'What do we have from Pathology, Sam?'

'Well, nothing much more than we would have expected, so far. Two bullet wounds: one to the chest and one to the head. The chest shot was not lethal; it somehow missed all vital organs. The killing shot was the one to the head, administered while the victim was incapacitated, lying on her back.'

'9 mm rounds, I presume?' said Prendergast.

'Yes … both fired from the same gun. The markings on the bullets are apparently quite distinctive. Forensics are pretty sure they would be able to match them to the weapon … if we can find it, that is.'

'Hmm … that's a big "if". Anything else?'

'Afraid not, sir.'

Prendergast turned his attention to DS Kevin Brown and DC Kate Evans. 'OK, Kevin, Kate …. What do we know about Professor Maddocks … professional and personal?'

Kevin exchanged a slight nod with Kate before responding to the question. 'We've spoken to most of her work colleagues, and the picture emerging is of a dedicated professional, driven almost to the point of obsession in her determination to deliver a vaccine against the coronavirus. Apparently, she was a great leader, if very demanding. Everyone says she was well liked and respected, and no-one can think of anyone who might have had a grudge against her. Not much help, I'm afraid.'

As Kevin paused for a moment, Prendergast interjected. 'OK … what about possible rivals from other vaccine development programmes?'

'Ah, yes,' said Kevin, 'I was just coming to that. I've spoken to a' – he glanced at his notebook – 'Doctor Peter Simmons … he's her immediate deputy. One of the first things he asked me about was the victim's laptop. Apparently, she always took it home with her at night, and used the front pocket of the case to carry all her personal effects like phone, keys, etcetera … saved her bringing a separate handbag to work. But here's the thing … the laptop case, and everything in it is missing, apart from her car key which was in her hand. She must have been just about to get into her car when the killer struck.'

'Interesting …' mused Prendergast. 'So it's more than likely that the killer took the laptop.' He paused for a moment, stroking his chin. 'Could this be a simple mugging after all?'

'Well, it's possible,' said Kevin, 'but the victim was wearing an expensive diamond ring and a Rolex watch, and those were left on the body. My guess is that it was the laptop the killer was after.'

'Hmm …' muttered Prendergast, 'what kind of information would be on that machine?'

'Well … it seems that there could be all manner of vital data relating to the vaccine, so it's quite possible that theft of that data could be a motive for the murder.'

'Hmm … to sabotage the Thomas Lewis programme, or enable someone else to catch up, I wonder?'

'I asked Doctor Simmons about that. It seems that all data on that laptop is backed up in real time on the university mainframe computer, so the programme won't be compromised in any way by the loss of the machine.'

'So,' concluded Prendergast, 'it's more likely that the machine was stolen to give the killer – or the killer's paymaster – access to the data it contains.'

'Seems that way,' agreed Kevin.

'OK … do you have anything else?'

'Well,' replied Kevin, 'that's all I've got so far on the work side of things, but Kate has been digging into her personal life.' He nodded to her. 'Go ahead, Kate.'

'OK … she was forty-two years old, divorced some ten years ago. Seems she's had a couple of relationships since then, but as far as anyone knows, nothing too serious. Since the work on the new vaccine development started, she's been utterly dedicated to that, with no time for anything else. She rarely socialised with any of her work colleagues, but they think she had two or three fairly close friends outside of work.'

She paused, flipping back and forth through the pages of her notebook. 'That's about all I have so far.'

'OK guys … good work,' said Prendergast.

Kevin stepped in. 'There's some obvious follow up work to do here. I'm going to investigate what's going on with each of the parallel vaccine development programmes to see if there's a possibility that someone out there might be prepared to kill for the data contained in that laptop.'

'Meanwhile,' added Kate, 'I'll track down the ex-husband and the previous boyfriends to investigate whether any of them might have a possible motive. I'll also talk to her female friends to see if there's anything there.'

DI Prendergast nodded, giving a small grunt of approval. He started to sum up.

'OK … good work everyone. On the face of it, it seems pretty unlikely that we're going to get much more from the crime scene investigation, Forensics, or Pathology. I think we should focus on the motive: was it someone desperate to steal vital data on the vaccine development, an ex with a grudge, or maybe something else?

'Kevin … where are the other main vaccine development programmes located?'

He consulted his notebook. 'One other here in the UK … at the University of Oxford; three in the USA; one in China; one in Russia; one in Switzerland; one in Germany; one in—'

'Christ,' interrupted Prendergast, 'how many of these programmes are there?'

'Well, those in the UK, USA, and China are the main ones but there are about thirty in total.'

His heart sank. 'OK … Kevin, you're going to need some help.' He paused, massaging his forehead between thumb and fingers, as he considered the task at hand. 'Kate, I suggest you press on with your investigation of the victim's personal life, while Priti and Sam join forces with Kevin to investigate the other vaccine development programmes.'

'Thank you, sir,' said Kevin. 'Uh, about the overseas programmes … how do you think we should—?'

Prendergast had anticipated the question. 'Use Interpol to liaise with local law enforcement. We don't want any international rows over stepping on local toes. But if you come across something that you feel warrants a personal visit, let me know and I'll try and obtain the relevant permissions.'

He scanned the four faces in front of him. 'Any questions?' There were none. 'Then let's press on.'

Chapter 4

A week had elapsed since Professor Maddocks's shocking death. Doctor Peter Simmons, her youthful number two, had been appointed to head the programme. Peter had worked hand-in-glove with Felicity, and despite his youth and relative inexperience, he was the natural choice to take over. When offered the post, he did not hesitate to step up.

The sense of loss among the team was palpable; somehow, all the energy and enthusiasm had evaporated. He had to do something to revive the programme. He was not a natural public speaker, but he decided to gather the team together for a briefing. It wasn't just for a pep talk, though that *was* sorely needed: he had some important information for them.

'OK guys ... it's been a week now. No-one's talking about it, but we're all feeling it. Felicity was such an inspiration that it's natural we're all feeling ... well, kind of empty inside.'

He paused for a few moments to let his words sink in before continuing.

'But she's gone, and we have to accept that. As well as grief, you may be feeling all kinds of other emotions: maybe anger, a desire to avenge Felicity's death, even. But bringing her killer to justice is a matter for the police.'

The room was deadly silent as he surveyed the sea of downcast faces before him; not even a cough or a shuffling of feet disturbed the stillness.

'For our part, the best thing we can do to honour Felicity's memory is to bring her project to fruition just as quickly as we possibly can. We're 99% of the way there to the first vaccine now. I will be submitting the final data to the regulators tomorrow. The main ones have promised to fast track the approval process. We could see the vaccination programme start to roll out within weeks. We'll soon be saving thousands of lives. Now that's something to be proud of, isn't it?'

He paused again, waiting for some sort of response. Finally, a few murmurs of approval could be heard, and one or two heads were nodding. He seized the moment and pressed on.

'But our work will not be done when the rollout begins. This disease will not be defeated until the majority of the entire world's population has been vaccinated ... that will take *billions* of doses. Saturn Pharmaceuticals will only be able to produce a maximum of three million doses per week even when they have ramped up to full capacity.'

More subdued murmuring as people began to engage with what he was saying.

'You all know that there is no other vaccine development programme in the world which is anywhere close to where we are, so we can't rely on others to pick up the slack ... for many months to come at least. We have to get *our* vaccine produced by several other pharmaceutical companies while the other development teams catch up and bring some alternative vaccines on stream.'

Finally, someone felt emboldened enough to ask a question: it was Alok Patel, one of the more experienced members of the team, who raised his hand. 'But surely, Peter, Saturn is never going to agree to share intellectual property with competitors?'

Peter smiled. 'Felicity had anticipated we might find ourselves in this situation and had laid the groundwork for a possible solution. She had been lobbying the UK government to work with other governments around the world to work out some financial arrangement to compensate Saturn for any lost income and provide incentives for several other companies to manufacture the vaccine. In the week since Felicity's death, I have been doing my damndest to push that project through to a conclusion.'

'So what's the situation now then?' asked Alok, eagerly.

'I'm pleased to tell you that, in addition to Saturn Pharmaceuticals, we have agreements – or at least letters of intent – in place with both Fenmore Sciences and Novagen in the USA, and Schwartz Pharmaceuticals in Germany.'

There was a stunned silence.

'Folks ... we will soon have no fewer than *four* major drug companies manufacturing our vaccine.'

After another second or two of silence, Alok put his hands together and began to clap. Then another pair of hands joined in – and another. Within seconds the entire room was filled with enthusiastic applause.

Peter waited for the noise to subside before continuing. 'Doctor Sofía Méndez, project leader at Saturn, will be the main technical liaison with the other drug companies, assisted by me where necessary.'

A subdued buzz of conversation began to spread around the room.

'Wait,' said Peter, patting the air with his hands to restore silence. 'As I'm sure you all realise, rolling out the vaccine, even with expanded manufacturing capacity, is not the end of the story. Like all viruses, this particularly evil little bastard is spawning new variants all the time. It can only be a matter of time before one or more variants proves to be able to evade our vaccine. We need to step up the programme for development of adjustments to the vaccine to combat those vaccine-resistant strains which will surely emerge.'

Most of his audience were now nodding enthusiastically.

'Any questions?'

One hand went up. 'This is great news Peter, and you know we'll all step up to the challenge, but I have a different question: is there any news on the police investigation into Felicity's murder … and is there any likelihood that the rest of us are in danger?'

Peter had not anticipated that question, and he didn't have an answer. 'I'm afraid, at this point, I don't have any more information on that front.'

And that sombre question rather killed the euphoria which had persisted just a few minutes previously.

***

DI Prendergast was holding a further task force meeting to take stock of the current status of all the various strands of the investigation.

'Priti … any further progress on the tyre tracks?'

'Well, we've checked all the cars belonging to staff who use that car park and cross referenced against the identifiable tracks. There is just one set of tracks which doesn't match any of those cars. The tyre is a Michelin Pilot Sport 5 – width 225 mm.'

'And does that narrow down the type of car significantly?'

'Not really, I'm afraid ... it's a common enough tyre used as original equipment on many mainstream models, and frequently used as an aftermarket fitment on others, too.'

'Hmm,' muttered Prendergast, 'so that's not going to help us much. And of course,' he added, 'the fact that a particular car was there that evening does not make it by any means certain that it was used by the killer. What about the shoe prints?'

'No change ... we just have the one set of prints from the size ten Timberland boots, but we're no closer to knowing who they belong to.'

'OK,' concluded Prendergast, 'it doesn't look as if any of the crime scene evidence is going to help lead us to the killer.'

Priti must have picked up on his downbeat tone. 'Sorry sir,' she murmured.

'Don't be,' he replied, keen to keep the motivation level up. 'This evidence may not lead us directly to the killer, but if we get to a suspect by other means, and if it's a man who owns such boots and a car whose tyres match the tracks, then it will be valuable additional evidence.'

Priti gave a small nod.

'Kate, how have you been getting on digging into the victim's private life?'

She cleared her throat. 'Right ... the ex-husband has remarried and has a child with his new wife. As far as I could judge, he and Professor Maddocks parted on amicable terms, and he seemed genuinely shocked and saddened to learn of her death. I could be wrong, but I think it's very unlikely that he had anything to do with it.'

Prendergast nodded. 'You're good at reading people, Kate ... I trust your judgement on this. What about the boyfriends?'

She visibly brightened at her boss's compliment. 'OK, as far as her colleagues are aware, she only had two other relationships after her marriage broke down, neither especially serious. One of the men is now married and doesn't appear to have had any grudge against the victim. The other guy emigrated to Australia around two years ago. I've spoken to him on the phone ... he's moved on and made a new life out there … I can't see that he would have any reason to have harmed Professor Maddocks.'

This line of investigation didn't seem to be too promising, but he pressed on. 'OK … uh, anything with friends or colleagues?'

'Nothing, I'm afraid, sir. All her colleagues seem to have liked and respected her, and she only had a very few friends outside of work, none of whom seem to me to be likely suspects.'

'OK, Kate … good work.'

He paused for a few moments, his brow wrinkled in thought, before continuing.

'OK, guys … as we suspected, it's not looking as though forensic or crime scene evidence is going to lead us to the killer, so we need to concentrate on motive. Kate's investigation seems to point away from any personal relationship that we know of as providing a motive, so it brings us back to a work-related issue.' He turned to DS Brown. 'Kevin, what's the score on the other vaccine development programmes?'

Kevin spread out several sheets of A4 paper on the desk in front of him. 'Right … well, both Priti and Sam have been helping me with this. With over thirty other programmes underway it's a pretty big task, and it doesn't help that they're spread all over the world.'

Prendergast felt a stab of impatience with this preamble when he wanted to get to the meat of the findings. 'I get that,' he interjected, his voice sounding a little tetchier than he had intended, 'so what do you have so far?'

Kevin came to the point. 'Right … well, with the help of Interpol we've made an initial contact with around half so far.'

'And?' prompted Prendergast.

'OK … it seems that even the most advanced of the other programmes are still several months away from having a vaccine they could submit for regulatory approval.'

'Could be all the more reason,' surmised Prendergast, 'why someone on one of those programmes might be prepared to go to extraordinary lengths to try to catch up.'

'Well,' replied Kevin, 'that's what I thought too, at first. However, it seems there are several radically different approaches to developing a vaccine, each using a different technology. The thing is, the Thomas Lewis Group's approach is unique … none of the other programmes we've looked at so far are using the same technology.'

He paused, looking up expectantly.

'Which means what, exactly?' said Prendergast.

'It means they would have nothing to gain by accessing Professor Maddocks's data ... or at least that's what they are all saying.'

'Well, if someone's guilty, that's what they would say, isn't it?'

'I guess so,' admitted Kevin, 'but Doctor Simmons has confirmed that the data would only be of value to someone pursuing a similar technology to Thomas Lewis ... and as far as he knows, no-one's doing that.'

'Well, *someone* thought it was worth taking the laptop,' muttered Prendergast.

'True,' said Kevin. 'After discussing it with Doctor Simmons I think there are two possibilities. First,' he said, tapping the forefinger of his right hand against the palm of his left, 'there could be one of the less prominent programmes that we haven't yet contacted which *does* use a similar technology to Thomas Lewis. Doctor Simmons was at pains to point out that, while the scientific community in the west is open and transparent, we have much less visibility of what is going on in Russia and China.'

'Hmm ... good point ... and the second possibility?'

'Someone could be intending to start from scratch – literally copying all of Professor Maddocks's work, and perhaps cutting some corners.'

Prendergast fell silent as he digested what Kevin had said. After some seconds he summed up.

'OK, so far we have nothing conclusive from Pathology or Forensics. There seem to be no promising leads related to the victim's private life. I think our working hypothesis has to be that Professor Maddocks was murdered in order to steal vital data on the vaccine development programme. I want the whole team on that line of investigation now. We need to check out every single one of the parallel development programmes and be alert for any clue that there's a new one starting up that we don't know about. I'm going to assign two more DCs to help with the effort.

'Let's get to it.'

***

DI Prendergast lingered after the team had dispersed. He was consumed by that awful sinking feeling in his gut which characterises an investigation which is going nowhere. His instincts told him that this was most likely a professional contract killing; the person behind the killing was very unlikely to be the one who had actually pulled the trigger. However, his years of experience told him that the best chance of success in such cases was to first find the killer and then get that person to lead him to the paymaster. Furthermore, if the killer was not identified within forty-eight hours of the crime, the chances of getting to the person behind it were much reduced.

In this case, the crime scene investigation and the pathology report had yielded precious little which might lead him to the killer, and a full week had elapsed since the murder. He was now having to rely on a protracted and speculative investigation into possible candidates who might have a credible motive.

It wasn't looking good.

Chapter 5

Fifteen months later

It was his day off, and Detective Inspector David Prendergast was tending to the numerous plants in his conservatory. The rain hammering on the glass roof beat out an unrelenting rhythm, while the water streaming down the windows rendered the view out over his garden a wavering, indistinct blur. The gloomy scene matched his mood.

The unsolved Felicity Maddocks murder had turned out to be, effectively, the end of his career with the Metropolitan Police. He had always known it would be a very high-profile case, given the intense media and public interest in the development of the coronavirus vaccine, and it was no surprise that his superiors were extremely upset that the case had never been solved.

Nevertheless, he felt he had been dealt with harshly when it was suggested that he take early retirement at the age of just forty-nine. He had been offered a severance payment of £300,000 on condition that he sign a non-disclosure agreement, precluding him from sharing any of the details of the case with the press. It was a tempting offer; £300,000 was a very substantial sum, and he was still young enough to make a fresh start in some other field of work. But what? Police work was all he really knew, and something – call it professional pride – prevented him from admitting he had failed. He could not accept the offer.

He hadn't, however, expected the way his superiors would react when he rejected the offer: he was immediately taken off front-line duties and given a back-office job. Although he retained his rank and his salary, the work was mind-numbing. Nevertheless, he accepted his lot with good grace. Maybe at some point he could get back to proper, front-line policing.

He tipped the last few drops from his watering can into one of the plant pots before refilling it from the tap above the sink he'd had installed in the conservatory. The irony of using purified drinking water to irrigate his plants, while there was a downpour of biblical proportions cascading down outside, was not lost on him. Not for the first time, he resolved to install a water butt outside so as to take advantage of nature's own water supply.

He continued absently on his routine watering circuit while contemplating his future. The following week would see his fiftieth birthday, but there was little to celebrate; he was single, had few friends, and now, no job satisfaction.

He shook his head, tucked the watering can underneath the sink, and retreated to the living room to watch some mindless daytime TV as a respite from fretting about the future.

***

Doctor Peter Simmons was feeling upbeat. The Thomas Lewis/ Saturn vaccine had been swiftly approved by regulators in the UK, the European Union, Australia, and the USA. Regulators throughout most of Africa and Latin America soon followed suit. Russia, India, and China remained the only large countries reluctant to approve the vaccine, each still racing to develop their own versions.

Manufacturing was now underway in four major drug companies, which together provided a capacity to produce almost twenty-five million doses per week. The rollout of the vaccine to the public was continuing at pace, and little by little, lockdown restrictions in most developed countries were beginning to be relaxed.

In short, the vaccine programme was an absolute triumph.

The motivation of the Thomas Lewis development team had suffered a devastating hammer blow when Felicity had been so brutally murdered, and the shadow hanging over the team persisted for weeks. As well as being a brilliant vaccinologist, she had also been a great leader and motivator, and her loss had affected many of the team profoundly. There was also the lingering fear that perhaps other members of the team might be in danger, though no-one could begin to imagine why.

And yet Peter, in spite of his youth and relative inexperience, had succeeded in lifting them up.

'What would Felicity have wanted us to do?' he had asked, answering his own rhetorical question by insisting she would have wanted them to press on and deliver the lifesaving vaccine to the world.

Before long, the team had put their fears and doubts behind them and launched themselves back into their work with renewed vigour.

And now, fifteen months after Felicity's death, her work had come to fruition: many thousands of lives had been saved and, once again, science had come to the rescue of mankind. The war wasn't over yet, but the end was in sight.

Yes, Peter had every reason to feel elated. And it didn't hurt that he had now become something of a celebrity, frequently asked to appear on national TV to proffer his expert opinion on matters pertaining to the coronavirus, the vaccine, and indeed to disease control in general. There was no doubt that he could, whenever he chose, quit the world of scientific research for a far more lucrative career as a TV personality.

No hurry, he thought. *In any case, there's unfinished business to attend to first.*

Chapter 6

Tessa Blackmore lay on her back, legs apart and knees raised, encouraging her husband, James, with increasingly urgent moans as he thrust into her, faster and faster. As she sensed he was about to reach his climax, she gave a cry of ecstasy, digging her fingers into his buttocks and pulling him to her; this spurred him on even further. Finally, he released a last shuddering groan, and she felt his full body weight ease down on her for a moment before he rolled off to one side, panting heavily.

As her husband's breathing gradually settled to a steady rhythm, she reached for the spare pillow which lay on the floor alongside the bed, raising her hips and slipping the pillow beneath her bottom.

'That was wonderful,' she breathed, huskily, easing herself back to begin the thirty minutes which she would spend in that position to allow the millions of sperm now inside her to do their work. 'Maybe we'll be lucky this time,' she whispered.

James did not respond; he had already drifted off to sleep.

This was the seventh consecutive night they had had intercourse, and probably the last time it would be worth trying during her current cycle.

She had to admire her husband's patience for three weeks out of every month, and his stamina during the fourth, but in spite of all her encouraging moans and words, the truth was that she derived little enjoyment from sex of late, and not once in the past eight months had she experienced an orgasm during intercourse. Sex had become nothing more than a means to an end: to conceive a second child.

It was almost a year since Zoe's tragic death at the age of just three months, but she remembered it as though it were yesterday. Sudden Infant Death Syndrome was the diagnosis, or 'Cot Death' as it is more commonly known. According to the doctors, such deaths were incredibly rare, a fact that offered Tessa and James no solace whatsoever, and neither did the assertion that no-one could say for sure what were the causes of such tragic events. Tessa was consumed by guilt, however; she was convinced that she was somehow responsible for Zoe's death. Had she laid her baby down in the wrong position? Wrapped her up too warmly? Or not warmly enough? In spite of the doctors' assurances that none of these things could have caused her baby's death she continued to torture herself, trying to explain the inexplicable.

James had been incredibly supportive during those dark days, and although she could never, ever, fully come to terms with Zoe's death, she finally came to accept that her baby was gone and there was nothing she could do to bring her back. As she and James talked it through, they gradually reached the conclusion that the best way forward for both of them would be to have another child and try to move on.

But it just wasn't happening for them.

Before conceiving Zoe, Tessa had been on the pill for around four years, while she and James established themselves, bought their modest two-bedroomed apartment, and ensured they were financially equipped to bring up a child in comfort and security. They were frankly astonished, but delighted, when Tessa fell pregnant within a month after coming off the pill. Yet now, eight months after she and James had started trying again for a child, it seemed destined not to be.

Chapter 7

In the early days of the pandemic, the government had been heavily criticised for its handling of the crisis. It was said that they had learned nothing from the mistakes made during the original coronavirus outbreak, some years earlier.

They were slated for being too slow to introduce lockdowns, too quick to lift them, and too casual about enforcement.

They were slammed for not acting hard and fast enough on international travel restrictions.

The test, trace, and isolate system introduced was widely perceived as chaotic and ineffective.

And the seemingly knee-jerk reaction to opening and closing schools was deeply unpopular with the public and the teaching profession alike.

As the infection rate surged, the National Health Service came under intense pressure, with hospital intensive care wards overflowing, and profoundly sick patients having to be treated in regular wards, operating theatres, and even corridors. Erratic and insufficient supply of personal protective equipment such as gowns and masks exacerbated the problem, and when doctors and nurses themselves began to fall sick in ever-increasing numbers, the government was, again, roundly criticised.

The opposition, while professing to offer a constructive and supportive approach during a time of national crisis, had in fact milked the situation for every shred of political advantage that they could. The government's thirteen-point lead in the opinion polls had, in the space of just a few short months, turned into a three-point deficit.

Peregrine Hartley-Briggs, Junior Health Minister, had done his best to keep his head down during those dark days, preferring to allow his boss, the Secretary of State for Health and Social Care, and *his* boss, the Prime Minister, to take the flak.

Now though, finally, there was a good news story to tell. The game changer was the vaccine: it had proved to be outstandingly effective against the original strain of the virus and, so far, almost all of the variants which had subsequently emerged. Around eighty percent of the UK population had been fully vaccinated, and the worst of the lockdown restrictions had been lifted. The public were finally starting to feel good again.

Peregrine was, if he said so himself, a smart political operator, and he judged the shift in public mood perfectly, picking just the right moment to start relieving his boss of the onerous task of leading the regular televised public briefings at Downing Street. He did so with great aplomb, invariably preceding his answers to the often-inane questions from journalists and the public alike with something like 'That's an incredibly important question'. Having puffed up the questioner with such a prelude to his answer he would then make sure he addressed them by their first name. His final tactic in cementing his image as 'one of them' was to downplay his upper crust, double barrelled name, insisting he preferred to be known as simply 'Perry Briggs'. Before long, 'Perry' had become the public face of the outstandingly successful vaccination programme.

***

'Perry' had just come off set after leading the government's latest televised TV briefing on the status of the fight against the coronavirus.

'Fucking journalists …' he muttered to his waiting assistant, as soon as he was off set and out of sight of the cameras, 'barely got a handful of brain cells between the lot of them.'

She took his papers from him without passing comment.

In spite of his irritation with the press – and the public – he knew his strategy was working well. His boss, the Health and Social Care Secretary, was deeply unpopular with the public, and it was only a matter of time before he would be thrown to the wolves. Peregrine's star was in the ascendency, and he would clearly be first choice as a replacement. And then it would be just two years until the next general election. The Prime Minister's public standing had also taken a big hit over his perceived ineptitude in the handling of the pandemic, and the party would surely want to ditch him before the election. With his new-found public profile and popularity, 'Perry' would be in with a good shot at the top job.

Yes, things were panning out very nicely indeed.

***

Amanda Frobisher was head of the ONS, the Office for National Statistics, and a key member of SAGE, the Scientific Advisory Group for Emergencies.

The ONS provided the UK government with statistics on any number of subjects ranging from air pollution to performance of the economy, and everything in between. But during the pandemic, the vast majority of its resources were devoted to the study of the statistics related to the spread and control of the disease: number of new cases, number of hospitalisations, number of deaths, prevalence of new variants, progress of the vaccination programme, and so on. These data were collated every day and submitted to SAGE, who in turn would advise the government to assist them in their decision making.

Amanda was sometimes called upon to stand in front of the TV cameras alongside the Prime Minister or Health and Social Care Secretary, or – increasingly of late – Junior Health Minister, Peregrine Hartley-Briggs. She would go through the latest data, presented in simplified form by means of multi-coloured charts for the consumption of the British public. She wasn't a natural presenter, and hated these public appearances, unlike Peregrine, who seemed positively to revel in them.

Although she didn't particularly like him, she realised that Hartley-Briggs was an up-and-coming star in the government, and that he had the ear of the PM. She would sometimes seek his advice about what items, amongst the plethora of data collected every day, to highlight for government attention. Some of it was obvious; the headline figures in relation to the pandemic were always eagerly awaited, but what about the myriad of other data, unrelated to the spread of the virus?

One thing, in particular, had caught her attention in recent weeks. It seemed that, over the past few months, there had been something of a decline in the birth rate in the UK. It wasn't a huge drop, and analysis of the data indicated a statistical significance of only 90%. That meant there was a one in ten chance that there were no underlying causes at work at all, and the apparent drop in birth rate was merely a statistical fluctuation which would, in time, correct itself. She was a scientist, and her scientific brain told her 90% significance was not sufficient for reliable conclusions to be drawn. Yet her instincts told her otherwise. She decided to discuss the matter with Peregrine.

'Thank you my dear,' he said, in typically superior, condescending tone, 'for coming to me with this matter. You've done exactly the right thing.'

Patronising bastard, she thought, but she was still glad to have shared her concerns.

'Now, as you have explained,' he continued, 'it is quite possible that there's nothing in this at all … that it's just a chance wobble in the figures.'

'Well, yes, but—'

He raised a finger, cutting her off mid-sentence. 'Even if that's not the case, it's hardly anything to get too excited about, is it? The birth rate has been soaring in recent years, so a little levelling off might actually be a good thing.'

'Well, I wouldn't disagree with that, but if there *is* an actual causality at work here, we should at least find out what it is … in case it results in some other – perhaps much more undesirable – effects.'

'Yes, yes … of course,' he soothed, 'and I'm not for one moment suggesting we ignore the data, but it's a matter of priorities. Right now, the government's bandwidth is fully occupied on dealing with the pandemic, and that's the issue which the public want us to be concentrating on.'

She knew he was right … perhaps she should have kept this to herself for the moment.

'Look,' he said, placing a hand on each of her shoulders – an unwelcome gesture which made her involuntarily recoil – 'you have fulfilled your obligations by bringing this to a government minister. It's down to me now to judge when and whether to raise it further.'

In spite of her instinctive dislike of the man, this was, indeed a comforting thought.

'Now,' he continued, 'I suggest you keep this matter under observation at a low level and if it *does* prove to become statistically significant, come and see me again. I'll take full responsibility for deciding if and when it's appropriate to escalate the subject.'

She came away from the meeting feeling that some of the weight had slipped from her shoulders, yet still there was an underlying uneasiness.

Chapter 8

Tessa Blackmore stared in disbelief at the bespectacled doctor sitting opposite as he summarised the results of the tests that she and James had undertaken.

'Well, I'm pleased to say, Mrs Blackmore, that there are no indications of any problems or abnormalities in your reproductive system; as far as I can see, everything looks perfectly normal.'

'And what about me?' said James.

'No problems there either,' said the doctor. He pushed his spectacles up his nose a little as he scanned the papers on the desk in front of him. 'Your sperm count is in the upper quartile of all men in the UK and the sperm themselves are of good quality.'

Tessa shook her head, puffing out her cheeks as she expelled a long, steady breath. 'Then why on earth can't I get pregnant?'

The doctor removed his glasses, biting thoughtfully on one of the arms for a moment before laying them on the desk. 'Well, there's every reason to suppose it may yet happen. How long did you say you've been trying for a baby?'

'Ten months,' she sighed.

He tipped his head to one side, pursing his lips. 'That's not so very long,' he opined. 'Many couples take much longer than that to conceive.'

'But when we had Zoe ...' she began. But even as she uttered the words, she felt the tears well up, burning her eyes. 'I – I'm sorry ...'

James took her hand, giving it a comforting squeeze. 'What Tessa is saying is that, last time, she fell pregnant within a month of coming off the pill. So what's different now?'

The doctor pushed a box of tissues across the desk towards Tessa, who took a couple, dabbing her eyes.

'Try not to upset yourself, Mrs Blackmore. It's still relatively early days. The tests all look satisfactory, so it may just be chance that you conceived so quickly last time while it's taking longer now.'

She nodded, sniffing as she regained her composure. Deep inside though, she just *knew* that something wasn't right.

The doctor gave a reassuring smile – which somehow gave no reassurance at all. 'I suggest you just keep trying for a while longer. Now, you know how to identify your most fertile days, don't you?'

'Yes, of course,' she replied, a little more sharply than she had intended.

'Well, you should have a window of around six days every month in which you could conceive, so keep trying on those days and, with a little luck, I'm sure it will happen for you.'

Tessa remained unconvinced as she and James left the hospital.

***

As they drove home, James and Tessa barely exchanged a word. All Tessa's instincts told her that merely carrying on in the same way as they had been doing for the last ten months just wasn't going to work, and she could tell from James's demeanour that he knew it too.

Once they arrived home, James made them some coffee and they sat together on the couch to talk things over.

'You know,' said James, 'it would almost have been better if the tests *had* identified some problem. At least then there might be something positive which could be done about it. This way it's just … oh, I don't know … unresolved.'

'I know,' she replied.

'I guess all we can do is keep trying … like the doctor said.'

'We both know there's no point,' she sighed.

'Oh, I don't know … I rather look forward to our special week each month,' he said, leaning over to nibble her ear.

'Idiot!' she laughed, grabbing a cushion and playfully thumping him over the head with it.

'Ha! Knew that would raise a smile,' he said.

She kissed him on the cheek. 'Well, we can carry on with that anyway, but I think we should reconsider some of the other options we discussed.'

He pulled back in surprise. 'You mean adoption? But you know how difficult that is just now ... we already looked into it. For whatever reason, the demand for children to adopt seems to have gone through the roof just recently.'

'I've been looking into some other ways ... ways which could enable us to jump the queue.'

His brows knitted together. 'I'm not sure what you're getting at.'

'Take a look at this,' she said, reaching for her iPad which was lying on the coffee table in front of them.

She flipped open the case and, with a few taps and swipes called up the website she sought.

'See,' she said, passing him the device.

On the screen was a photograph of a beautiful baby girl, olive skin, probably Asian. The name of the website was 'babiesnet1437.onion'; the strapline was 'The child you always wanted'.

Chapter 9

'How on earth do you even know how to access this "dark web" thing?' spluttered James, as he struggled to come to terms with what his wife had put to him.

'Ruben showed me,' she said. 'Please don't be angry with me.'

Ruben was Tessa's brother. He worked in I.T. and was something of an expert on computers and all things to do with the internet. He and Tessa had always been very close, but even so, James was surprised that Ruben would have helped her embark on a road which he felt sure she shouldn't be going down. In truth, all James knew about the dark web was what he had picked up from the media, but what he *had* heard, he certainly didn't like. He kept his feelings in check, though, and decided to give his wife a chance to explain.

He emitted a deep sigh before asking, 'So what exactly *is* the dark web anyway?'

'Well,' she said, 'as far as I understand from Ruben, it's basically a huge collection of websites that you can't find with a standard search engine like Google.'

'O...K – well, how do you even find the kind of sites you're looking for then?'

'You have to have a special browser called "Tor" ... Ruben put it on my iPad for me and showed me how to use it to find what I was looking for.'

A hollow, empty feeling swept through him at the realisation that his wife had resorted to this dubious course of action without even feeling able to discuss it with him. He swallowed back the urge to give voice to his disappointment and decided instead to try to understand what was involved.

'But is this ... I mean is it actually legal? Everything I've heard about this "dark web" suggests it's used for all sorts of criminal activity.'

'Well, Ruben says it's not illegal to access the dark web, and in fact there's quite a lot of perfectly legal activity conducted on it, but ...'

'But what?' said James.

'While it's true that although there *are* plenty of legitimate activities on the dark web, there are also a hell of a lot which are certainly *not* legitimate. Look, I only want to find a way that we can have a family again. I don't want to even go near any of the really scary stuff.'

He fell silent, taking some moments to digest what his wife had told him. But now it was time to move on from the generalities of this murky underbelly of the internet and address the real issue facing them.

'But *buying a baby,* must surely be illegal.'

The tears welled up in her eyes and, seconds later, the dam burst; she dissolved into an uncontrollable fit of sobbing, her shoulders heaving.

He moved to put his arms around her, but she pulled back sharply, pushing him away. 'How can you be so cruel as to put it like that? As if a baby – a beautiful human being – can be regarded as a mere commodity to be bought and sold.'

'I ... I'm sorry,' he whispered, his heart pierced as he saw the anguished look in her eyes, 'I just ...' He couldn't find the right words.

His wife was in full flow now. 'How is it any different from a legal adoption? Tell me that.' Her eyes challenged him for a response.

'Oh Tessa ... it *is* different. Children who are put up for adoption have no proper home. For them, to be taken into a loving family environment is a lifeline.'

'And why do you think these babies are in any better position? If you could open your mind and take the time to read all the details on the website, you'll see that they only offer babies who have no other chance in life. Most have lost their parents in wars or have been born into violence and mistreatment. For them, a loving family environment *is* their only lifeline.'

For James, such words of reassurance on a website – particularly one operating in the shadows like this one – held little credence. But with his wife in such obvious distress this was not the time to voice such concerns. Once again, he moved to put his arms around her; this time she relented, laying her head against his chest, sobbing softly.

'I'm sorry Tessa … it's just a hell of a lot to take in all at once. Just give me a little time. I *will* read all the details on the website, and then we'll talk about it some more.'

'You mean it?' she breathed, lifting her head and searching his eyes.

'Yes … I do,' he said, brushing back a few strands of her hair and kissing her lightly on the forehead.

***

They did talk about it some more – lots more. Now, three days later, James's initial shock and resistance had softened somewhat, though he still had significant reservations.

'Are you sure you want to go ahead with this?' he said. 'Shouldn't we just keep trying for a baby ourselves as the doctor suggested?'

'It's not going to work, James. I don't care what the tests showed or what the doctor said … I just *know* that something's wrong.'

'You can't *know* … maybe it's just—'

She cut him off. 'I *do* know. Call it women's intuition … call it what you like, but I know it's not going to work. Now do you want to have a family or not?'

'Of course I do … you know I do.'

'Then this is the only way,' she insisted.

When he saw the fierce determination in her eyes, he knew it would be useless to argue; he emitted a deep sigh. 'OK, look … *if* we're going to seriously consider doing this, there are a lot of things we need to look into.'

Her expression softened. 'Like what? Let's go through it all together.'

'Well,' he replied, 'for a start we need to understand whether it's legal.'

'OK,' she said, leaning forward, 'I've already checked all that out.'

'You have?'

'Uh huh … I've checked out a lot. Look, it's true that offering a baby for sale on the internet is not strictly legal, and the same goes for buying one …'

James couldn't help reflecting on his wife's furious reaction some days ago when *he* had dared to refer to the arrangement as buying and selling of human beings. He let it pass.

'… but there are ways to get around this,' she continued.

'Hmm,' he muttered, tilting his head enquiringly, 'and how does that work?'

'Well … it's all explained on the website. We present the whole thing as surrogacy, which *is* legal. We say that your sperm has been implanted in a surrogate mother and then the baby can be legally registered to us.'

'But surely a DNA test would prove that wasn't true.'

'Yes, but apparently, no-one normally asks for a DNA test to be done. As long as both we, and the surrogate mother, have an agreement, the authorities just accept that.'

'But there *is* no surrogate mother,' he protested.

She broke eye contact. 'The company – Babiesnet – can provide all the necessary paperwork.'

'Oh, Tessa … this all sounds pretty shady.'

'Maybe, but it's not like we'd be doing anything really criminal is it?'

'W…ell, I—'

'I mean who's going to get hurt?'

He didn't have an answer to her question, and he knew full well she wasn't expecting one; he changed tack. 'Alright, assuming all that works OK, there's still the question of payment … I mean, is it legal to be paying for surrogacy?'

'Yes, it is. For a UK surrogate it's considered to be "expenses", but in some countries it's OK to pay a fee on top of expenses. Babiesnet can sort out the relevant arrangements for the country that the baby comes from.'

He fell silent, astonished that Tessa had gone into this whole thing in such detail. It was obvious, by now, that she would not be easily dissuaded. And, actually, he was just as keen as she was to rebuild their family. Nothing could replace little Zoe, but another child might ease the pain and allow them to move on. Maybe she was right: maybe this *was* the best way.

'Alright,' he said, 'suppose we *were* to go ahead with this … how much would it cost?'

He saw the hope blossom in her eyes as she leant forward. 'It varies according to age, sex, and ethnic origin of the child, but …'

'But what?' he asked, puzzled at her sudden reticence.

'Here,' she said, grabbing her iPad, 'take a look.'

A few taps and swipes later, she tilted the device towards him. The photograph on the screen was of a beautiful baby, probably just a few months old, pale skinned, with an improbably dense mass of dark hair for such a young baby. A delightful picture, but why was she showing him this?

'She's gorgeous, isn't she?' enthused Tessa.

'Well, yes but …'

And then it dawned on him.

'You … you've actually chosen the baby you want?' he gasped, in disbelief.

'Only if you want her, too,' she said.

'But … oh, I don't know, Tessa. This is all so sudden.'

'Not for me, it isn't. I've been looking for ages, and … well, she's just perfect, isn't she?'

He fell silent, gazing at the image on the screen. The child was undeniably beautiful, but the thought that his wife had gone so far down this road, without even consulting him, was deeply unsettling.

'She's beautiful,' he agreed 'but—'

Before he could complete his sentence, it all came tumbling out. 'Her name is Luriana … but that's only temporary … we can choose whatever name we like. She's only three months old … born in Albania, but her mother is a prostitute and cannot care for her. We could give her a much better life here in England. What do you think?'

James puffed out his cheeks, expelling a long, steady stream of air. 'Oh wow, Tessa … I don't know … this is a hell of a lot to take in. Why didn't you talk to me about this earlier?'

'Well she's only just become available.'

He shook his head. 'Not just this particular child … I mean the whole idea.'

'I wanted to research it properly before we discussed it, but then when Luriana became available, I … well we're discussing it now, aren't we?'

'I guess we are,' he sighed.

Tessa grasped his hand. 'Look, we need to make a quick decision … I'm sure there will already be other couples interested in her right now. We'll have to be the first to pay a deposit if we're not to lose her.'

He still had a myriad of questions, but when he met her gaze, the way her eyes shone with hope melted him; he knew a tipping point had been reached.

'You're really set on this child, aren't you?' he murmured, still not quite able to take it all in.

'She's perfect, isn't she?'

There was no going back now. 'How much would we have to find?'

She fixed him with a pleading expression. 'The deposit to secure her is twenty-five thousand pounds.'

He had really had no idea what to expect, but that figure rocked him back. 'Twenty-five *thousand* … that's just a *deposit*?'

She nodded. 'And another twenty-five thousand on delivery of the baby.'

He was reeling now. 'So fifty thousand total?'

She gripped his hand more tightly, locking eyes with him. 'I know it's a lot, but … well, just look at her, James – she would make our lives complete.'

'Alright, alright,' he whispered, hugging her to him, 'but where are we going to find that kind of money.'

'We have the inheritance from my father … that's over seventy thousand.'

'Well, yes,' he agreed, 'but that was earmarked to help us move up from this apartment to somewhere with more space.'

'But that's the whole point … if we are unable to start a family, we won't *need* more space. I'd rather spend some of the money to get our family started. We can always wait a little longer to trade up … maybe take a bigger mortgage than we were planning, when the time comes.'

He smiled, giving a resigned shake of his head. 'You've got it all worked out, haven't you?'

'What do you think?' she pleaded.

He finally relented. 'Let's do it then.'
She flung her arms around his neck. 'I knew you'd love her.'

Chapter 10

Peregrine Hartley-Briggs had just dealt with the final question from journalists at the daily public coronavirus briefing on national TV. He hadn't actually answered the question but, in evading doing so, he had at least managed to slip in one of the soundbites calculated to feature in all of that evening's news bulletins.

'And so, as you can see,' he oozed, 'we are winning not only the battle, but also the war.' He liked that one. 'Thank you, Lucy,' he said, shutting up the hapless journalist before she could have another go at extracting an answer from him, 'for your incredibly important question. And that's it for this evening.

'But let me close,' he added, looking directly into the camera, 'by thanking the public for the Herculean efforts that each and every one of you has made in complying with government guidelines to help defeat this invisible enemy.'

He gathered his papers and turned away from the camera followed by Amanda Frobisher, head of the Office for National Statistics. She had been alongside him throughout the briefing, and he had constantly praised her for her 'invaluable expertise'. In truth though, she had been way too honest and open about the public health risks still remaining; he would have to reconsider the wisdom of putting her in front of the cameras in future.

'Fucking journalists ...' he stormed, as he passed his papers to his waiting assistant, 'they couldn't dream up more crass and stupid questions if they tried. Still, I got the strapline about the battle and the war in ... that'll be all over the news this evening.'

'It will ... a masterstroke if you don't mind me saying,' replied his assistant.

He wasn't entirely sure whether there was a hint of sarcasm in her voice, but he gave her the benefit of the doubt. Anyone with tits like that and such an enticing smile deserved the benefit of the doubt.

'Why, thank you my dear,' he said. 'It was rather good, if I say so myself.'

***

As he settled into the back seat of the taxi, he loosened his tie, releasing a heavy sigh within the surgical mask he was obliged to wear on any form of public transport. It had been an exhausting day: most of his morning had been spent in the House of Commons, attending a particularly fractious debate on a forthcoming bill aimed at giving the police greater powers to control public disorder at demonstrations and other mass gatherings.

In his opinion, such legislation was long overdue: since the advent of the pandemic there had been a disturbing upsurge in such demonstrations. The loony left were objecting to just about every measure the Government had implemented in an effort to control the disease. They didn't like the lockdown measures, they didn't like the travel restrictions, and they especially didn't like the vaccination certificates introduced to allow a cautious re-opening of theatres and sporting events. Fucking morons didn't even see the irony inherent in their actions: crowding together, yelling and screaming, spreading the virus even as they objected to the very measures designed to protect them from it.

Naturally, the Labour opposition were opposing the bill, citing infringement of civil liberty and other such liberal-minded poppycock. And, predictably enough, the various minor parties were lining up with Labour: as usual, they'd seize on absolutely any opportunity to try to inflict a defeat on the Government, regardless of the subject at hand.

He'd had to miss the afternoon session in the Commons in order to prepare for the public coronavirus briefing which he'd just led, but the debate was scheduled to continue the following day, before the vote was cast. In spite of the mischievous tactics of the opposition parties, he was pretty sure the Government had the votes they needed to get it though.

Yes, it had been an exhausting day; weren't they all? There was no doubt about it, the meagre salaries paid to MPs were in no way commensurate with the gruelling workload which they had to endure. Still, if things panned out as planned, he would soon be Conservative Party Leader, and hopefully, Prime Minister. Even that lofty position didn't come with the sort of salary it deserved, but the real rewards would come later, after he stood down from politics. Ex-prime ministers could earn millions from after-dinner speeches, conference addresses, and so on. And Peregrine was, leaving all false modesty aside, an extremely accomplished public speaker.

However, that was all in the future. He needed a way of garnering sufficient income right now to fund his extravagant lifestyle. He had come from a wealthy family and had inherited a considerable sum from his late parents, but it was surprising just how easily he had burned through that money.

To begin with, his elegant three-story town house in Kensington had set him back over fifteen million pounds. The customised Rolls Royce which sat in its underground garage, and rarely saw the light of day, had set him back another two million. And then there was the gambling: somehow, every time he was on a winning streak, some bad luck would turn up just at the wrong moment. His sexual preferences did not come cheaply either. He could only achieve real sexual satisfaction when a certain degree of pain was inflicted on him: not too little, but not too much. It was a skill which few of the call girls he had experienced had truly mastered. Furthermore, in his position, it was essential to maintain the utmost discretion. The high-class girls who could provide the services he required, and could be relied upon for such discretion, were very expensive indeed.

No, if he were to rely entirely on his MP's salary, even supplemented by inflated expense claims, he would not be able to maintain his current standard of living. Fortunately, though, he had found a way to turn the current public health situation to his advantage.

***

As he approached his glossily painted Georgian front door he glanced at his watch: just after 8 p.m. Plenty of time to check up on his non-ministerial business interests before settling down to watch himself on the 9 p.m. news bulletin. He always made a point of watching himself back on TV after every public appearance; it helped him hone his already-formidable public speaking skills. He knew just how important it was to keep the pace of delivery measured, judge the right moments to pause for effect, know when to inject a little humour, and when to look humble or contrite. Yes, Peregrine knew only too well the importance of style over substance for an ambitious politician, and he was determined to become the absolute master of his craft.

He fumbled in his pocket for his door key, inserting it into the lock and turning it, before pushing the heavy door inward. He stepped into the expansive hallway and punched in the code to silence the insistent bleeping of his intruder alarm before shrugging off his jacket and hanging it over the newel post at the foot of the stairs.

He made for his study, which led directly off the hallway, heading straight for his desk and pressing the power switch on his laptop. As he waited for the device to complete its power-up sequence, he stepped over to the cocktail cabinet in the corner of the room, pouring himself a generous measure of his favourite Islay single malt whisky, adding a dash of water from the crystal decanter alongside.

He took a sip of the amber fluid, swirling it around in his mouth, savouring the smoky, peaty flavour for a few moments, before allowing the fiery liquid to course down his throat. Issuing a satisfied sigh, he moved back to his desk and sat down in the deep-buttoned leather-upholstered chair.

The laptop had, by now, finished its start-up routine and settled on the home screen. He tapped in his password – *PM2besoon* – and navigated his way through a couple of layers of protection to the website he sought - *babiesnet1437.onion.*

On this occasion there was only one new enquiry – a little disappointing when compared with the two or three which usually came in every day. However, it was a very promising enquiry: instead of the usual tentative first approach, this woman – one Tessa Blackmore – had actually chosen the baby she wanted and had indicated she was ready to pay the full asking price. He checked his database containing details of all the babies he had procured: ah yes – the Albanian child, named Luriana. He had paid the equivalent of just seven hundred pounds to her desperate mother: a comparative bargain for such a photogenic baby. With an asking price of fifty thousand pounds, even after all the costs associated with importing the child and sorting out all the paperwork, his profit would be over forty-five thousand pounds. However, since this client appeared to be so eager to procure this particular baby, there was no harm in pushing things a little further. He composed a response to her enquiry.

Dear Mrs Blackmore – Thank you for your valued enquiry. As you will appreciate, a beautiful baby such as Luriana has attracted considerable interest. In fact I already have two other prospective clients who wish to adopt her. One has offered to pay sixty thousand pounds, a figure which the other bidder has been unable to match, so unless you are able to improve on that figure, I'm afraid I will have to let Luriana go to a new home with that client. Somehow, though, I sense that you and Luriana would be the perfect fit, so I do hope you will be able to come up with a suitably improved offer. – Best wishes, Babiesnet.

He pressed 'send' before settling back in his chair and taking another sip of his whisky. He called up the spreadsheet which set out his profit and loss account. Over the past month he had sold thirty-one babies, generating income of just over £1.4 million. After deducting all expenses, his net profit for the same period was around £1.1 million. He smiled; a million-plus per month was a decent enough return, but it was only going to get better. With the gradually falling birth rate, the number of enquiries he was receiving was slowly but steadily increasing. It wouldn't be long before he would be netting £2 million or even £3 million a month.

He was, however, concerned about Amanda Frobisher, Head of the Office for National Statistics. She had already detected the initials signs of a fall in the birth rate and, although he had placated her for the moment, it wouldn't be long before she established a statistically significant downward trend. She was no idiot, and if he didn't act on her advice, she would quickly realise he was stalling. Then who knew what she might do? If this matter could not be kept quiet, then the full weight of available government resources might be brought to bear on it. If that happened, it would become increasingly risky to continue with his operation.

As he contemplated this disturbing potential sequence of events, he began to gravitate towards the inevitable conclusion that Amanda would somehow have to be dissuaded from spilling the beans.

His thoughts were interrupted by a ping from his computer, alerting him to an incoming message on the Babiesnet site. He clicked to open it.

Re. Luriana – I have discussed the matter with my husband, and we are willing to pay £65,000 ... £30,000 deposit and the balance when she is delivered to us – Tessa Blackmore

He smiled – she had taken less than twenty minutes to respond, coming up with an additional fifteen thousand pounds. He decided not to risk pushing it any further. He composed a reply.

Tessa – you have made a very wise choice. I confirm that Luriana will soon be yours. I will shortly send you details of how to place your deposit and get the ball rolling – Best wishes, Babiesnet.

He checked the clock on the wall: 8.47 p.m. In less than one hour he had earned himself around sixty thousand pounds, and all in good time to settle down and watch himself on the 9 p.m. news.

Chapter 11

Sofía Méndez smiled as she read, for the third time, the email on the screen in front of her. The job offer was from Novagen in California, one of the four pharmaceutical companies now manufacturing the vaccine jointly developed by Thomas Lewis College and her own company, Saturn Pharmaceuticals. Novagen was around three times the size of Saturn Pharmaceuticals, with huge global reach, and now they wanted Sofía to head up their entire vaccines division. They were offering to more than double her current salary, and that was before any negotiation.

If she accepted the position, it would mean a move to the USA, but that was not a problem. Although Sofía had lived all her life in the UK, she had no major ties; she was single, and both of her parents had passed away. Actually, the prospect of starting a new life in the Californian sunshine, away from Scotland's miserable climate was pretty exciting.

The initial rollout of the vaccine in the UK was nearing completion, and the only new project on the horizon at Saturn Pharmaceuticals was to liaise with Peter Simmons at Thomas Lewis College on the development of various tweaks to the vaccine to address new variants of the Coronavirus which would inevitably continue to arise over the coming months and years. That was not a particularly exciting prospect, particularly as Peter had become something of a media star and would probably soon quit his scientific career to become a TV pundit.

She would take a little while to consider her options but, inside, she was 90% of the way there already. Still, it wouldn't do any harm to give the impression that she was on the fence and would take a lot of persuading. Who knew? Maybe Novagen might improve their offer even further without any overt efforts at negotiation on her part.

Her thoughts turned to the late Felicity Maddocks, Peter's predecessor as head of the Thomas Lewis Vaccine Group. She had been a brilliant scientist, and Sofía had liked her too. The mutual professional respect between the two women had eventually grown and developed into more of a friendship, but when it came to crunch time, the issue which faced them surpassed mere friendship. In the end Sofía had accepted the inevitable: Felicity had to die for the greater good.

**

Peregrine Hartley-Briggs was sitting at his home laptop, busy checking the accounts of Babiesnet.com. Things were going very well indeed. In the last two weeks alone, he had generated income of almost £1 million with a net profit of over £800,000. If the growth of the business continued at this rate, he'd be looking at a first full year net profit of around £20 million, completely dwarfing his meagre MP's salary and comfortably funding his lavish lifestyle. He sighed with satisfaction, rising from his chair and making for the cocktail cabinet to pour himself a generous measure of single malt whisky. Just as he raised the crystal tumbler to his lips, his phone rang. He moved over to his desk and picked up the handset. It was Amanda Frobisher, head of the ONS.

'Why, hello, Amanda,' he said, 'to what do I owe the pleasure of this call?'

'It's about the stats relating to the birth rate which we discussed the other week.'

Shit ... thought I'd kicked that one into the long grass for the moment, he thought. 'Oh ... well, we've already discussed that, haven't we? We agreed the figures are not conclusive.'

'Well,' she replied, 'at that time, they weren't ... but having compiled and analysed the latest data, I can now say there is 98% confidence of a real drop in the birth rate.'

'I see,' he said, adopting his best caring, interested tone. 'So what does that actually mean?' He knew full well what it meant, but he needed to give himself time to think about how he would respond.

He thought he detected a sigh on the other end of the line before she replied. 'It means there is only a 2% chance that the dip in the birth rate is merely a random chance fluctuation. It is far more likely that there is an underlying causality … that something has happened to affect the birth rate.'

'Hmm … and do you have any idea what that "something" might be?'

'At this stage, no … but I've assigned some of my team to look for correlation with possible causal factors, such as diet, lifestyle, medication, and so on. The interesting thing, though, is that the change has happened so rapidly and affected such a large proportion of the population. It points to a whole-population causal factor rather than a factor affecting only certain individuals. We'll be thoroughly investigating that possibility.'

'This is all very interesting,' said Peregrine, 'but do we really need to worry about a bit of a drop in the birth rate? After all these Islands are already very crowded.'

Now he definitely detected a noisy expulsion of breath at the other end of the line.

'Well, it matters to couples who are trying for a baby, and it matters if the causal factor also affects some other aspect of human health. At the very least we need to *understand* what's happening; if not, we risk the possibility of failing to spot some new, emerging public health crisis.'

He realised he had badly misjudged his reply and moved to mitigate his error. 'Of course … you are absolutely right to bring this to my attention.'

'Good,' she sighed, more than a hint of sarcasm in her tone. 'I'm glad we are on the same page. So, I will continue with the investigation to gather more data and try to identify the causal factor or factors. The question is what are *you* going to do.'

Insolent bitch, he thought. *What way is that to talk to a government minister?* But this wasn't the time to pick a fight with this irritating meddler. He needed to buy some time to decide how to handle the situation.

'I will, of course, raise the matter to Cabinet level. Right now, they are fully occupied dealing with the coronavirus crisis, but they will be made aware of the invaluable work you and your team are doing on this emerging situation. Meanwhile, let me know at once of any new information you are able to discover.'

'OK,' she said. 'Please let me know how the Health and Social Care Secretary and the Prime Minister react. As I'm sure you are aware, my remit allows me direct access to the PM if I judge it necessary in the light of any situation which I judge to be injurious to the public good.'

Now he was boiling: this wretched woman was actually threatening to go over his head. He realised he had previously underestimated her.

'Of course,' he soothed, '… and absolutely right that you should have such access, in light of the critical importance of your role. But have no fear; you can count on me to ensure the PM is kept fully apprised of the situation.'

'So we're clear then?' she pressed.

'Crystal, my dear.'

She hung up without further comment.

'Goddamit!' he muttered, out loud, taking a large mouthful of his malt whisky, wincing as he swallowed too much, too quickly. 'What the fuck do I do now?'

That was a question which was to cost him most of that night's sleep.

Chapter 12

DI David Prendergast was working on a proposal to review and update National Health and Safety Guidelines for detention of suspects held in police custody. Well, at least, that's what he was supposed to be working on; in truth he was gazing beyond his computer screen at the oak tree just outside his second-floor window.

The thrush which had been coming and going for much of the last hour flitted into view and settled on the branch alongside its almost-finished nest. The creature had a bundle of what looked like dried-up grass in its beak; it hopped onto the rim of its nest and began depositing the grass inside, carefully spreading it out and working it into position. Eventually, it settled inside the nest, wriggling down and fluttering its wings, as though testing whether the structure was to its liking. Evidently it wasn't, for almost immediately, the bird took off once more; perhaps it had decided a little more padding was required.

David sighed. At least that thrush was working on something worthwhile; it had a clear objective and, it seemed, some definite idea of what constituted a successful result. That was more than he could say about his own miserable situation.

He had known, from the moment he was taken off front line policing duties, that he would become saddled with a host of pretty unsatisfying projects, but he could hardly have foreseen just how desperately tedious the work would be. He was born to do proper detective work, and he knew he was good at doing so. During his career he had chalked up an impressive record of solved cases – until that wretched case of the murder of Professor Felicity Maddocks. No detective, however good, is going to solve *every* case they encounter, but it was his misfortune that there was such intense media and public interest in that particular case which had, effectively, finished his career.

Now, though, as he contemplated the depressing prospect of working on these tiresome projects for the rest of his time in the police force, he was wondering whether he should have taken the generous early retirement package previously offered to him. Maybe, if he approached his superiors, the offer would still be on the table. Perhaps he could start afresh as a private investigator; he would be giving up a decent, regular salary for a much more uncertain income stream, but at least he'd have interesting and challenging work once again. And if the £300,000 payoff was still on offer, that would go an awfully long way to compensate for loss of income for several years.

His wistful reflection was interrupted by the trilling of the phone on his desk.

'Hi, David … it's Mark here … Mark Stevenson. Remember me?'

Mark was an old colleague of David's. They had joined the Metropolitan Police as young rookies at around the same time and progressed through the ranks at a similar rate, but their paths diverged some years ago, when Mark moved north and joined the Greater Manchester Police. David hadn't seen him or heard from him since then.

'Mark? Long time no see … how are you?'

'Oh, not bad … always busy up here … always plenty of bad guys to put away.'

David gave a wry smile, which was, of course, lost on his old friend, some two hundred miles away.

'How about you?' said Mark.

'Oh … so-so, I guess. To be honest, since I failed to solve the high-profile case of the murder of the scientist heading up the vaccine programme in London, they've put me on a load of back-office work … not really my thing.'

'I guess not. Look, actually that's why I'm calling: I've got something that might be of use to you.'

'Go on,' prompted David, his interest piqued.

'Well, you've probably heard about the bloke shot dead by our guys up here in Manchester on Monday.'

'Uh, huh … you involved?'

'No ... well not in the shooting incident itself, but I'm investigating what the dead guy was up to and why he pulled a gun on a copper. Turns out he was a professional hit man ... he knew he'd be going down for life if he was arrested, so he tried to shoot his way out of a corner, even though there were firearms officers present.'

'Oh, I see ... but why do you think that this case would be of interest to me?'

'I was just coming to that. Among his possessions was a mobile phone ... registered to a Professor Felicity Maddocks. That's your vaccine scientist, isn't it?'

Now his friend had David's full attention; he sat bolt upright in his chair, pressing the phone more tightly to his ear. 'Yes, it is. You think he might be her killer?'

'Well, it's got to be a strong possibility, don't you think?'

'Absolutely ... I've always suspected her murder was a professional hit. Anything interesting on the phone?'

'Well, it looks as though he's never bothered to do anything with it since he acquired it, because it still seems to have all Professor Maddocks's contacts, data, etcetera on it.'

'Such as?'

'Well, it could be nothing, but Professor Maddocks's calendar shows that she was due to meet with a Sofía Méndez on the very day of her murder.'

'Sofía Méndez?' said David. 'She's head of the vaccine programme at the pharmaceutical company manufacturing the vaccine in Scotland.'

'Well, according to the calendar, the meeting was to be down there in London, so presumably Doctor Méndez was meant to travel down to meet Professor Maddocks.'

'Hmm ...' mused David, 'curious ... I don't recall Méndez mentioning *that* during the investigation. I'll need to check back over the notes.'

'Well, here's something else for you to check: she had *another* meeting with Professor Maddocks scheduled for the following morning, but obviously that one never took place as the professor was murdered that evening. Now why would she need to have two meetings with the same person on two successive days rather than cover whatever they needed to in a single meeting?'

Now David's antennae were well and truly twitching. 'I don't know, but it's certainly interesting.'

'Isn't it? Look, I've had a word with my super and he's agreed that as the professor's murder was your case, I can pass the phone to you and let you and your guys decide whether to reopen the investigation.'

'Wow … that's great, Mark. I owe you one.'

'I've arranged a courier to get the phone to you by tomorrow. I just hope it opens some doors for you and helps get your career back on track.'

'Thanks again Mark.'

'No worries.'

***

It was around three hours since the courier had arrived with the phone, and David Prendergast was buzzing with what he had discovered.

The meeting between Doctor Méndez and Professor Maddocks on the day of her murder had been scheduled for 9.00 a.m. The second meeting was scheduled for 10.00 a.m. the following day. Why two meetings on two successive days? He could think of only two possible explanations.

Firstly, they could have simply run out of time and arranged to continue the following day, but with a 9 a.m. start, it would have to have been a very long agenda indeed to have overrun into a second day.

The second possibility was that something unexpected had cropped up resulting in the two scientists needing to arrange another meeting. He decided to contact the mobile service provider to check for records of calls made by Professor Maddocks around the time of her murder.

Jackpot! She had called Sofía Mendez at 9.41 p.m. on the very day of her murder. The duration of the call was just four minutes and seventeen seconds. For her to be calling her colleague so late in the evening after they had already been together that day, it must have been something very important or urgent. Maybe this was the call which set up their meeting for the following morning. Except she would never live long enough to make that meeting.

Why on earth didn't we check her phone records at the time of the original investigation? David chided himself. *Anyway, what's done is done ... the question is, what to do now?*

David knew that Doctor Méndez was one of the people interviewed during the original investigation into Professor Maddocks's murder. He called up the notes of the interview, which had been conducted by Kate Evans, one of the members of his original task force.

Doctor Méndez was not thought to be a key witness, based as she was in Scotland, far from the scene of the murder, and for that reason she had only been interviewed by phone, rather than in person.

It seemed she was Professor Maddocks's main contact at Saturn Pharmaceuticals, but as far as could be seen, the relationship between the two of them was purely professional. She had been unable to furnish Kate with any suggestions as to who, if anyone, might have had a motive for the murder. She had been ruled out of the investigation early.

But here was the thing which really stood out: there was no mention in the interview notes of any meeting between the two women in London on the very day of Professor Maddocks's murder. Neither was there anything about the phone call or the further meeting arranged for the following day. Odd.

He picked up the phone and dialled Kate's number. She picked up after two rings.

'Oh, hi sir ... good to hear from you.'

'No need for the "sir" bit anymore, Kate: on paper I may still hold the rank, but I'm certainly not doing the job.'

'Oh ... I ... well, to me you're still "sir" ... sir.'

He chuckled. 'As you wish, then. Look, I've come across some new evidence which may be relevant to the Felicity Maddocks murder.'

'You have? But that case is closed, isn't it?'

'Officially, yes ... but I'd like to follow up this lead anyway ... just in case ... and I'm hoping you might be able to help.'

'Me? Well, if you think so ... how can I help?'

'Do you remember Sofía Méndez ... the scientist at Saturn Pharmaceuticals.'

There was a momentary pause before she replied. 'Yes ... she was head of their vaccine programme.'

'And you interviewed her as part of the murder investigation, right?'

'Yes, but only on the phone. As far as I recall, she wasn't able to shed any light on motives or possible suspects, and she certainly wasn't a suspect herself. Why do you ask?'

'Bear with me for a moment and I'll explain. Look, do you recall if she said anything about when she last saw Professor Maddocks?'

She fell silent for a few moments. 'I don't know … it was quite a while ago and she wasn't really a key witness. Have you checked my interview notes?'

'I have … and there's no mention of when they last met.'

'Oh … I guess it's a question I should have asked. Rather remiss of me … I'm sorry. Is it important?'

'Well, the new evidence I've turned up indicates that she had a meeting with the victim on the very day of her murder … down here, in London.'

'What? Well, I'd certainly have remembered if she'd told me *that*.'

'I'm sure you would, Kate … and you would undoubtedly have explored what the meeting was about. And there's more … the two of them had arranged to meet again the following morning, except that Professor Maddocks was murdered before that meeting could take place.'

'Wow! You think Méndez might be implicated in the murder somehow?'

'I don't know, but in any event, it seems very strange that she didn't mention any of this when interviewed, even if you didn't ask the direct question.'

'Hmm … what should we do about it?'

'Look … the case is officially closed. I'll only be able to get it reopened if there's a compelling reason to do so.'

'Well, yes … I suppose. But the fact that she didn't mention the meetings …'

'I know … all my instincts tell me that something's not right here. Even so, the super may still take some convincing to authorise the reopening of the case. After all, the public have long since forgotten about it, and the vaccine rollout is going well. He's not going to want to commit resources to a cold case unless there's a very good chance of getting a positive result.'

'You have to try, sir.'

'I will … let's hope he's in a receptive mood.'

'Well, good luck … I hope you can convince him.'

'I'll let you know. Oh, and Kate … might be best not to mention any of this to anyone until we know whether the case is going to be reopened.'

'Of course … I won't say a word.'

Chapter 13

David was sitting opposite Detective Superintendent Damian Willcox in the spacious office which his rank conferred upon him. On the desk between them lay Felicity Maddocks's phone, open on her calendar app.

'So, as you can see,' said David, 'it seems that Doctor Méndez met with – or at least was scheduled to meet with – the victim, here in London on the day of her murder.'

'Hmm …' muttered the DSU, 'that's certainly interesting, but as you have pointed out, the two of them worked closely together on the vaccine programme. There could have been any number of legitimate reasons for such a meeting.'

'But on the very day of the murder? And for Doctor Méndez not to even mention it when interviewed?'

'Well, from what you have told me, your DC didn't even ask the question as to when Doctor Méndez had last met with the victim.'

'I know, and she realises that was a mistake … but even so, doesn't it strike you as strange that Doctor Méndez didn't volunteer that information?'

'Maybe, but it's hardly evidence of any actual wrongdoing, is it?'

'I suppose not,' admitted David, 'but what about the late evening phone call between them and the plan to meet again the following day?'

The DSU shrugged. 'It could be anything … I can't imagine a complex vaccine development programme can proceed without a few bumps in the road.'

David exhaled slowly, trying to contain his frustration at his boss's apparent complacency. 'I'm sorry sir, but this seems to me to be more than just "a bump in the road". Why would Professor

Maddocks need to call Doctor Méndez so late in the evening when they had been together anyway earlier in the day? I suspect the two of them had some major issue to resolve and arranged to meet the next day to thrash it out.'

'Sorry David but, notwithstanding your years of experience, that's nothing more than supposition on your part.'

'Maybe, but the fact that Professor Maddocks was murdered before they could even meet again … well, it sounds pretty suspicious to me.'

'Well, it may sound suspicious, but it's not hard evidence, I'm afraid.'

By now, David was boiling inside. Did his boss actually care about getting to the truth? He bit his tongue and framed his response carefully.

'I appreciate that sir, but surely it has to be worth following up.'

Willcox exhaled a weary sigh. 'So what are you asking of me, David?'

'I'd like to have the case reopened. Give me my old team back and let me dig into this new information. If Sofía Méndez is implicated, I'll find out.'

'That's one hell of an ask, David. You know how tightly resources are stretched at the moment.'

'I know, but if a highly respected scientist is implicated in the murder of a close colleague, it begs the question of motive. Who knows what the bigger picture might be?'

The DSU planted his elbows on the desk, interlacing his fingers and resting his chin on them as he expelled a long, steady stream of breath. He maintained this posture for several long seconds before responding.

'Look, David … I accept that this is interesting information, but whether it has some bearing on Professor Maddocks's murder is pure speculation.'

'So let me look into it,' persisted David.

The DSU disentangled his fingers and placed both hands flat on the desk, shaking his head. 'This is not enough to reopen the case, but I *will* allow you to do some further informal investigation. Then, if you can give me enough reason to do so, I'll consider formally reopening the case.'

David's heart leapt; it wasn't what he wanted, but it was as much as he could reasonably have hoped for. He nevertheless decided to press further.

'Thank you, sir. And can you allocate a couple of other officers to help me?'

'My God, David … you are really pushing your luck now. I already told you resources are stretched thinly.'

'Even so …' pleaded David.

'Enough!' said the DSU, his tone hardening. 'I'll tell you what I can do: there are a couple of students who have just graduated from the "Police Now" National Detective Programme who need to be allocated to their first placements. You can have one of them to help you in your preliminary investigation.'

'A complete rookie? But sir—'

'No "buts", DI Prendergast.'

The fact that the DSU had addressed him by his formal title made it clear that he would not be pushed any further. 'Of course … thank you sir. I'll get right on it.'

***

The person allocated to assist David was Neil Parker. Prior to enrolling on the National Detective Programme, he had obtained his first degree from Leeds University. Now, following completion of the two-year National Detective Programme, he was ready for his first assignment as a fully-fledged detective constable.

He was tall and skinny, with a thin, bespectacled face and short, brown hair. He looked younger than his twenty-five years. David's first impression was that he seemed rather shy and lacking in confidence. Nevertheless, this was all the help David was to be afforded so he would have to do the best he could with the hand he had been dealt.

David briefed him fully on the original case and the new information which had come to light. The young man listened intently, interrupting occasionally to seek clarification of one point or another.

'So that's the case we'll be working on,' concluded David. 'Any questions?'

'Er … so how are we going to approach it, and what part do you want me to play?'

'OK … obviously we need to know what the meeting on the day of the murder was all about, so I intend to start by interviewing Doctor Méndez.'

'Er … sir,' he said, raising his hand.

'No need for the hand up thing, Neil … you're not in a lecture class now.'

'No … right … well, as you said, this meeting could have been completely legitimate, but if Doctor Méndez *is* involved in the murder, it might be best not to let her know that you are coming to see her. I mean, you wouldn't want to give her time to fabricate a story.'

David raised an eyebrow; maybe this lad was not as wet behind the ears as it first seemed. 'That's a very good point, Neil. I intend to travel up to her place of work in Scotland and arrive unannounced to interview her.'

'That's good, sir; they made quite a thing on the training course about the value of surprise and interpretation of the suspect's reactions.'

OK, he's definitely no idiot, thought David. 'Well, I'm not sure that Doctor Méndez can be considered a "suspect" just yet, but you're quite right.'

'OK, so what do you want *me* to do?'

'Right … to begin with, I want you to stay right here while I go to interview Doctor Méndez. Depending on what I find, I may need you to access various resources or obtain information for me.'

The young man's face fell; clearly, he was hoping for a more meaningful involvement than this, but until David had spoken to Doctor Méndez he couldn't possibly decide how to utilise his inexperienced assistant. In any event, Neil did not question the instruction.

'Yes sir … anything you need … just call me.'

***

Saturn Pharmaceuticals headquarters was situated on a modern business park: the sort with predominantly low-rise buildings, generously spaced and interspersed with plenty of green spaces. The building itself was a single-story affair, clean and unfussy, with vast areas of smoked glass windows punctuating the pale grey cladding on the walls. The company name and logo were proudly displayed on an imposing marble monolith set in the centre of the immaculately groomed lawn which fronted the building. David followed the gently curving, paved path up to the main entrance, whose glass doors slid obediently open at his approach.

Inside, the spacious reception area looked more befitting a five-star hotel than an industrial unit. The floor was tiled in highly polished marble which picked up the sheen from concealed lighting around the walls. There were four informal seating areas towards the edges of the space, each set on a dark blue, circular rug. The focal point was the reception desk, above which was a large plaque bearing the words, 'Saturn Pharmaceuticals – dedicated to making lives better'.

Dedicated to making bucketloads of money, more likely, thought David as he surveyed the opulent surroundings.

Behind the desk sat an attractive young woman, with flawless makeup and dark hair, styled in an updo. She looked up and flashed him a warm smile, revealing two perfectly even rows of dazzlingly white teeth.

'Good morning, sir … how can I help you?' Her soft, Scottish burr was warm and welcoming.

He reached into his pocket and produced his warrant card. 'Detective Inspector David Prendergast, Metropolitan Police. I'd like to speak to Doctor Sofía Méndez please.'

The well-practised smile which adorned the young woman's face faltered for a moment; he guessed she wasn't used to police officers turning up out of the blue.

'Oh, I'm afraid Doctor Méndez is not here today.'

Damn it, he cursed, inwardly. This was always a possibility, and the major downside of arriving unannounced, but he had judged it a risk worth taking to retain the element of surprise. On this occasion though, it hadn't paid off.

'I see … well, can you tell me where I can find her?'

'She's attending some business meetings in London'

London? For Christ's sake, that's where I've just come from. He couldn't suppress the weary sigh which escaped his lips.

'When will she be back?'

The receptionist consulted her computer screen and, after a couple of clicks on her mouse, replied. 'Not until next Thursday, I'm afraid. I'm so sorry you've had a wasted journey … I can give you Doctor Méndez's mobile number if you want to speak to her.'

That was absolutely not what he had in mind; he needed to see her in person, look into her eyes, check her body language, assess whether she was lying. Still, her number could well be useful – already, he was beginning to formulate a plan.

'Thank you,' he said, 'that would be much appreciated.'

'Of course,' she said, looking up at her computer screen and scribbling the number on a post-it note, before handing it to him. 'Shall I let her know you'll be calling?'

That was the very last thing he wanted; once she knew he wanted to talk to her, whether by phone or in person, she would be forewarned, and the element of surprise would be lost.

'Oh, no ... that won't be necessary,' he said, though, anyway, he doubted that this girl would be able to resist letting Doctor Méndez know that the police had come calling. 'Thank you for your help.'

***

The moment he was outside the building, David called his new assistant, back in London.

'Neil, there's something I need you to do for me. It's urgent, so listen carefully.'

'Yes, sir ... what do you need?'

'If you go down to the tech department, they should be able to issue you with an IMSI catcher device. It's a—'

'I know what it is, sir: an International Mobile Subscriber Identity Catcher ... also known as a "Stingray".'

David was completely taken aback that this young man would know about such devices.

'So you know what it does?'

'Yes ... essentially, it acts as a fake mobile tower, which intercepts calls between a target mobile phone in the area and the real tower, allowing eavesdropping without the target being aware. Who are we listening in to?'

'Doctor Méndez ... turns out she's down there in London right now for some meetings.'

'Oh, so you weren't able to see her then?'

'No, but now, before I catch up with her, I want to know who she's meeting in London and what they are discussing.'

'Does she know you tried to see her?

'Not yet, but I'm guessing she'll find out soon enough.'

'Then I'll get right on it, sir; best if we can intercept some calls before she finds out you want to talk to her. We may already be too late. Give me her number.'

'OK,' said Prendergast, after reading out the number, 'let's not waste any more time talking about—'

'Click' … 'Buzz'. His young assistant had already hung up.

Chapter 14

David gazed out of the window of the aircraft at the unbroken layer of white cloud below, bathed in brilliant sunshine, in contrast to the dull and drizzly day which he knew lurked beneath. He was lost in thought, grappling with the tricky decision of how to approach his first meeting with Sofía Méndez.

His plan to catch Doctor Méndez by surprise in Scotland had been thwarted, and by the time he caught up with her, she would almost certainly be aware that he wanted to speak to her. Maybe that didn't matter: maybe she had nothing whatsoever to do with Professor Maddocks's murder; maybe her meeting with the professor on the day of her murder was completely above board and she'd simply forgotten to mention it when Kate had originally interviewed her. Maybe … but all his instincts told him otherwise. If she was forewarned of his visit, however, she would have had more than enough time to construct a perfectly credible explanation for all of her actions.

Much would depend, now, on whether David's keen young assistant had been able to set up the IMSI device and intercept some of her calls before she became aware of the fact that the police wanted to talk to her.

His thoughts were interrupted by the voice of the captain announcing that they were about to begin their descent. Moments later the engine note eased a little, and he sensed the familiar gentle change in pace and inclination of the aircraft as it approached London's Heathrow airport.

As soon as they were on the ground he switched on his mobile and called Neil Parker. He didn't waste any time on unnecessary pleasantries.

'So what have you got so far?' he barked, realising too late that his tone was far sharper than he had intended.

The young man sounded unfazed. 'OK ... she has made three calls since I began monitoring her phone. The first was to Doctor Peter Simmons, the head of the vaccine programme at Thomas Lewis College. It was a short call just setting up a meeting for tomorrow morning.'

'Nothing unusual there,' muttered David. 'They obviously work closely together on the vaccine programme. What about the other calls?'

'Right ... the second was to a Professor Julian Chambers. I've googled him and it turns out he is a virologist who worked at the University of Oxford.'

'"Worked"? Past tense?'

'Yes, he's been retired for some years.'

'So he's not involved with the vaccine programme then?'

'As far as I can ascertain, no,' replied Neil.

'Hmm ... interesting,' mused David. 'What was the call all about?'

'Sounded like confirmation of another meeting – day after tomorrow. Not much info. I'm afraid, but I got the impression that there would be several others present at the meeting.'

'OK I'll listen to the full recording later ... we're just about to get off the plane, so I'll have to sign off for a bit. Quickly though, what was the third call?'

'A Doctor Matthew Turner ... he's head of Environmental Sciences at the University of Hampshire.'

'So, another scientist or academic, but in a different field. Does he have any involvement in the vaccine programme?'

'No, I don't think so.'

'Hmm ... odd. OK, look, we're getting off the plane now. I'll call you again on my way back to the station. Then, when I get there, we can go through the full recordings together. Keep monitoring her phone for any further calls. Oh, and good work Neil,' he added, anxious to mitigate his earlier fractious tone.

'Thank you, sir.'

***

Sofía Méndez was settling into her hotel room, unpacking and hanging up the clothes she would need for the next few days in London when the trilling from her handbag announced an incoming call on her mobile. It was from the receptionist at Saturn Pharmaceuticals.

'Oh hi, Suri … what can I do for you?'

'Well, I just thought you would like to know that there was a policeman here earlier today; he said he wanted to speak to you.'

A cold chill slithered down her spine. 'A policeman? What did he want?'

'He didn't say … just that he needed to talk to you.'

Shit! Whatever this was, it couldn't be good. Nevertheless, she did her best to sound totally unconcerned. 'Did this policeman give you his name?'

'Yes,' she replied, pausing for a moment before replying, 'Detective Inspector David Prendergast.'

'Did he sound Scottish?' She doubted it with a name like 'Prendergast'.

'No, he said he was from the Metropolitan Police, in England.'

Oh shit, shit, and treble shit! If he'd travelled all the way up from London without giving any advance warning, it was a pound to a penny that he had hoped to catch her by surprise. OK, she needed to think fast now.

'Is he still up there in Scotland?'

'Well, to be honest, I don't know. I'm surprised he hasn't called you.'

'You gave him my mobile number?'

'Well yes … he seemed very keen to talk to you.'

She expelled a deep sigh. If he'd been so keen to talk to her, yet having obtained her number had not called, it could mean only one thing …

She did her best to conceal her irritation. 'Well thanks for letting me know Suri. I'm sure he'll be in touch in due course.'

She hung up.

What to do now? It was entirely possible – indeed likely – that her calls were now being monitored by the police. She wasn't completely sure about the legality of such surveillance, but she couldn't afford to take any chances. If they were listening in, when did they start? Impossible to say for sure, but the chances were that it could only have started after Suri had foolishly handed over her mobile number. She looked back through her call log; since the approximate time of the detective's visit to Saturn she had only made three calls, none of which would have contained any really damning information. It could have been worse. Now though, she needed to make quite sure that no further incriminating information could be intercepted.

The group of which she was a member generally used WhatsApp to communicate sensitive information as it was encrypted in such a way as to make it impossible – even for the police – to intercept the content of the messages. This latest development made it even more vital to exercise maximum caution. She delved into her handbag to retrieve her back-up, pay-as-you-go mobile and opened WhatsApp, selecting the group chat, and composing the following message …

Suspect my usual phone may have been compromised. I don't think anything important could have been intercepted, but as a precaution I am switching to this number until further notice. For further security all of us should communicate only by WhatsApp until we know for sure. I will explain further at our meeting this week.

Now she needed to prepare for the visit from the detective which she was sure was coming.

***

David Prendergast was back at the station with his young assistant. He listened intently to the recordings of the three phone conversations which had been intercepted. Frustratingly, he had to agree with Neil's assessment that, other than revealing the recipients of Doctor Méndez's calls, the recordings yielded little else of any value.

'And there have been no further calls since these?'

'No sir … these three were all made within thirty minutes of each other but there's been nothing in the past three and a half hours.'

'Hmm … could be nothing, but …'

'Could be that she now knows you want to speak to her and suspects that we might be listening in to her calls,' suggested Neil.

'She may have stopped using the phone or switched to some other means of communication.'

This lad certainly wasn't stupid, displaying an instinct for detective work which belied his lack of experience.

'Exactly,' agreed Prendergast.

'I'll keep monitoring her phone, just in case, but I don't think it's going to help us any further,' said Neil. 'So what do we do next?'

'Well, Doctor Méndez is most likely expecting a visit from me, so I won't disappoint her. Trouble is she'll have had time to prepare; I'll bet she's got a perfectly credible explanation for her meeting with the victim on the day of the murder, and for not mentioning it when Kate interviewed her.'

'What about the people she phoned today?' said Neil.

'Well, *if* she's guessed we intercepted the calls, she'll have tipped them off and agreed a common story.'

'I agree ... so maybe there's not much mileage in interviewing them.'

'No ... but I've been thinking about this on the drive from the airport.'

'So what's the plan?' said Neil, eagerly.

'Well,' replied Prendergast, 'there seems little point in talking to Peter Simmons: he and Doctor Méndez obviously work closely together and would have any number of perfectly valid reasons to arrange a meeting.'

'True,' said Neil, nodding.

'However, this Professor Julian Chambers character is interesting: he's been retired for some years and is apparently nothing to do with the current vaccine programme, so why would Sofía Méndez be meeting with him?'

'And,' added Neil, 'it sounded as though there would be others at the meeting too.'

'Right, but rather than interview him after he's had time to prepare, I think we should put him under covert surveillance ... if, that is, the super will commit the resources to do so.'

'Couldn't *I* do it?' pleaded Neil.

Prendergast shook his head. 'We'll need a team of at least three to mount 24/7 surveillance ... let me talk to the super and see where we go from there.'

But David wasn't optimistic; he knew Detective Superintendent Willcox only too well. His boss would want a lot more evidence than they had so far to commit the resources for a full-blown surveillance operation. He would almost certainly have to resort to the alternative plan he had come up with.

Chapter 15

Sofía Méndez had been expecting the call.

'Doctor Méndez? This is Detective Inspector David Prendergast – Metropolitan Police.'

'Oh,' she said, effecting her best impression of surprise, 'the police? Er … what's this about?'

'We have come across some new evidence pertaining to the murder of your colleague, Professor Maddocks.'

'Felicity? But that was well over a year ago.'

'Indeed … but a few new questions have now been raised. I understand you are here in London as we speak.'

'Yes, I am, but I'm not sure how I can help.'

'It would be best if we could meet in person rather than discuss it on the phone; could I come and see you today?'

'Well, yes … I suppose so, but I really can't see how I could possibly be of any help after all this time. I mean … I already spoke to one of your people at the time.'

'I appreciate that, Doctor Méndez, but as I mentioned, some new evidence has come to light.'

'Well, OK then … if you think it will help.'

'Thank you. It may or may not help but best to leave no stone unturned, as it were.'

'Of course … let's see now … I have meetings this morning, but I'm free from 1 p.m. onwards; you could join me for lunch if you wish.'

'I'd prefer not to mix business with pleasure, Doctor Méndez … how about I meet you at your hotel at around 3 p.m.?'

'Of course … I certainly wouldn't want to go against police protocol. I'm staying at the Hotel Du Vin Cannizaro House, in Wimbledon.'

'I know it,' replied David

'OK, well shall I meet you in reception then?'

'Yes, that would be fine … see you at 3 p.m. then.'

She hung up. Shame he hadn't taken up her suggestion of meeting over lunch; she had hoped a few glasses of wine might take the edge off the detective's perceptive faculties. She would have to rely instead on her own guile. She was, leaving all false modesty aside, an attractive woman, and could generally win most men over when she turned on the charm.

Now then … how best to prepare for the interview?

OK, so he said he had some 'new evidence'; what could that be? She had no idea, but she had to prepare for every eventuality. It was more than likely that he'd have recordings of the three phone calls she'd made the previous day so she would need a good explanation for each of these, but she couldn't for the life of her see how he could have made any link between these calls and Felicity's murder. If he came up with something unexpected, she would have to improvise.

***

DI Prendergast arrived a little early. Apart from two men sitting and chatting in a corner, the reception area was deserted. He identified himself to the girl at the front desk and then took a seat in a quiet corner well away from the pair who were already seated. There was some wallpaper music playing softly in the background: not loud enough to interfere with conversation but sufficient to afford them a little privacy should anyone else turn up and sit down nearby. This would be a perfectly satisfactory location for the interview with Doctor Méndez.

It was around ten minutes later that an attractive woman appeared, picking her way down the elaborate staircase taking the due care that her high heels demanded. Aged around late thirties he guessed; long, dark hair; dusky complexion; slim, shapely figure, which her close-fitting emerald-green dress showed off nicely. *Not your stereotypical image of a scientist,* thought David.

She glanced around, swiftly establishing eye contact across the room. She approached with a slight sashay: nothing too overt, but just enough to provoke male interest. The detective smiled inwardly;

if only she knew that he was gay she would have realised she was wasting her time.

David stood up and extended his hand. 'Doctor Méndez?'

She nodded, flashing him a dazzling smile and widening her dark eyes a little. 'And you must be Detective Inspector Prendergast.'

'Thank you for seeing me at short notice.'

'Oh, please … Sofía,' she said, taking the seat opposite and crossing her legs, causing her dress to ride up her shapely thigh a little.

'So, Detective … how can I help?'

In spite of her Latin appearance, and Spanish-sounding name, there was no trace of an accent; she could easily have been born and brought up in the Home Counties.

'You said,' she continued, 'that you had some new evidence relating to Felicity's terrible murder. What have you found after all this time?'

'Unfortunately, I can't go into details of the new evidence, but it has raised a few questions which I believe you may be able to help me with.'

'Of course … anything I can do to help. Fire away.'

So far, she looked and sounded relaxed and confident; there was nothing to suggest that she was at all uncomfortable.

'Do you mind if I record our conversation? It just saves me having to take notes and speeds things up a bit.'

'Not at all … go ahead.'

Still no chink in her demeanour.

He set down the pocket recorder in the centre of the table and switched it on.

'When was the last time you spoke with Professor Maddocks before her death?'

There it was: for the first time, a flicker of doubt in her eyes. She swiftly recovered.

'Oh goodness, it was such a long time ago. Felicity and I worked closely together so we were always on the phone, online, or meeting in person. Now, let me think …'

And she clearly was – thinking that is, but not simply searching to recall something. She placed a forefinger against her chin, tilted her head, and pursed her lips. It was a good act, but Prendergast wasn't fooled; he'd lay bets she was furiously assessing the possibilities of what he might know and how best to respond.

It was several seconds before she spoke. 'Oh, you know I'm really not sure after all this time.'

He decided to give her a helping hand. 'Did you by any chance see her on the day of her murder?'

There it was again: that slight shadow flitting across her eyes. She was good; most people wouldn't even have spotted it. But he was better; he knew she was lying about being unable to recall the meeting. He could only guess what she had concluded about what had prompted his question ... she wouldn't know, of course, that he had acquired the victim's phone. It took her but a moment, though, to decide how to respond.

'Ah, yes ... I remember now. I was here in London for some meetings, and I *did* meet with Felicity that day.'

'So what did you discuss?'

'Well, we were about to submit the trial results on the vaccine for regulatory approval, but at the last minute we discovered a few slightly disturbing data in the trial results. We were discussing whether to delay the submission until these had been thoroughly investigated.'

'And ... what did you decide?'

'Well, you'll appreciate, Detective, that these things are all about balance of risk. You don't want to release a drug which may have bad side effects, but at the same time every day's delay in rolling out the vaccine would cost more lives.'

She was playing for time, and he knew it.

'So what did you decide?' he repeated.

The subtle flirting had now stopped completely; she was definitely rattled.

'Well, we ... er ... didn't reach a firm conclusion.'

'So what did you do?'

Her hesitation in replying was momentary but telling. 'We were both very tired, so we agreed to meet again the following day, but ...'

'But she was murdered before you could do so.'

'Yes ...' she whispered, grabbing a tissue from her bag and dabbing away an imaginary tear, 'absolutely tragic.'

Prendergast wasn't buying her sudden show of emotion, but he didn't want that to be obvious. 'Please ... take your time, Doctor Méndez.'

'I'm OK,' she sniffed, apparently composing herself. She screwed up the tissue and dropped it in the small waste bin alongside the coffee table between them. 'It was just such a terrible time.'

'Indeed,' said David, happy to play along with her charade. 'Are you OK to continue?'

'Yes, of course ... but I don't really see what any of this has to do with Felicity's murder.'

'Just trying to establish all her movements and contacts in the hours leading up to her death. Sometimes it helps.' He didn't elaborate further.

'Well, I hope so,' she said. 'Now, is there anything else I can help you with?'

She was fidgeting in the chair now, looking as though she was anxious to wrap this interview up as quickly as possible. The calm, self-assured confidence had evaporated.

'Just one thing: how did you eventually resolve the dilemma about whether to delay the submission of the vaccine for regulatory approval?'

There it was again: the momentary flicker of uncertainty in her eyes.

'Well, after Felicity's death, Peter took over ...'

'Doctor Simmons?'

'Yes ... we went through all the data again and came to a decision to go ahead with the submission while doing additional trials in parallel to ascertain whether there was any substantive risk of side effects.'

'And was there?'

'No ... no, it turned out the previous data were spurious.'

'Well at least that was a positive outcome.'

'Yes.' She gave a weak smile.

'Well thank you. Doctor Méndez. You've been most helpful. I won't take up any more of your time.'

They both stood up, she smoothing down the creases which had formed in the front of her dress, and he buttoning his jacket.

As they shook hands, he delivered his parting shot. 'Sadly, Professor Maddocks is no longer with us, but I assume Doctor

Simmons will be able to corroborate your account of the discussions leading up to the final submissions to the regulators?'

Her eyes flared. 'Of course. Good afternoon then.'

She turned and headed for the stairs; the studied sashay had disappeared completely now.

Chapter 16

James and Tessa had paid the thirty thousand pounds deposit, and it was now time to collect their new baby. Tessa was consumed by a melting pot of conflicting emotions: she was buzzing with excitement, but at the same time nervous as hell; overflowing with maternal instinct, yet apprehensive about whether she could really love this child like her own.

In addition to the emotional turmoil she was dealing with, both she and James were deeply uneasy about the arrangements for the physical transfer of the baby. They were to meet a representative of Babiesnet underneath a specified railway arch at midnight, which, in itself, seemed highly suspicious. Furthermore, Babiesnet now insisted that the balance of thirty-five thousand pounds be transferred to a nominated bank account before the baby could be handed over. Despite their protestations, no flexibility on these conditions could be negotiated. The only concession which was offered was that the couple would be allowed to see the baby, and the accompanying paperwork, before transferring the money. A gentle reminder that, should they back out of the deal, the deposit was non-refundable, left them with no choice but to accept.

They arrived at 11.50 p.m. The archway under the bridge was dark and forbidding; their headlights providing the only illumination. There was no-one else there and no sign of any vehicle. Tessa was immediately on edge.

'Why aren't they here?' she whispered.

'We're early,' replied James. 'Let's just wait.' He was probably just as nervous as she was, but if so, he was trying not to show it.

And they did: they waited, and waited, in a tense silence. Midnight came and went; still no-one came.

By 12.15 a.m. James had clearly had enough. 'Right – that's it. Let's get onto these bastards to find out what's going on. What's the phone number?'

'I don't have one,' Tessa wailed. 'All communication has been via the website.'

'Shit!' muttered James. 'In that case give me your—'

'Look,' she cried, clutching his arm and pointing.

As his eyes followed her pointing finger, he saw a faint pool of light reflecting from the damp brickwork under the archway. It was bouncing up and down erratically and gradually getting brighter. While they couldn't see anything beyond the bend in the road ahead of them, a vehicle was obviously approaching.

The next few seconds seemed to stretch for ever, but finally the blinding headlights rounded the bend and shone full in their faces. Both of them instinctively shaded their eyes as the vehicle approached. It slowed to a crawl and finally, with a squeal of brakes, came to a halt about thirty feet away. The driver killed the engine and extinguished the headlights, leaving just the parking lights on. As her eyes adjusted, Tessa was now able to discern that the vehicle was a dark-coloured SUV.

The tense silence which now ensued was deafening. What should they do? Get out of the car? Wait for the occupants of the SUV to emerge? The two of them exchanged an anxious, wordless glance. Eventually, James switched his own parking lights on, trying to cast a little more light onto the other vehicle. It looked as though the driver was a man, but there was no-one in the front passenger seat. Still nothing happened.

'Oh, sod this,' he muttered, reaching for the door handle, 'I'm going to—'

His words caught in his throat as the interior light of the SUV came on and the driver's door opened; the man who stepped out was tall, shaven-headed, and heavily built. James opened his own door and stepped out to face the other man.

'You Mr and Mrs Blackmore?' grunted the stranger.

'Yes ... do you have the baby?'

He did not reply but turned to open one of the back doors of his vehicle. A young woman stepped out cradling a blanket-wrapped bundle in her arms.

Tessa flung open her door and jumped out of the car. 'Is that her ... is that Luriana?'

The man did not answer her directly, instead growling, 'You got the money ready to send?'

James intervened. 'We've got the money, but we need to see the baby first.'

The man waved the young woman carrying the baby forward. As she stepped into the glow cast by the car lights, Tessa was able to see that the woman had a dark complexion and black hair. Her eyes looked haunted, anxious. A thought struck Tessa like a hammer blow: could she actually be the child's biological mother? Would these people be heartless enough to drag her all the way from Albania only to see her baby handed over to another woman?

Whether James had had the same thought she did not know, but she lost no time in approaching the other woman and asking, 'Can I hold her?'

The woman did not respond.

'She doesn't speak English,' muttered her minder.

Tessa held out her arms, as though to hold the baby, while the big man gestured for the woman to hand over the child. She hesitated for a moment, but then held the baby forward.

Tessa took the baby, gently pulling the folds of the blanket away from her face.

The flood of emotion was almost overwhelming. 'It's her ... it's Luriana. Oh, James, come and look; she's beautiful.'

He stepped towards her and gazed at the child she was holding. She did, indeed, look just like the baby they had seen on the Babiesnet website.

They were to be allowed very little time to savour the moment as the big man growled, 'OK, you need to send the money now.'

'What about the paperwork?' said James. 'We need to see that's all in order.'

The man shrugged, turning and reaching inside the car. After a few moments he withdrew a large, brown envelope, proffering it to James.

'OK, I need a few minutes to check all this.' He turned around, intending to get back in his car to take advantage of the interior light.

'Uh uh ...' muttered the man, waving a finger from side to side, 'you check it out here.'

'What the fuck ... you think I'm going to drive off, leaving my wife and the baby here?'

'You might have a weapon in the car.'

'A weapon?' cried James. 'Christ, what do you take us for? We're just ordinary people, paying a small fortune to adopt a child.'

The man was unmoved. 'Check the papers out here.'

James sighed in obvious frustration. There was no point arguing so he knelt down in front of one of his car's parking lights and began scanning the papers.

After a minute or two of tense silence, Tessa could contain herself no longer; she moved forward to look over his shoulder. 'Are they all OK?' she whispered.

'I think so, but without studying them properly, I'm not sure I can really say.'

The big man was getting impatient. 'Happy now?' he grunted.

'I guess,' muttered James, rising to his feet.

'Then let's get on with it ... the money.'

'Go on, James ... do it now,' said his wife, a slight quaver in her voice.

He withdrew his mobile from his pocket and tapped to wake it up. As he did so, his face fell; he looked crestfallen.

'What? What is it? What's wrong?' cried Tessa.

'There's no signal.'

Chapter 17

'No signal? There must be,' wailed Tessa.

James held up the phone to show her. As she stared in disbelief at the words on the screen, a giant fist clenched her stomach.

James raised the phone above his head, and then to the side, waving it around desperately as though this would somehow capture a stray wave. It was to no avail.

The big man's expression hardened. 'What the hell are you playing at? If you're trying to fuck with me, I'm warning you …'

He took a couple of steps towards Tessa, reaching out to grab the baby.

She jumped back hugging the child tightly to her breast. 'No!' she screamed.

'Wait!' yelled James, grabbing the man's arm in an attempt to restrain him. 'I'm telling the truth … look for yourself.' He thrust the phone in front of the man's face.

It took a couple of seconds, but finally his expression morphed from one of rage to one of puzzlement. 'Hmm,' he muttered, standing down from his attempt to grab the child. 'OK … use mine.' He withdrew his phone from his pocket and tapped the screen, whose glow now illuminated his face, revealing an expression of utter bewilderment. After a few moments he looked up. 'Mine's the same. Don't make sense … I made a call to the boss just before stopping here.'

This was not a good situation, but at least the moment of crisis had passed.

'Look,' said James, 'maybe it's just the immediate location: we're in a bit of a cutting here and the railway bridge is above us … could be blocking the signal.'

The other man took a few seconds to process this suggestion before replying. 'Hmm,' he grunted, 'alright then … we can walk up to the end of the bridge up there' – he indicated the spot with a nod – 'and try again.'

'Yes,' interjected Tessa, 'go on … I'll wait here with Luriana.'

'Oh no you won't … I'm not having you jump in the car and take off with the baby. You're coming with us.'

'For heaven's sake,' hissed James, 'do you seriously think she's going to just drive off and leave me here?'

The man's tone hardened. 'Look … you want this kid or not? If you do, you'd better stop fucking arguing and do as I say.'

'For Christ's sake—' began James, but Tessa cut him off. The last thing she wanted was to antagonise this man and jeopardise the whole thing.

'OK … OK … I'll come,' she said.

The big man turned to the other woman, who had been watching the whole tetchy exchange in nervous silence.

'You … get in the car and wait.'

He had apparently forgotten what he had told them just minutes earlier: that she did not speak English. She shook her head, her frightened eyes flitting back and forth between her tormenter and the baby.

'Oh, for fuck's sake,' muttered the man. He stepped towards the car, wrenching the back door open and shoving the woman towards it. 'Get in,' he shouted, gesturing towards the open door.

She got the message.

'Wait there,' he ordered, slamming the door shut as soon as she was inside.

'Right,' he grunted, turning back to James and Tessa, 'come on … let's do this.'

So, the three of them set off, James and Tessa – still holding the baby – in the lead, the big man shepherding them from behind.

With each step, James continued scanning his phone as though willing the vital signal bars to appear. They did not.

They trudged onward; by now they had covered about fifty yards. Tessa turned around to see that the other man was also studying his phone. So intent was he that he almost walked straight into her.

'Keep going,' he growled, waving her forward with the back of his hand.

The little procession resumed its forward march in silence, the tension now almost unbearable.

They had covered about another twenty yards when it finally happened. 'Yes,' cried James, 'I've got a signal!'

'Thank God,' breathed Tessa.

'Well, I haven't got one,' muttered the other man. 'Oh wait … yes … got one now …only one bar though.'

'Let's go on a bit further,' said James '… make sure we've got a decent signal.' They moved forward a few more yards and, suddenly, James called out, 'Yes … I've got three bars now … should be enough.'

'OK,' grunted the other man

James opened his banking website and pulled up the payment page. 'OK, I'm ready … I'm making the transfer now.'

James's fingers were trembling as he haltingly called up the account details. Finally, he entered the amount – £35,000 – and hit 'confirm'. After a few anxious seconds, he declared, 'payment confirmed.'

He looked up at the other man. 'It's done. You should have the money.'

Tessa's heart was pounding as she watched the man gazing intently at his own screen. Several seconds passed; no response. She couldn't stand the tension. 'Well? Have you got it?'

'Shut up!' he snapped back. 'I'm checking.'

'Listen,' said James, his tone menacing now, 'if you're playing some kind of trick on us, I'll—'

He was cut off by the other man raising his hand, palm-forward. 'Got it.'

Tessa felt a wave of relief wash over her; she uttered a loud but unintelligible – even to her – sound: a sort of cross between a sigh and a whimper. She felt her knees starting to buckle. James had spotted it; he rushed to her, steadying her, lest she and the baby should fall.

'It's OK … it's done now,' he soothed. 'Let me take the baby.'

She gently passed the child to him.

'OK, we're done here,' muttered the big man. 'Let's get back to the cars.'

The walk back to the cars seemed considerably quicker, the crushing tension having eased and no-one anxiously scanning their phones. No words were exchanged though. When they arrived, the woman was still obediently sitting in the back seat of the car. The man opened the tailgate and withdrew a large sports holdall. His demeanour seemed somehow less disagreeable now. Maybe even *he* had been feeling the tension.

'Here are some of the essentials to get you started: nappies, clothes, milk and so on.'

'Thank you,' whispered Tessa.

In an uncharacteristic display of apparent empathy, he replied, 'Yeah, well I hope you enjoy your new baby. She'll have a better life here with you.'

With that, he stepped back into the car, starting it up and executing a three-point turn. As he did so, Tessa caught a fleeting glimpse of the haunted eyes of the woman sitting in the back seat. Seconds later they were gone, leaving James and Tessa alone in the gloom of the railway arch together with their new baby.

Chapter 18

Professor Julian Chambers, retired University of Oxford virologist, sat back in his armchair, watching with keen interest the TV news report on the latest statistics relating to the pandemic. He took a sip of his Cognac, nodding his approval.

Julian's PhD thesis, completed some thirty years earlier, had been on the subject of viral pandemics: how they take hold and spread through populations. In the course of his research, he had spent a considerable time investigating the influence of population density on the transmission of viruses. But, while it was not the primary objective of his research, his findings had made him acutely aware of the devastating effect that population growth, even then, was having on the environment. In the years since then, the situation had only worsened, with global population growing out of control and the environment being destroyed at an alarming rate.

Dismayed at the appalling lack of action by heads of government throughout the world to tackle the issue, he eventually decided to make it his personal mission to do something about the existential threat facing the planet.

His research had made clear three inescapable facts: first, that the earth's population had grown way beyond any level which was sustainable in the long term; second, that human activity was rapidly destroying the environment; and third, that such overpopulation provided ideal conditions for the spread of a global pandemic.

This third factor offered the obvious solution: release a highly transmissible disease with a significant fatality rate upon the world. As the disease spread, the population would be gradually reduced, and as the population reduced, so, eventually, would the rate of transmission of the disease. At the same time, those people who had caught the disease and survived would develop immunity. When population density was low enough, and when most of the remaining population had developed immunity, the disease would eventually die out. The world would be left with a more sustainable level of population and mankind could start anew. The elegance and simplicity of the 'herd immunity' concept was nothing short of beautiful.

It had taken Julian some years to develop such a disease, but eventually he came up with a new virus within the coronavirus family which, according to his trials, met the requirements. It was predicted to be highly transmissible, often fatal, particularly in older age groups, and there was no vaccine available which could constrain its spread.

When Julian had developed the original virus, some ten years earlier, he had taken care to release it far away from his home in Surrey. Instead, he travelled all the way to China and introduced the virus at a wet market, throwing the world's suspicion on this as the original source. The World Health Organisation had conducted an extensive investigation to try to determine the exact source, but it had proved inconclusive. The Chinese authorities had been less than fully co-operative with the investigation, and in the absence of hard evidence, most commentators concluded that the outbreak probably had indeed jumped from some animal species to humans at the wet market.

There were however two problems with Julian's plan.

Firstly, the death rate turned out to be considerably lower than he had predicted: just 1%. This was simply not high enough.to make the radical impact on population growth which he considered necessary.

The second problem was that Julian had underestimated the extraordinary capabilities of his peers in the scientific community. Within one year of the outbreak first having been detected, no fewer than five effective vaccines had been approved for use throughout much of the world. Within two years, the majority of the population of the developed world had been fully vaccinated and the rollout to the developing world was well underway. Just three years after the original outbreak, the disease had been brought under control, its severity now no worse than the common cold for most people. All that was necessary to keep it under control was a programme of annual vaccination with vaccines tweaked each year to combat any new variants which might emerge.

With the vaccinologists of the world now adept at modifying the vaccines to deal with any new variants which might develop, Julian realised that nothing short of a radically new vaccine-resistant virus with a significantly higher fatality rate could defeat the efforts of the scientists. It had taken him over three years to develop such a virus in the well-equipped laboratory hidden away within his large, sprawling Surrey home.

He would never have had the money to set up such a facility had it not been for a very substantial inheritance from his late parents, who had also bequeathed him the extensive mansion in which he now lived. It had not been easy to keep his work secret, but he lived alone and kept himself very much to himself. He had never formed any sort of relationship with a woman – or a man, come to that – and he rarely entertained visitors. The only people who regularly entered his home were the two cleaners he employed to maintain the vast property, and they were never allowed to enter his laboratory, which was always kept locked when he was not working there. As a consequence, he had succeeded in preventing his project from being discovered.

When it came to deploying the new virus, he had, once again, seeded the infection far away from home, this time choosing the *favelas* of Brazil: an environment highly conducive to the spread of infection and sorely lacking in healthcare or medical resources. The disease had taken hold and spread rapidly, and by the time it caught the attention of the world's public health authorities, it was already out of control. Before long it had spread throughout much of the world.

Initially, the infection was thought to be due to yet another variant of the original coronavirus. However, when the virus was subjected to genomic sequencing to determine the nature of the variant, it became apparent that this was, in fact, a completely new coronavirus.

He had expected that this virus would prove too much of a challenge for the vaccinologists around the world to overcome. He was wrong; disturbingly, one research team, based at Thomas Lewis College, University of London, had made outstanding progress towards developing a vaccine in a much shorter time than he could possibly have foreseen. If they succeeded in developing an effective vaccine, and their technology were to be shared with other research groups around the world, it could only be a matter of time before, once again, his efforts would be thwarted by the scientific community.

Considering this situation had led him to two conclusions: first, that he could not hope to defeat the efforts of the world's vaccinologists in the long term, and second, that he could not succeed on his own – he needed help.

With these thoughts in mind, he had set about finding a small number of other like-minded people in the worlds of academia, science, and politics who would work with him to find a way to realise his objectives. This was very dangerous indeed, for if he were to make an error of judgement about any of these people it could result in his work being exposed to the authorities.

But it didn't. He had taken great care when approaching potential allies and had now assembled a small team who were as committed as he was to the cause. Their work remained a closely guarded secret.

Between them, this group of people had come up with an alternative strategy to suppress, and eventually reverse population growth. This time it was not dependent on defeating the efforts of the vaccinologists, but rather it would take advantage of their work. The new plan wasn't ideal, as it would take longer than he would have liked to achieve the objective, but it had the potential, in the long term, to achieve a higher percentage reduction in global population than even his improved virus could. Furthermore it would not be derailed by the development of vaccines.

Yes, all in all, Julian was pretty pleased with the way things were going.

However, the message he had recently received from Sofía Méndez was troubling him. It would need to be discussed with the whole group at the following evening's meeting.

Chapter 19

As David had expected, his superintendent had declined his request for a surveillance team to monitor Professor Julian Chambers 24/7, based on such flimsy evidence as he had so far.

From Sofía Méndez's intercepted phone calls, he knew that she was due to meet with Chambers that evening. He had no idea what the meeting was about, but he was quite sure that Méndez had been lying to him when he interviewed her. If she was implicated in Professor Maddocks's murder, was it possible that Chambers was too? His instincts told him that this meeting might well hold the key.

Denied the facility of a full surveillance team, David's only option was to carry out some limited surveillance himself.

***

David didn't know what time Chambers and Méndez were due to meet or who else might be in attendance, so he began his stakeout early: at 5 p.m. He parked some distance away and approached the residence on foot, positioning himself among the trees opposite the main gates. He took with him a small, folding, camping stool, a vacuum flask full of hot coffee, and a pair of binoculars.

The time dragged by painfully slowly as he sat waiting for something to happen. Now it was almost 8 p.m. and the daylight was starting to fade; the evening chill began to seep through his clothing and into his joints. He was beginning to lose confidence that this meeting was ever going to happen.

His thoughts were interrupted by the vibration of his phone – set to silent – in his pocket. It was his assistant, Neil, who had valiantly offered to stay on at the station for as long as he was needed, to respond to any requests which David might have for information or other assistance.

'Anything happening yet, sir?'

'Unfortunately no. There's no sign of any activity and no vehicles have arrived or left. In fact, it's such a quiet road that there have only been a handful of cars even driving past since I arrived. I'm beginning to think … Wait! I can see another car approaching … I think it's slowing down.'

The car which came into view was a dark coloured Toyota. It was, indeed, slowing down, and came to a halt right outside the gates.

'Hold on,' whispered David, 'I'm going to try to get the registration number.' He kept the phone to his ear and lifted the binoculars to his eyes. 'Yes, here it is …' He read out the number. 'Get a trace on that will you?'

'On it, sir.'

A woman got out of the car and spoke into what looked like an intercom system alongside the gates. He couldn't positively identify her in the prevailing poor light, but her height, build, and hairstyle matched those of Doctor Méndez. He waited to see what would happen.

Within a few seconds, the huge gates began to swing slowly open, and the woman got back into her car. When the gates were fully open, she drove through, disappearing from view as she followed the curving, gravel drive around to the far side of the house.

He was still holding the phone to his ear when Neil came on the line again. 'OK, I've traced the car … it's an Avis hire car.'

'Can you find out who's got it at the moment?'

'Already on it, sir … I'm just waiting for them to come back to me on the other line. Oh … hold on, it's them.' The line went silent for a few moments, and then he came back on. 'It's our target: Doctor Sofía Méndez.'

He felt a surge of relief; perhaps his evening wasn't going to be wasted after all.

'OK, thanks Neil … I'm going to stay here to see who else shows up. Wait for my next call.' He hung up.

Now things started to happen fast. Within a couple of minutes, a silver BMW arrived. Neil identified it as belonging to Doctor Peter

Simmons, Head of the vaccine development programme at Thomas Lewis College.

Before Neil had even hung up, the next car arrived: a blue Audi SUV.

'Neil, stay on the line … I've got another registration number for you to check.'

He held the binoculars to his eyes once more and read out the number.

A couple of minutes later, Neil came back with an answer. 'It belongs to a … Joanna Prentice. No idea who she is.'

'Me neither,' replied David. 'Never mind, we can check later when … Wait! Here's another car … a black Renault.'

David read out the registration number and waited for Neil to come back with an answer. When he did, the excitement in his voice was unmistakeable.

'It's Doctor Matthew Turner … that's the lecturer at the University of Hampshire … one of the people Sofía Méndez spoke to on the phone the other day.'

'OK, good,' replied David. 'Can't see any other cars just now but stay there for a bit longer in case I need anything else.'

After the brief flurry of activity, everything went quiet again. After another fifteen minutes of inactivity, David concluded that all the attendees of the meeting had probably arrived now and that there was little to be gained by waiting any longer. He stood up, his knees creaking with the combination of the stiffness which had set in and the cold.

Just as he was about to fold up his stool, however, he heard another car approaching. This was no ordinary car though; he recognised the cultured growl of a twelve-cylinder internal combustion engine – a comparative rarity, even before new car sales had gone all-electric. A few seconds later a silver Rolls Royce hove into view and pulled up at the gates. He grabbed his phone and called Neil.

'Neil … you still at the station?'

'Yes sir, of course.'

'I've got another number for you to trace.' He grabbed his binoculars and read out the number. 'OK, looks like a personalised plate … yes, it's "PHB 1".'

'I'll get right on it,' said Neil. 'Hold the line.'

As the car pulled through the gates, the gravel crunched noisily beneath its huge tyres. Just as it moved out of sight, Neil came back on the line. 'It belongs to a ... Peregrine Hartley-Briggs. Any idea who that is?'

Stunned, David replied, 'Yes I do ... Hartley-Briggs is a government minister. What the fuck is *he* doing here?'

Chapter 20

The meeting took place in Professor Chambers's spacious dining room. The oak-panelled walls, cut-glass chandeliers, and original oil paintings leant the room an air of opulence. A faint aroma reminiscent of cigar smoke, musty books, and ancient leather hung in the air.

The professor surveyed the expectant faces of the five other people seated around the huge, oval dining table before calling the meeting to order.

'Good evening, ladies and gentlemen. Thank you all for coming. Let me first check, as usual, that everyone has taken all the customary precautions to ensure that their presence at this meeting has remained secret.'

A subdued murmuring and nodding of heads ensued.

'Good ... before we move to the matters on the original agenda, I think we should ask Doctor Méndez to apprise us of what was behind the somewhat disturbing message she sent us just recently.' He turned to Sofía. 'Please ... Doctor Méndez.'

She cleared her throat before replying. 'OK ... well, just after I flew down to London a couple of days ago, I got a message to say that a Metropolitan Police detective had visited the plant in Scotland, wanting to speak to me—'

'The police?' he gasped. 'That is indeed a very worrying development. What did he want?'

'Seems he's turned up something which has prompted him to take another look into Felicity Maddocks's murder.'

A hollow, sinking feeling eviscerated his stomach; this was even worse than he could have imagined. He needed to ascertain whether the group was in imminent danger.

'Did he say what it was that he had come across?'

'No, he was a bit cagey on that point, I'm afraid.'

'This is a real concern,' opined the professor. 'When we instructed the contractor to take the laptop from the murder scene, we thought it would be enough to send the police down a blind alley, assuming theft of the data it contained was the motive for the killing. And it seemed – until now – that the strategy was successful. But if this detective is digging into the case again after all this time, it suggests he must have discovered something to cast doubt on such a scenario.'

'I'm not so sure,' said Sofía. 'I don't think it's as bad as it sounds. He's already been in contact and interviewed me. From the way the discussion went, I don't think he has anything solid at all.'

'So what did he have to say?'

'OK … let me go through it all in detail and we'll see what everyone thinks.'

'Please … go ahead,' said Julian, doing his best to calm himself and assess logically whatever she had to say.

She spent the next twenty minutes or so running through her encounter with DI Prendergast, stopping occasionally to respond to questions raised by the others. When she had finished, Julian felt a little less anxious. He summarised his thoughts for the rest of the group.

'Hmm … from what you have said, it does indeed sound as though he has nothing concrete to link you with Professor Maddocks's murder, though it's puzzling that he would be looking into it again after all this time. And he wouldn't reveal the nature of this "new evidence" he claims to have?'

'I'm afraid not. I'm not at all sure he really does have actual new evidence; I almost got the sense he was just fishing.'

'Well,' muttered the professor, 'something has clearly caught his attention.'

'Well, whatever it is,' replied Sofía, 'I don't think it can be anything definitive, or I'm sure he would have pressed me further. It's been a couple of days since he interviewed me, and he hasn't followed up at all.'

'Let's hope you're right, but in any event, we should treat this development seriously and redouble our efforts to ensure absolute secrecy.

'Now then, if, as you suspect, he has intercepted your recent calls he will be aware of your contact with some of this group.

That's not necessarily a huge problem in itself: academics and scientists working in related fields frequently collaborate. We should, however, make sure we have our stories completely straight as to how we are working together should he choose to investigate further. Meanwhile, we should continue with the precautions regarding communications which you have already recommended.'

The next person to speak was Doctor Matthew Turner, Head of Environmental Sciences at the University of Hampshire. 'Agreed ... however, I think it's particularly important that Sofía and I have a convincing reason to be in contact, as my field of study is not so clearly related to hers.'

'Matthew's right,' interjected Sofía, 'but I've been thinking about that, and I think I have a credible story we can use. I think it would be quite plausible that we could be researching the possible effects of an individual's environment on the efficacy of the vaccine.'

'That could work,' agreed Matthew. 'Let's talk it over separately after the meeting.'

'Very good,' said Julian. 'Hopefully no serious damage has been done, but clearly we must all remain vigilant.'

A round of coughing and chair shuffling signalled that everyone was ready to move on.

'Perhaps we can now move on to the main part of the agenda. Peter, what are the latest data you have on the effectiveness of the vaccine?'

Doctor Peter Simmons, Head of the Vaccine Programme at Thomas Lewis College, began his summary. 'The latest statistics continue to indicate an efficacy of around 96% against the virus is conferred by two doses, and—'

'Yes, yes,' interrupted Julian, irritated that Simmons had seemingly wilfully misinterpreted his request, 'we all know this ... the number barely ever changes. What I mean is, how effective is our additive at suppressing fertility?'

'I was just coming to that. We have now conducted extensive trials with women of childbearing age who have volunteered to take part, thinking they were participating in a trial of a new version of the vaccine designed to give even greater protection against the virus.

'The results indicate that female fertility is reduced by approximately 70%. In other words, there were 70% fewer pregnancies among the women given the modified vaccine – which of course is the version being rolled out globally – compared to the control group.'

'OK,' breathed Julian, 'that's very good. Any indications of birth abnormalities among the other 30%?'

'Too early to say. We've done everything possible to guard against such side effects but … well, as you know, this compound was developed on a very tight timescale to make sure it was ready in time for the mass rollout of the vaccine. We can't be as sure as we would ideally like to be.'

'No matter,' said Julian. 'The question of possible birth defects is of secondary importance.' He scanned the faces around the table, his expression grave. 'You all know that that I had reservations about the strategy of suppressing the birth rate as a means of population control. I would originally have preferred to let the virus run its course, eliminating a significant proportion of the population within a few years rather than waiting decades for this approach to have a significant impact. However, I have to acknowledge that a 70% reduction in birth rate is an excellent result, and in the long term it should lead to an even greater reduction in global population than could be achieved by fatalities due to the virus. There is, though, a downside …'

He paused, ensuring he had everyone's full attention.

'With such a significant downturn in birth rate it can only be a matter of time before such a trend is picked up by government statisticians around the world. In fact, I understand from Doctor Prentice that our own Office for National Statistics may have already done so.'

Doctor Joanna Prentice was Chief Statistician at the ONS, and effectively, deputy to Amada Frobisher, Head of the ONS. She sat at the table directly opposite Julian, who then addressed her.

'Doctor Prentice … perhaps you can apprise us of the situation?'

She pushed her spectacles a little further up the bridge of her nose. 'Yes, of course. One of my team picked up the first indications of a reducing birth rate some weeks ago. At that time the figures were not statistically significant, so I tried to gently steer him away from pursuing it further. Unfortunately, it seems I was insufficiently forceful, and he continued monitoring the relevant data, which gradually built up to a more significant level.'

'How significant?' interjected Julian.

'The current figures show a statistical significance of around 90%.'

This revelation prompted a collective intake of breath from those around the table.

'Although I tried to downplay the issue, my boss, Amanda Frobisher, eventually got to hear of it. Even 90% significance is not really high enough to conclude that the trend is real; it could still be just a chance fluctuation in the figures. However, it's enough to pique her interest. Consequently, she has instructed me to put some of my team on trying to establish any correlation with possible causal factors.'

'Hmm … that doesn't sound good,' muttered Julian.

'Well actually,' she replied, 'it's probably not too much of a problem.'

'How so?' he enquired.

'Look, the ONS deals only in analysis of statistics. The only way that a link with the vaccine could be established would be if we were able to compare the birth rates of vaccinated and unvaccinated women of childbearing age. In the UK, the vast majority of people have already been vaccinated; there are just not the numbers of unvaccinated women in the general population to allow such data to be collected and analysed.'

'Makes sense,' opined Julian, his analytical, scientific brain immediately grasping the veracity of Joanna's assessment. 'So it would take a controlled, clinical trial to verify the causal link with the vaccine.'

'Exactly … you would first need a reason to hypothesise a link with vaccination and then set up a controlled, clinical trial comparing birth rates between vaccinated and unvaccinated women.'

'Similar to the trial that Peter has already conducted to arrive at the assessment of a 70% drop in birth rate due to vaccination,' said Julian.

'Indeed,' she replied, 'and that's just not the kind of work the ONS does. I'd say we're safe, for the moment, from detection, however much time the team spends on analysing population-wide statistics.'

'OK,' said Julian, 'but what about other agencies around the world?'

'Well,' continued Joanna, 'in developed countries such as the USA and most of Europe, a similar situation pertains: with more or less whole-population vaccination having been achieved, they'll pick up the fall in birth rate, but not be able to ascertain what's causing it. When it comes to developing countries like most of those in Africa, there's still a large enough percentage of the population unvaccinated to, potentially, establish a correlation, but they simply don't have sophisticated analytical agencies like the ONS to conduct the analyses necessary.'

'In other words,' concluded Julian, 'it's unlikely that anyone – worldwide – will realise that the vaccine is responsible … for the foreseeable future at least.'

'That would be my assessment,' she confirmed.

***

Peregrine Hartley-Briggs, who had hitherto remained silent throughout the entire meeting, could contain himself no longer. 'May I add some information which I believe is relevant here?'

Julian turned to him. 'Of course … what's on your mind?'

'Joanna has already mentioned the interest which her boss, Amanda Frobisher, has taken in the data relating to the birth rate. Well, I have to tell you that Amanda has already approached me on the issue, and despite my efforts to divert her from pursuing it further, she has refused to let it go … she's like a dog with a bone.'

Joanna interrupted him. 'I know she's been to see you, but I don't really see how that changes the situation which I have just outlined.'

'She's threatening to go over my head and inform the PM of her concerns.'

'So what if she does?' replied Joanna. 'How does that change the situation?'

Peregrine paused for a moment, struggling to suppress the surge of anger rising within him. How could this wretched woman be so complacent, not to mention disrespectful?

'Well, for a start, it undermines my authority, and also—'

'With respect,' interrupted Joanna, 'that is hardly a consideration for this group.'

Now he was boiling. 'Well, it might just become one once I am elected as PM … then you'll all need my help.'

Julian intervened in the tetchy exchange. 'Peregrine ... while we all obviously support your bid to reach the highest echelons of power, it is not germane to the immediate issue at hand here.'

'But—' protested Peregrine.

'The point is ...' persisted Julian, 'do you have any logical reason why Doctor Frobisher would be able to expose the vaccine's hidden purpose?'

'Well, not specifically,' spluttered Peregrine, 'but once the PM has been informed, who knows where it could lead.'

'That's hardly a coherent argument,' said Joanna.

He could have cheerfully throttled her, there and then.

Julian added insult to injury. 'I'm afraid I have to agree ... Doctor Prentice has explained why the risk posed by her boss's interest is unlikely to threaten our cause at the present time. I suggest we listen to her professional advice. We should, of course, remain vigilant but, unless something changes, I think we can afford to remain relatively sanguine about this particular development.'

Bloody scientists, thought Peregrine, *all they seem to consider are their logical analyses, and statistical significance, and probabilities, and so on. They just don't have any kind of instinct for political realities.*

As the matter of Amanda Frobisher's meddling appeared to have been put to bed, for now at least, the meeting moved on to other issues.

Peregrine had by now, however, pretty much tuned out. Every fibre in his body told him that Amanda Frobisher was going to be a problem, and he needed to decide how to deal with her.

Chapter 21

The following morning, David and Neil were in the station early to go over what they had learned from the previous evening's stakeout. David winced as he took a sip of the scalding hot coffee which he had just obtained from the vending machine. Neil had wisely settled for a glass of cold water.

'Damn!' muttered David. 'Catches me out every time ... why on earth can't they just turn the temperature down a bit?'

Neil chuckled. 'Well, has anyone asked them to?'

'How should I know?' grumbled his boss.

'I'll get onto maintenance,' said Neil.

'Never mind about that just now,' said David. 'So, what do we know so far?'

He began scribbling names on a whiteboard.

Doctor Sofia Méndez – Head of vaccine programme at Saturn Pharmaceuticals

Professor Julian Chambers – Retired Oxford virologist

Doctor Peter Simmons – Head of vaccine programme at Thomas Lewis College, London.

Doctor Joanna Prentice – Head Statistician at ONS

Doctor Matthew Turner – Head of Environmental Sciences at University of Hampshire

Peregrine Hartley-Briggs – Junior Health Minister

'Hmm ... so what do these six people have in common ... what could be the connection?'

'Well,' ventured Neil, 'apart from the minister, they are all academics or scientists.'

'True,' said David, 'but the only two with an obvious need to be working together are Sofía Méndez and Peter Simmons: they are both intimately involved with the vaccine programme.'

'But this Julian Chambers,' said Neil, 'is also a virologist. Even though he's retired they could be consulting him for his expertise.'

'OK, that's three out of six, but what about the others?'

'I agree it's a puzzle,' mused Neil.

'Look,' said David, 'I'm convinced that Sofía Méndez knows something about Professor Maddocks's murder. Whether these other people are implicated I don't know, but somehow we need to find out what the connection is.'

'Would you consider interviewing some or all of them?'

David shook his head. 'If they *are* implicated in some wrongdoing, I don't want them to know we're investigating them.'

'Well, what then?' said his young assistant, spreading his hands.

David hesitated for a few seconds before replying; he knew that what he was about to suggest was a huge risk, given Neil's tender years and lack of experience, yet this young man had already demonstrated a keen intellect and an uncanny instinct for police work.

He judged it was worth the risk.

'OK,' he began, 'this is what I'm thinking ...'

Chapter 22

Amanda Frobisher lived alone. She had never formed any long-term relationships; her dedication to her work had proven to be a major turn-off to all of the men she had fleetingly dallied with. Most of them seemed only to be interested in sex: an activity which she found strangely unsatisfying. In the end she had accepted that she would probably never find the sort of meaningful relationship she sought and resigned herself to a solitary life devoted to work and public service. Maybe it was better that way.

It was 7 p.m. Unusually, she had left work on time that day; there was something on her mind, and she just couldn't concentrate at work until she could come to some sort of resolution. That 'something' was the unexplained drop in the birth rate. The latest data had indicated 99% confidence that the change was real: that this was no random statistical fluctuation. No, it was almost certain, now, that there was some causal factor which had significantly reduced the birth rate across a broad swathe of the population. Although her team were working furiously on trying to identify what that causal factor might be, they had, so far, come up with nothing.

Although she had reported the situation to that pompous arse, Peregrine Hartley-Briggs, she had the distinct impression that he was not going to act on it. She had already dropped some very strong hints that she was prepared to go over his head if necessary, but still he kept hedging on the subject.

Conflicted about what to do, she stood up from her armchair and headed for the kitchen. She opened the fridge and withdrew the bottle of Pinot Grigio which she had opened the previous evening; it was still around half full. She poured herself a glass and returned to her chair, taking a welcome sip of the cooling liquid, relishing the sharp, tangy flavour as she swirled it in her mouth before letting it course down her throat.

So, what should she do? She knew full well that Hartley-Briggs, obnoxious though he might be, was a rising star in the government. There was even talk of him as, potentially, a future party leader. Crossing swords with him would not be good for her career prospects. And yet, if this data on the birth rate was not taken seriously, who knew what public health crisis might be creeping up on an unsuspecting population?

Amanda did not consider herself to be a heavy drinker, but she regularly enjoyed a glass or two of wine in the evening after a busy day at work: just enough to relax her a little but never sufficient to get her feeling tipsy. This evening, though, she felt surprisingly vague after consuming barely half a glass. Strange.

And yet she could not relax; the effects of the alcohol could not banish the stress of dealing with the dilemma she was facing. She knew she needed to make a decision, and there was only one decision which would sit comfortably with her: she would have to go over Hartley-Briggs's head and approach the Prime Minister directly. Only with the PM's backing would she be able to devote sufficient resources to pin down the cause of the unexplained fall in birth rate.

With the decision made, some of the weight slipped from her shoulders. She drained the remainder of her wine and stood up to go and get a refill. As she did so, a wave of nausea swept over her; she steadied herself on the arm of the chair for a moment until the feeling passed.

As she made her way to the kitchen, she felt a strange tightness in her chest and her breathing became laboured. *Oh God ... hope I'm not coming down with something.* She shook her head in an effort to dispel the feeling and made for the fridge.

She opened the fridge door and took the wine bottle, but, strangely, there was no strength in her grip. She struggled to even hold the chilled bottle, slippery as it was with condensation. She slammed the door shut and made to take the couple of steps to the nearby countertop to set the bottle down, but suddenly her legs felt weak. Her fingers stiffened and the bottle slipped from her grasp, shattering on the hard, tiled floor, spraying its contents far and wide. Now her legs felt as though they were not her own, she was unable to exercise any control as her muscles went into a spasm before her legs buckled and she fell to the floor. As she reached for the edge of the countertop to try to haul herself upright her fingers were curled into a bizarre claw which she was unable to straighten. Now she was struggling to breathe.

What the hell is happening to me?

She knew she needed medical help – and fast – but her phone was in the living room alongside the chair where she had been sitting. She made one more attempt to drag herself to her feet, but it was useless. The only thing for it was to try to crawl. As she began slowly, painfully dragging herself across the floor, the several yards she needed to cover became an unbridgeable chasm. She had virtually no muscle control in her legs and now even her arms would not respond to the signals her desperate brain was sending. She was struggling for every breath now, and she knew she just wasn't going to make it.

'H…elp!' she cried, but what was intended as a piercing scream emerged as a weak, strangled croak. It was the last sound that Amanda Frobisher ever uttered.

Chapter 23

It was over twenty-four hours later when Peregrine learned that Amanda's body had been discovered. Apparently, when she didn't show up for work that day and failed to respond to any calls, one of the ONS staff went over to her ground floor apartment on her way home from work. No-one answered the doorbell, so the girl who had gone round peered through the window and saw her lying on the floor. She called for an ambulance and the police, who forced entry to her flat, but Amanda was declared dead at the scene.

It's a shame, thought Peregrine. *If she hadn't meddled so much, this wouldn't have been necessary.* He had actually quite liked her, and she wasn't a bad looker either; given different circumstances, he might even have made approaches to see whether she was up for the kind of sexual practices that he favoured. However, this was business, and in spite of all the assurances given by the scientists and statisticians, he was concerned that, should she go directly to the PM, it might lead to further investigation, possibly culminating in the discovery that the vaccine was responsible for the sharp reduction in the birth rate.

Not that he gave a toss about population control and the supposed destruction of the environment, but he had a very lucrative business supplying babies to desperate couples; that needed protecting at all costs.

Anyway, the deed was done now; he just hoped that the information provided to him by the toxicology expert he had hired – at great expense – was accurate.

The poison chosen was Batrachotoxin, an extremely potent compound found only in certain species of frogs in South America. It was, he was told, used by a number of tribes to tip the poison darts which they used in their blowpipes for hunting. Just a couple of drops was apparently enough to stop a creature such as a monkey in its tracks. For a full-grown human being, the toxin would take a little longer to take full effect, but, depending on dosage, it could still kill within minutes. The mechanism by which this poison works, his adviser had told him, was by inducing extreme muscle spasms which would quickly incapacitate the victim by causing seizure of muscles in arms and legs. Before long the muscles controlling heart and lungs would be compromised leading to difficulty in breathing and erratic heartbeat. The eventual cause of death was usually catastrophic heart failure.

The great advantage of this poison was that it was extremely unlikely to be identified in a post-mortem. To detect it would take a very special type of test looking specifically for this particular toxin. Routine toxicology in the UK would only look for common poisons such as arsenic, strychnine, and so on; no-one would dream of looking for a poison derived from a frog native to the tropical forests of South America. No, the victim's death would almost certainly be put down to natural causes: a massive heart attack.

It had been an expensive exercise to dispose of Amanda. By the time he had paid the toxicologist to obtain the rare poison and the intruder skilled enough to gain entry to her flat and lace the wine bottle without leaving any tell-tale signs, it had set him back well over £70,000. Still, that was a drop in the ocean compared to his potential losses if his baby smuggling enterprise were to be compromised.

The phone rang: it was Joanna Prentice. When she spoke, her voice held a tremor.

'Peregrine ... it's Joanna. We need to talk ... urgently.'

'Oh, Joanna ... I guess you'll have heard the terrible news about Amanda.'

There was a hitch in her voice as she replied. 'Of course I have ... she's ... she *was* ... my boss for Christ's sake.'

'Indeed ... very upsetting for you.'

'Upsetting? That's a bit of an understatement.'

'Of course ... absolutely tragic.'

'Did you have something to do with this?' she blurted, her tone accusatory.

He adopted his best impression of a deeply wounded tone. 'Why, Joanna ... how on earth could you even suggest such a thing?'

'I heard what you said at the meeting … you wanted to shut her up … one way or another.'

'Well, it's true that I was concerned, but your case for calm was so well-argued that it considerably reassured me.'

There was venom in the brief silence which preceded her reply. 'Well you certainly didn't sound very reassured at the time.'

'Well no … I was very concerned about the possible consequences if Amanda decided to go directly to the PM … you know as well as I do how exposed we might all be if our group were to come under the spotlight.'

'Of course I do. You think I'm stupid?'

'Oh, far from … you know I have the utmost respect for your expertise and professionalism. That's my whole point … now I've had time to digest what you said, and … well, it was a most cogent argument.'

She didn't sound convinced. 'You'd better not be bullshitting me, Peregrine, because if I find that you *did* have something to do with Amanda's death—'

'Please … please … calm yourself.' He was patting the air in a calming gesture, which was, of course completely lost on Joanna, on the other end of the telephone line. 'Look, I imagine they'll probably do a post-mortem, which should establish the cause of death. I'm as keen as you are to know what happened.'

She finally began to sound a little less agitated. 'OK … well, I guess we'll find out soon enough, but—'

He interrupted her, 'Look, tragic though Amanda's death is, it does present some opportunities.'

'Opportunities? How the fuck can you even think like that right now?'

'Well, think about it … who is going to replace her as Head of the ONS?'

'I … I don't know. I haven't even thought about it.'

'Oh, but you are too modest, my dear. Surely you are the obvious choice.'

'Me? Don't be ridiculous. In any case I absolutely couldn't countenance profiting from Amanda's death.'

'Oh no … you mustn't look at it like that. None of us would have wanted this awful situation, but we are where we are. The question is … who is best qualified to take over?'

'Well, I guess I'm qualified, but I'm not the only one ... there are several others who might equally step into the role.'

'But if I were to drop a few words into the right ears, I'm sure I could tip the balance in your favour.'

'Look, I don't want any favouritism from you, thank you ... especially on the back of Amanda's death. She wasn't just my boss; she was my *friend*.'

'Of course ... I understand. But what's done is done ... nothing can bring her back. But just think how advantageous it would be to our cause to have one of *us* in charge of the ONS.'

She fell silent for a few seconds before replying. 'W...ell, yes, I suppose I can see that, but ...' Her voice tailed off.

Peregrine smiled; he almost surprised himself with his smooth-talking powers of persuasion. Almost. Actually, he had such supreme confidence in his own abilities that he could never truly surprise himself at how good he was.

He pressed home his advantage. 'For a start, you could redirect the efforts of the team away from the investigation into the falling birth rate.'

'But I've already explained why that's not a problem. And you said yourself, just a short while ago, that you understood that.'

Oops – lost a little ground there. 'Of course, but it would do no harm to just gently pivot the team away from digging into that subject. Sort of belt and braces, if you will.'

'Maybe,' she muttered, 'but I think we're getting ahead of ourselves. I probably won't even get the job.'

'Let's see, shall we?'

'Look, I can't focus on that right now. I don't think Amanda has ... *had* ... any close family around. If not, then when her body is released, I'm going to take it upon myself to organise the funeral.'

'Oh, what a thoughtful thing for you to do,' he schmoozed.

'It's the least I can do,' she said, before adding, 'Will you be coming?'

'Of course ... I couldn't possibly pass up the opportunity to pay my final respects.'

'Thank you.'

'Well, I must go now ... take care.'

He hung up, very pleased at how he had talked this woman around and confident that he could pull enough strings to get her into the top job at the ONS.

He just hoped that what he had been told about the poison was accurate; if the post-mortem detected the toxin in Amanda's body, it would well and truly put the proverbial cat among the pigeons.

Chapter 24

Doctor Matthew Turner, Head of Environmental Sciences at the University of Hampshire, was about to deliver his first lecture to the new intake of students enrolled on his course.

'Welcome to the Environmental Sciences degree course,' he began. 'My name is Matthew Turner. I will be your course leader over the next three years and one of several lecturers helping you throughout the course.'

'The fact that you have chosen this field of study tells me that you care about our planet. That's good, because not enough people really do. It's true that, in recent years, awareness of the threats facing our environment has begun to increase, but the vast majority of people have no conception of the scale of the existential emergency facing our planet.'

He paused for a moment to assess whether his words had sunk in.

They had. Already, that introductory statement had silenced the few subdued mutterings at the back of the lecture theatre. He had everyone's full attention now.

'So,' he continued, 'over the course of the next three years we will explore the many clear and present dangers which threaten the health and wellbeing of our environment, and indeed that of humanity itself.'

That stark statement served only to deepen and prolong the expectant silence in the room.

'The course consists of twelve modules,' he continued, 'each addressing a specific aspect of Environmental Sciences, but before we get into those specifics, I'd like to get a feel for your current understanding of where the most significant threats to the environment lie.'

He paused for a moment, surveying the expectant faces before him.

'So ... to kick us off, let's have some thoughts on what you consider to be the greatest environmental threat currently facing our planet. Who wants to go first?'

Four hands went up; he pointed to a bespectacled young man in the front row. 'Yes ... your name is ...?'

'It's Martin, Doctor Turner.'

'Oh, no need for such formality ... you can all call me Matthew.' He paused for a moment. 'Go ahead Martin.'

'It has to be global warming. According to the stats I've seen, global temperatures, which remained more or less static for a full century from 1880 to 1980, have increased by more than one full degree Celsius since then ... that's just insane. The polar ice caps are melting, and sea levels all around the world are rising at an alarming rate.'

'Very true,' responded Matthew, 'and do you know what the projections are going forward?'

The student shook his head.

'Well without significant intervention, most experts forecast a rise of around two point five to three degrees Celsius over the next fifty years. Such an increase would be utterly devastating to mankind with widespread flooding of coastal communities and a huge increase in extreme weather events. We're already seeing the beginning of these consequences: an upsurge in hurricanes, tornados, wildfires, flooding, and so on.'

'But,' replied the student, 'at least, as I understand it, governments around the world have pledged to take urgent action to limit the increase in global temperatures.'

Matthew smiled. 'It's one thing to make a pledge ... it's quite another to make it happen. The official pledge, agreed as a global target, is to limit the increase to one point five degrees which, in itself, would still be disastrous, but I know of no respected, independent expert who thinks we are anywhere near being on course to achieve even that figure.'

The student nodded. 'So not much good news on that front, then.'

'I'm afraid not,' said Matthew. 'I believe it will come down to the efforts of a younger generation ... like those of you in this room, to really tackle this issue head-on. Some of you may, in the future, go on to become decision-makers on the world stage. Just think about that.'

The bemused expressions on the sea of faces looking toward him suggested that most of his students had never considered themselves likely to ever assume such a profound responsibility.

'OK,' continued Matthew, releasing a small chuckle, '... maybe a bit heavy for the moment ... let's move on. We have a full module on global warming later in the course, so we'll explore this topic in much more detail then.

'So ... any other issues we should be worried about?' he said, casting his eyes back and forth across the faces of those present. His gaze settled on a red-haired young lady in the second row with her hand raised. 'And you are, Miss ...?'

'Suzy ... Suzy Pope.'

'Go ahead, Suzy.'

'It's plastic pollution that really bothers me. We see so many reports of oceans absolutely choked with plastic waste ... with shocking consequences for marine wildlife.'

'Yes,' agreed Matthew, 'and it's not just wildlife which is affected; we now know that microplastics ingested by fish are being consumed by humans in dangerous quantities. Do you know how much plastic we have already put into the oceans?'

'I don't know exactly but ... well, far too much.'

Her answer prompted a subdued ripple of laughter from the other students.

'Well,' replied Matthew, 'you're not the only one who doesn't know exactly, but the general consensus is around a hundred and fifty million tonnes. And we're currently adding to that at the rate of around ten million tonnes every year.'

A collective gasp rippled around the room.

'OK, thanks Suzy ... we'll be dealing with the issue of plastic pollution later in the course.' He raised his gaze. 'Any more suggestions?'

A few more hands went up; he indicated a girl with close-cropped hair and multiple face piercings about halfway up the banked rows of seats.

'Yes, Miss ...?'

'Keely Roberts.'

'Yes, Keely ... what's *your* biggest concern.'

'I'm worried about deforestation. The massive destruction of rainforests is devastating the natural habitat of many species, threatening some with extinction.'

'Indeed,' cut in Matthew. 'Do you know how much rainforest is being destroyed every year?'

'I've read that it's equivalent to a football pitch every six seconds.'

'Yes, that's about right ... and some 25% of the world's rainforest cover has already gone. Bear in mind, also, that as well as the impact on wildlife which you mentioned, this deforestation cuts CO_2 capture and exacerbates the global warming problem which we discussed earlier.'

He moved to wrap up this line of discussion and move on.

'OK, so we can all agree that global warming, pollution, and deforestation are significant threats to our environment. We'll be covering each of these subjects and many more over the course of the next three years. But here's a thought for you ... I would contend that all of these issues are secondary ... that they all stem from one common underlying cause.' He paused for a moment before adding, 'Would anyone like to suggest what that might be?'

He searched the faces of the students for several seconds before the young man in the first row who had been first to speak earlier on raised his hand.

'Yes ... Martin, wasn't it?'

'Yes, sir'

'"Matthew",' he reminded his student.

'Right ... sorry ... Matthew,' he murmured.

'Go ahead, Martin.'

'I would say overpopulation is the key factor,' replied the young man.

'Yes!' cried Matthew raising a forefinger and jabbing the air. 'Overpopulation. All of the issues we have discussed are a direct result of human activity, and as the world's population grows, then naturally all these issues are exacerbated. Let me show you some statistics ...'

He tapped a few keys on his laptop and projected a chart onto the screen behind him.

'This chart shows world population from the year 1800 right up to the present day and projected growth up to the year 2060. As you can see, world population first passed one billion in 1804. It wasn't until 1930 – one hundred and twenty-six years later that it passed two billion. Now look at this ... it has taken just fifty years since then to reach almost *eight* billion, and it is projected to continue rising.'

He paused for a few moments to let the numbers sink in.

The student, Martin, raised his hand. 'That's seriously scary ... and it begs the question of just what *is* a sustainable level of global population.'

'Indeed it does,' said Matthew, delighted at the way this young man was asking all the right questions. 'Well, it depends on the level of consumption of human beings. At present, the developed countries like the USA and most of Europe consume vastly more resources and impact the environment much more per capita than developing countries like most of those in Africa. But it's a natural human desire to aspire to a constantly improving standard of living, and the developing world is gradually catching up.

'The best estimates we have are that if the majority of the world's population were to reach a level of consumption similar to Western Europe the planet could sustain a population of around two point five billion.'

'But we're already over three times that number,' gasped Martin, without waiting to be invited to speak.

'Yes, and it gets worse ... consumption levels in the USA are almost double that in Western Europe; if worldwide consumption were to rise to *that* kind of level, then a sustainable worldwide population would be around one point five billion at best ... less than one fifth of the current figure.'

A stunned silence pervaded the lecture theatre as the implications of these figures began to sink in.

'Now,' continued Matthew, after a few seconds, 'it may take a very long time for consumption levels in the developing world to reach those of Western Europe, let alone the USA. Nevertheless, even now, the planet is, by any rational analysis, already overpopulated ... and with population still rising, we are on a dangerous trajectory.'

A number of heads were nodding, and some subdued murmuring suffused the room.

'So,' he continued, 'I think you can see that whatever actions governments take to reduce emissions, pollution, deforestation, and other destructive factors, any comprehensive plan for the future of our planet must also address the issue of overpopulation.

'So here's your first assignment: a ten-thousand-word paper on the subject "Proposals for a twenty-year plan to curtail and reverse global population growth." I think you'll be surprised how readily that each of you, as an individual, will be able to come up with a number of feasible ways to help address the issue. The problem in the real world is that it requires many different governments with different ideologies and political considerations to come together to tackle the issue, and history tells us that individual governments are generally spectacularly ineffective at co-ordinating responses to global problems.'

He glanced up at the clock at the back of the room. 'OK, we're just about out of time now, so that's it for today … you have one week to hand in your assignments. I'm looking forward to seeing all your ideas.'

Chapter 25

Doctor Matthew Turner had been disappointed with the initial papers submitted by his students on the subject of global population control. They had, for the most part, been desperately unambitious. The suggestions generally revolved around public education, financial incentives to limit family sizes, and aid from richer countries to developing counties. These were all things which governments around the world had already tried, to a greater or lesser extent, with very little success.

Over the subsequent weeks he had revisited the subject with his students several times, but few had shown any inclination to widen their horizons and think more radically – with one exception. Martin Stanton was the student who, at that very first lecture, had been the one to identify overpopulation as a key factor in the gradual destruction of the environment. His initial paper had been barely more imaginative than those of his peers, but in subsequent discussions he had definitely shown a willingness to consider more radical approaches.

Matthew decided to explore the subject further with Martin away from the group pressure of his fellow students. He invited him for afternoon tea in his study.

'Thank you for joining me this afternoon Martin. Please ... take a seat.'

The young man did so, his face betraying the puzzlement and discomfort he was clearly feeling.

'Tea or coffee?'

'Er ... tea please, Doctor Turner.'

'Oh please, what have I told you? Call me Matthew,' he replied, as he poured the tea. 'And help yourself to biscuits.'

'Thanks,' murmured the student.

'OK,' continued Matthew, once they were both settled, 'I expect you're wondering why I invited you here this afternoon for this little chat.'

The student's Adam's apple bobbed up and down in his throat. 'Well, yes ... I mean, have I done something wrong ... or is my work not up to scratch?'

'Oh no,' replied Matthew, waving his hand dismissively, 'quite the contrary.'

'Oh ... what do you mean?'

'I'm interested in your views on population control. You have shown a more open-minded and enquiring approach than many of the other students. I'd like to explore that further with you.'

'Oh, I see. Well ...what exactly do you want to discuss?'

'I get the sense that you may hold rather more radical views than you have been happy to voice in a public forum.' He fixed the student with a steady gaze. 'Am I right?'

Martin broke eye contact. 'Maybe ... it's just that ...'

'... you're afraid of being judged?'

'Kind of, I guess.'

'Well don't be ... at least not by me. I want my students to feel free to express their views openly ... however controversial they may be.'

The student looked up, re-engaging Matthew with his eyes. 'Really?'

'Really.'

Martin sat a little more upright in his chair, relief washing over his face.

'So now we've got that clear,' continued Matthew, 'I have an interesting question for you.'

'OK ... what's that then?'

'What do you think about the ideas which have been put forward by your fellow students regarding population control?'

'Well, if I'm completely honest, I think most of them are too ... well ... insufficient.'

'Can you expand on that?'

Suddenly he became animated – the shroud of reticence and shyness began to fall away. 'Look, we are facing an existential crisis, right?' He didn't wait for a reply before continuing. 'The world is already populated beyond a sustainable level and the numbers just keep rising. All this stuff about education and financial aid may, at best, slow down the rate of population growth ... *eventually* ... but it's too little, too late. The increase in population needs to be stopped in its tracks right now and then reversed.'

He paused, sighing heavily.

'So what would *you* suggest should be done?' prompted Matthew, inclining his head a little.

'Look, did you really mean what you said ... that nothing is off-limits here?'

'Of course ... it's just the two of us, and we're only kicking around ideas ... no-one is breaking any laws or offending anyone's sensibilities. So what do you think?'

'OK, well when we were faced with an immediate emergency in the form of the pandemic, governments around the world didn't flinch from imposing what many would see as draconian measures, enforceable by law. All the moaning about infringement of civil liberties and so on was swept aside.'

'That's true,' encouraged Matthew. 'So your point is?'

'My point,' said Martin, stabbing the tabletop with his finger, 'is that population growth is arguably ... no, *un*arguably ... an even greater threat to humanity than the current pandemic. In fact,' he continued, on a roll now, 'it could be said that the pandemic is actually *helping* in the fight against the greater threat of population growth.'

Suddenly, he checked himself breathing heavily, the frustration evident on his face. He took a moment or two to compose himself before continuing.

'I – I'm sorry, maybe I've said too much.'

'On the contrary,' said Matthew, 'It's a breath of fresh air to hear one of my students thinking so radically.'

'You mean that?'

'I do. Look, let me summarise what I think you are saying: overpopulation is the greatest threat currently facing humanity. All the other factors, such as global warming, pollution, deforestation, and the rest are secondary ... they are fundamentally the results of overpopulation. Agreed?'

'Absolutely,' said the student, leaning forward, his eyes intent.

'So, given the scale of the crisis, it is justifiable to impose extreme measures, overriding conventional notions of civil liberties.'

'Yes,' added Martin, 'and perhaps more than just perception of civil liberties ... it may be necessary to fundamentally re-think what most people regard as right or wrong.' Once again, he checked himself. 'I just mean something which might seem wrong in the short term may actually be in the interests of the greater good … if you see what I mean.'

'I do,' agreed Matthew. 'So … if we accept that the scale of the problem justifies what might be regarded as extreme measures, the question is, what might those measures be?'

'I do have some thoughts, but …' ventured Martin. He froze, evidently uncomfortable about going further.

'Look,' said Matthew, rescuing his student from his obvious discomfort, 'perhaps that's enough for the moment. I have enjoyed our chat, and I am genuinely impressed by your analysis of the situation. Can I suggest we meet again shortly to explore the subject further?'

'Yes,' said Martin, 'I'd like that.' He raised himself from his chair before adding, 'If you don't mind me saying so, Doctor Turner—'

'Matthew'

'Yes, of course … Matthew … you're not at all like I expected you to be.'

'I'll take that as a compliment,' chuckled Matthew. 'Shall we say same time Thursday?'

'OK – that's great.'

'Oh, and maybe it would be best not to mention our little chat to the other students. We don't want any accusations of favouritism, do we?'

'Oh … right. No, I won't mention it.'

After his student left, Matthew sat down to contemplate the discussion they had just had. His sense about Martin Stanton had been spot on: this young man might well be the candidate – one of them, at least – he was looking for. If anything, he was perhaps even more in tune with his own thinking than he had expected. He took his mobile from the desk and tapped out a message.

Julian – I believe I may have identified a possible candidate for 'Operation Next Gen'. I will explore this young man's views further over the coming weeks to assess whether he is suitable to put forward. – Matthew

He hit 'send' before gathering his things and preparing to head for home. Before he could even make it to the door of his study, his mobile pinged with a reply.

Matthew – Good news, but don't forget that if he is introduced to the programme he will have access to extremely sensitive information, so before you introduce him, you'd better be sure he's 100% reliable – Julian

Chapter 26

The post-mortem on Amanda Frobisher's body concluded that she had died of natural causes: a massive heart attack. Unusual for an apparently healthy woman, just forty-one years old, but not unheard of.

Peregrine Hartley-Briggs hadn't really wanted to attend the funeral, but since he wanted to smooth over his rather fractious relationship with Joanna Prentice, he judged it was worth investing a couple of hours to show willing. Apparently, Joanna's assumption that there would be no close family to organise or attend the event was correct, so she had taken on the mantle of organiser and would also deliver the eulogy.

As Peregrine joined the small queue of people filing into the crematorium, he saw that Joanna was standing at the door shaking the hand of everyone who entered.

'Thank you for coming, Peregrine,' she said, when he reached the front of the queue. 'I know you're a busy man.'

Her eyes were puffy and red – too much so for her heavy eye makeup to conceal – and her voice a little tremulous. *I guess she must have been closer to her erstwhile boss than I realised*, he thought.

'Oh, please ... call me Perry. Look, I couldn't possibly have missed this opportunity to pay my last respects. She was my friend, too, you know.'

Her forehead crinkled in a frown for a moment, but she did not comment. If these two *had* been closer than he had previously realised, maybe she was aware that he and Amanda hadn't exactly been best buddies. No matter: the post-mortem had ruled out foul play, and it looked as though everyone – including Joanna – had accepted that.

'Er, perhaps you'd better go through,' she said.

'Of course … I don't want to be blocking the doorway for others.'

He moved through into the main hall, where that peculiar atmosphere, unique to funerals, pertained. Organ music played softly in the background while those already seated spoke to each other in hushed tones. He took a seat as far back as he reasonably could without looking as though he wasn't part of the modest congregation.

At length, the minister stepped up to the pulpit at the front of the room and the organ music stopped. After a couple of seconds of expectant silence, he began.

'Friends … we are gathered here today to celebrate the life of Amanda Celia Frobisher …'

Never knew about the 'Celia' bit, though Peregrine. But that was about as far as his attention lasted. He quickly tuned out from what the minister was saying, his mind turning to other matters.

As the service continued, he didn't even register the other speakers at all – including Joanna, who delivered the eulogy. It was only when the music started up again to accompany the slow, solemn journey of the coffin through the purple curtains which concealed the heavy doors leading to the incinerator behind, that he came fully back to the here and now.

After one more prayer, which he dutifully mumbled as requested, the ceremony was over.

On the way out, Joanna shook his hand once again. 'Thanks again, Peregrine.'

'Perry,' he reminded her.

'Yes, of course … are you coming to the wake?'

'Indeed I am … I'll see you there.'

***

The wake took place in a community hall just a hundred yards or so from the crematorium.

As he entered, Peregrine took a glass of sparkling wine from the tray held by an attractive young girl with dark hair, tied back in a ponytail. He lingered for a moment, offering her his best smile. As she seemed completely unmoved by this, he moved on into the room. It was rather shabby really: the varnish on the woodblock flooring had worn through in many places and the cream paintwork on the walls looked distinctly tired. They had made an effort to smarten things up with strategically placed floral displays, but overall, it all looked a bit sad. But then again, funerals were supposed to be sad, weren't they?

He took a sip of his drink. His nose wrinkled; this wasn't proper champagne – more like some cheap imitation such as prosecco. Oh, well, it was well chilled and nicely fizzy; it was better than nothing and would have to do.

He looked around the room; he didn't see a single person that he recognised. As there seemed to be no further mourners coming in, the young girl who had served him his drink now looked to be at a bit of a loose end so he decided she might be the best person to be treated to his charm and wit. He drained his glass and strolled casually towards her.

'Delicious, my dear … could I have another?'

She extended her tray towards him, and he took one of the last two remaining glasses.

'That's a most attractive outfit you're wearing, if you don't mind me saying.'

The outfit was a pretty standard black waitress's outfit with white collar and apron, but it fitted her curves nicely and Peregrine felt she was very easy on the eye.

The girl glanced down at herself looking a little thrown by his remark. 'Er, well … it's just my uniform.'

'Well, I suppose it's all down to the way you wear it,' he schmoozed.

'I … er … well, thanks,' she replied, awkwardly. 'Look, if you'll excuse me, I need to pick up some more drinks and circulate among the other guests.'

'Of course,' he muttered, rather irritated that he had been so rudely rebuffed.

She hurried off, leaving him on his own again.

Just at that moment, Joanna appeared at the door having apparently waited for all the other guests to make their way across from the crematorium first.

'Oh, hello,' he said, 'come on through, and let me get you a drink.'

'Thanks … I need one.'

He summoned the waitress, who had just refilled her tray, and took another glass of the cheap bubbly, passing it to Joanna, who gratefully took a generous swallow.

'Better?' he said.

'Yes … thank you. It's such a relief to get that over with … finally feels like some sort of closure now.'

'Indeed … it was a beautiful service, though.'

'Yes, it was … at least we've given her a good send-off.'

Oh heavens - not that old cliché.

'Indeed … and I have to say that your words, in particular, were especially moving.'

'Thanks,' she said giving a weak smile.

As she took another deep swallow of her drink, he noted that she was starting to look appreciably more relaxed. This was probably as good a time as any to give her the important news which he had for her.

'Look, Joanna …' – he didn't usually address her by her first name, but he judged that now was the right time – 'now that Amanda has sadly passed on, we need to talk about succession.'

'Oh … not right now … it can wait, can't it?'

'Well, I'm not so sure it can, really. The ONS is now rudderless, and the UK Statistics Authority is keen to get it back on course as soon as possible. I've been having a few words in the right ears and although you won't hear officially until tomorrow, I can tell you – unofficially of course – that you are going to be offered the top job: National Statistician and Permanent Secretary. Congratulations.'

She looked absolutely shellshocked. 'I … I don't know what to say.'

'Don't say anything just now, but when they approach you tomorrow, say "yes". It's a fitting reward for your talent and contribution, and I don't need to remind you how valuable your appointment will be to our cause.'

'I … I suppose so, but …'

As her words tailed off, Peregrine's phone chimed. He raised a forefinger, while he checked the phone. The WhatsApp message was from Julian Chambers.

'Excuse me for a moment,' he said, 'I'm afraid I need to attend to this.'

The message was short and to the point.

We need to talk – can you get to my place today?

Arrogant sod, he thought. Why should this man assume that a busy government minister can just drop everything at a moment's notice? However, he *did* need to respond and find out what the hell Chambers was stressing about.

'Look,' he said to Joanna, 'something's come up that I need to deal with. I have to go now, but just think about what I've told you … do the right thing.'

***

In the end, Peregrine did agree to meet Julian that same day. He was evidently very agitated about something and insisted that it could not be discussed on the phone or be resolved with an exchange of WhatsApp messages.

When Peregrine arrived at Julian's mansion, the professor did, at least, extend the courtesy of offering Peregrine a drink before getting down to business. He poured two tumblers of single malt whisky and ushered Peregrine towards one of the two deep-buttoned armchairs in the corner of his opulent study.

'OK,' began Peregrine, 'what's this about?'

'It's about,' replied the professor, 'the death of Amanda Frobisher.'

'Oh …yes, most unfortunate.'

'Please … don't treat me like an idiot.'

Julian Chambers was a man who normally chose his words with care and consideration; Peregrine was completely taken aback by the bluntness of his response.

'I'm sorry … I'm not quite sure what you mean.'

'What I mean, is that I don't believe in coincidence. It's pretty unusual for a relatively young woman, apparently in good health and with no history of heart problems, to just keel over with a massive heart attack and die.

'And when that woman just happens to be a person who has access to the Prime Minister and has threatened to bring the falling birth rate to his attention – a situation you have expressed deep concern about – well, that's quite a coincidence, isn't it?'

'Hold on a minute,' protested Peregrine, 'I hope you're not suggesting that *I* had something to do with her death. You have no

140

way of knowing what health problems she may have been suffering. For all we know, she may have had a long history of heart problems.'

'Ah, but that's the thing ...' said the professor, 'I *do* know. I have checked her medical records.'

Peregrine was completely floored by this revelation. 'But how did you get them? I mean medical records are supposed to be completely confidential.'

'You are not the only one who has contacts,' said Julian. He did not elaborate further.

'Well even if she didn't have any previous problems with her heart, that doesn't prove anything. Anyone can fall victim to a heart attack.'

'Indeed they can, but as I said, I don't believe in co-incidence. I'm a man who considers probabilities, and the overwhelming probability here is that you arranged to shut her up.'

'That's an outrageous accusation ... you have no right to—'

The professor held up his hand, palm-outwards, cutting Peregrine off mid-sentence.

'Wait ... hear me out. This is not necessarily such a bad outcome.'

Peregrine contained his indignant rage, intrigued as to what Chambers was going to say next.

'Look, I am well aware that you have pulled some strings to get Doctor Prentice appointed as Frobisher's successor as head of the ONS.'

'What?' exclaimed Peregrine, astonished. 'How could you possibly know that?'

'As I said ... you are not the only one who has contacts.'

Chambers reached for a wooden case on the coffee table between them. He opened it to reveal that it was full of cigars; he offered one to Peregrine, who shook his head.

'No ... I don't smoke. Where are you going with this?'

Infuriatingly, the professor paused to take one himself, trim the end, and light up, puffing until the tip glowed brightly. *Get on with it, you bastard.*

'It won't have escaped your notice that, with this appointment, we will have our own people in place in all the key positions. Sofía Méndez at Saturn Pharmaceuticals, Peter Simmons at Thomas Lewis Vaccine Group, Joanna Prentice at the ONS ... and of course your good self in government … possibly with a good shot at the top job in due course.'

'Well, nothing can be taken for granted of course, but if I say so myself—'

'Yes, yes. Anyway, we can both agree, I think, that this is actually rather a good outcome.'

'So what is your point?'

'Look, our cause is sufficiently important that no action is off-limits when it is threatened. Last year we all agreed that Felicity Maddocks would have to be eliminated if she would not come on board with our plans.'

'So … what are you saying?'

'What I am saying, is that that particular action was agreed by the whole group. Together we judged that the risk of Maddocks scuppering the programme outweighed the risk of the reasons behind her killing might come to light.'

Finally, it began to dawn on Peregrine where Chambers was headed.

'In the case of Amanda Frobisher, we all agreed that, in spite of her interest in the falling birth rate, she would be unlikely to discover the cause.'

'Not *all* of us,' interjected Peregrine.

'OK … a majority then. The point is that a collective decision was taken, and the success of our venture depends on us all acting in concert. Have you considered what the consequences might have been if it were discovered that her death was not from natural causes?'

'Look, I've already told you, I'm not admitting to anything.'

'Well, it really doesn't matter whether you admit it or not. We both know you did it.'

Finally, Peregrine accepted there was no longer any point in protesting his innocence.

'The point is,' continued Chambers, 'that killing her was judged by the group to be a risk not worth taking … and you went against that collective decision.'

He did not try to refute the accusation; he waited while the professor took a deep draw on his cigar, before exhaling a choking cloud of smoke and setting it down on the ashtray on the desk. *Come on you bastard – get to the point.*

'The thing is,' he concluded, 'what's done is done and, as it happens, the gamble has paid off ... *this time.*'

Peregrine was, by now feeling completely baffled by the professor's line of argument. 'So if we're all agreed that it's worked out well, what was the point of dragging me over here, and away from my important work in government?'

'I don't doubt that your work in government is important, but *our* work is even more important. If you ever do anything to jeopardise it again, there will be consequences.'

Peregrine was completely taken aback. Why, the jumped-up prick had actually got the audacity to threaten a government minister. A hot rage surged within him.

With some difficulty, he held his anger in check. 'Finished?' he muttered, tight-lipped.

'Finished,' said Chambers, 'just as long as we understand one another.'

Chapter 27

After Hartley-Briggs had left, Julian poured himself another whisky and sat down to consider the situation.

On the face of it, things were going well. Those who had presented the main obstacles to the success of the project had been eliminated without their deaths being linked to the group. They would soon have their own people in place at the heads of the Thomas Lewis and Saturn vaccine programmes, and the ONS. Not to mention Hartley-Briggs in the Department of Health and Social Care. The vaccine had now been rolled out to the majority of the developed world and even developing countries were making good progress. The modification to the vaccine to suppress female fertility was clearly very effective, as demonstrated by the trials carried out by Peter Simmons. The birth rate was now measurably dropping in the UK and probably also in other countries where the population had been widely vaccinated, though he didn't have access to the statistics to verify this. Yes, all in all, things couldn't have panned out much better.

He had his reservations though. As he had explained to the rest of the group, this plan would be slow to bring population growth under control. Although far fewer babies were now being born, this – in itself – would have little immediate effect on population numbers; it was not until a significant proportion of the population died through natural causes that global population growth would slow down and eventually reverse. It would have been quicker to just let the disease run its course until, eventually, 'herd immunity' brought it under control, by which time global population should be approaching a more sustainable level.

Unfortunately, due to the efforts of his erstwhile colleagues in the scientific world, this approach had failed. The vaccine looked set to strangle the spread of the disease and thwart his plan. In any case, the rest of the group had grave reservations about letting a lethal disease rip through populations; they considered it to be too harsh, too cruel. Didn't they understand that desperate situations call for desperate measures?

In the end, though, the birth control strategy had been the plan agreed among the members of the group and, this approach did, to be fair, have some advantages over his original plan.

Firstly, it did not depend on defeating the efforts of the world's vaccinologists, but rather took advantage of their work. And secondly, with a 70% reduction in birth rate, it had the potential, in time, to achieve a significantly greater population reduction than deaths due to the virus alone.

So far, the plan was working well. Given the long timescales involved, though, he knew he probably wouldn't live long enough fully to see it through. There were also signs that some of the others in the group might not be as committed to the long term as he would have liked. That was why he sought to recruit a select few young people to join the cause. For this purpose he was relying on Doctor Matthew Turner at the University of Hampshire to try to identify suitable candidates.

Although overall, things were pretty much on track, there were a couple of slightly disturbing developments. For a start, he didn't much like the way this detective was looking into Felicity Maddocks's death again, more than a year after the event. Although Sofia's account of the incident gave no cause for undue concern, he was nevertheless uncomfortable about it.

He was also concerned about Peregrine Hartley-Briggs. His action in arranging the murder of Amanda Frobisher had been reckless, and totally counter to what the group had agreed. Although, on this occasion, his gamble had paid off, and actually produced a positive outcome, there was no guarantee that whatever he might do next would be similarly beneficial. The man was a loose cannon. He just hoped their discussion that afternoon might curb Hartley-Briggs's excesses.

Julian was not naïve, though: he knew that there was every chance that the whole programme could be disrupted at any moment by an unwise move or a chance discovery. That was why he had, for some time, been working on an escape route and a plan 'B' should everything turn to shit.

He levered himself out of his armchair and moved over to the corner of the room, where he pressed an inconspicuous-looking feature on the carved wooden detailing on the oak panelling. A large section of panelling swung smoothly forward to reveal a tall safe behind. He punched in a code and opened the heavy steel door. Inside were a Heckler and Koch submachine gun, and a Glock handgun. But it wasn't one of the weapons which he withdrew; it was a hefty-looking pile of documents. He took them over to his desk and laid them down.

He had already studied the documents extensively and didn't need to read them again. He only needed to make a final decision as to whether to proceed.

And now he had: he turned to the signature page and scribbled his signature above that of the supposed witness who was, in fact, completely fictitious. If all went well, the transaction would be completed within days.

***

Peregrine Hartley-Briggs was still fuming as he drove down the slip road and joined the traffic crawling along the M25. Neither the silken ride of his Rolls Royce, nor the soothing tones of Mendelssohn's Violin Concerto in E minor, could mollify his anger. No, there was only one thing which would do it; he tapped a button on the touchscreen on his dashboard at which point the music was automatically muted to allow him to make his call.

It was more than an hour later that he finally pulled into his underground garage. He checked the clock on the dashboard: 8.05 p.m. In spite of the horrendous traffic, he still had almost an hour and a half in hand.

He locked the car and moved upstairs into his house. The first thing he did was to go into his study and pour himself a generous measure of single malt whisky. The second was to go to his desk drawer and pop out a little blue pill from the silver foil card within. He put it in his mouth and swallowed it, washing it down with a mouthful of the whisky, wincing as he realised he had swallowed a little too much.

He moved through into the bedroom, undressed, and slipped into his dressing gown. Feeling much more comfortable now, he went into the living room, put on some soft music, and settled down to wait.

Just before 9.30 p.m. the doorbell rang; his heart jumped at the anticipation of who was there. When he opened the door he was met with the sight of a very attractive young woman with long dark hair. She was wearing a full-length raincoat and high heels. Her heavy makeup was possibly a bit over the top, but he liked them like that. She was carrying a leather holdall.

'Hello Perry,' she purred. 'I understand you have been a bad boy.'

'Yes ...' he replied, 'very bad indeed. That's the reason I called you.'

'Well, you'd better let me in then.'

He stood aside to let her past him; she made straight for the stairs, for she knew the layout of the house well. He followed her up to the master bedroom. Once inside she set down the holdall on the couch in the corner of the room.

'Now then,' she said, 'you know what happens when you've been a bad boy.'

He nodded.

'You are going to have to be punished.'

She loosened her belt and slowly unbuttoned her coat, slipping out of it and letting it fall to the floor. His mouth felt as though it were full of sand as his eyes roamed up and down her body. She wore dark stockings with lacy tops, supported by a black suspender belt, over which was stretched the tiniest of thongs which failed fully to conceal the top of a strip of dark pubic hair. Her ample breasts bulged over the top of a black peephole bra, through which her nipples proudly protruded.

He grabbed the glass of water, which was on the bedside table, taking a long swallow to lubricate his parched throat.

'I ... I'm sorry, Miss Belinda.' It wasn't her real name, but that was how he always knew her.

She tutted. 'Dear, dear ... won't you ever learn to behave? I'm afraid, Perry, that I'm going to have to give you a very severe reprimand.'

She turned to the holdall and bent over, very slowly, as she unzipped it, making sure she gave him ample time to take in the sight of her shapely buttocks and the plump, black satin mound peeping out from between them. When she turned to face him, she was holding a riding crop. She slapped it against the palm of her hand.

'You like what you see?'

He nodded dumbly.

'You want to touch?'

He nodded again

'Well come here then,' she whispered, beckoning him.

He stepped forward, holding out his hand, desperate to feel those hard nipples and the soft warmth of her breasts.

Suddenly he felt the sharp bite of the riding crop on the back of his knuckles.

'You bad, bad boy,' she scolded. 'You know you're not allowed to touch.'

'I … I'm sorry,' he gasped, massaging his throbbing hand.

'Get that thing off,' she ordered, slipping the tip of the riding crop inside the collar of his dressing gown and flipping it to the side.

He obediently shrugged out of it, letting it fall to the floor. The pill he had taken earlier, and the heat of the moment had, by now, taken full effect; he was sporting an impressive erection, visible to him even over his pot belly.

She looked down at it, tutting as she stroked the tip of the riding crop along its length. 'Now you know you're not allowed to get too excited until I say so, don't you?'

'I know … I'm sorry.'

'Get over there,' she commanded, gesturing towards the bed with the riding crop. 'I'm going to have to punish you very severely indeed.'

He moved over to the bed and sat on the edge.

'Bend over,' she barked.

He turned to face away from her, bent over the edge of the bed and waited; the anticipation was almost too much. Nothing happened for several long seconds and then … *Thwack* … the sharp sting of the crop across his buttocks made him cry out in pain, but it was a delicious kind of pain.

'Silence!' yelled Miss Belinda, 'you know you're not allowed to make a noise.'

She struck him again; in spite of his best effort, he could not suppress another cry of pain.

'Oh dear,' she muttered, 'I'm going to have to take additional measures. Wait there.'

She was silent for a few moments, but then he felt something like a rubber ball being rammed between his teeth and then a cord or strap being fastened behind his neck. Now he could not speak at all.

'Hands out in front of you,' she commanded.

As he stretched his arms forward, she secured his wrists together with a pair of handcuffs, looping a chain through them and securing it to the metal headboard of the bed.

'Now then,' she said, walking around to the side of the bed where he could see her, 'this is going to hurt …'

Chapter 28

Sofía Méndez was torn. Novagen had now increased the salary on offer, if she agreed to join them, to almost three times her current salary at Saturn Pharmaceuticals. The promise of year-round sunshine and an exciting new life in California, with a salary she could never dream of making in the UK was almost overwhelmingly tempting. And yet, she believed passionately in the cause of population control, and felt she would be letting the group down if she took the job. As Professor Julian Chambers was leader of the group, she wanted to seek his advice. Given the importance, complexity, and sensitivity of the issue it just couldn't be dealt with by exchange of WhatsApp messages or calls; she arranged a one-to-one meeting with him at his opulent Surrey mansion.

'So,' she sighed, after spending some twenty minutes outlining the position, 'that's my situation.'

Julian had barely interrupted her at all during her account, but she could tell from his face that he was taking it all in, processing it, weighing up options.

'Hmm …' he mused, stroking his chin, 'I can see why you would be conflicted, but possibly … just possibly … this could present us with an opportunity.'

'What do you mean?' she said.

'Our mission is a truly global enterprise … agreed?'

'Well yes, of course, but I don't see—'

He held up his hand to curtail her question. 'I'm thinking out loud here but …' he placed a forefinger against the side of his chin, falling silent for a few moments.

This time she did not interrupt him. This man had a formidable intellect; if he was taking time to process some possibilities, it was worth waiting.

Finally, he articulated the train of thought that he was pursuing. 'OK, look … it was always going to be challenging to orchestrate a worldwide campaign from here in the UK.'

'But we've been doing well,' she said.

'We have,' he agreed, 'but luck has been with us … so far. Now that the vaccine programme is rolling out worldwide, the possibilities for our activities to be discovered are expanding exponentially. Imagine how beneficial it would be to our cause if we had a foothold in the USA … arguably the most technologically advanced nation in the world. Even if – God forbid – the UK operation were to be shut down we might well be able to continue with our work from the USA.'

At last she began to understand where he was going with this. 'You want *me* to establish that foothold in the USA?'

'Who better?' he said. 'You have an impeccable reputation within the vaccinology world; you are fiercely committed to our cause, and you have the persuasive skills to convince others of its righteousness.'

Suddenly it all fell into place. Hitherto, she had seen this situation as a binary choice: a choice between furthering her career and lifestyle or furthering the cause of population control. Julian had helped her see she could possibly do both.

'You think I could do it?' she said, '… set up a satellite group in the USA?'

'It doesn't matter what *I* think … do *you* think you could do it?'

'I don't know … I need some time to think about it.'

'OK … take that time, but there are other factors which we also need to consider.'

'Such as?' she said, somewhat distracted by the unexpected possibilities now on the table.

'Well, there is no doubt that having you in place in the USA would be highly beneficial to our cause, but I'm a little concerned about losing your influence at Saturn Pharmaceuticals. Saturn was the original manufacturer of the vaccine and, as you well know, there are a number of people there, apart from your good self, who worked closely with the development team at Thomas Lewis.'

Suddenly the cause for his concern became clear to her. 'You're worried that without me there, someone else in the team might discover what is going on.'

'Exactly … how likely do you think that is?'

'Well …' she ventured, 'I don't think it's very likely at all. Now that we are in mass production, the manufacturing people are just working to a formula. They don't get too involved in the clinical mechanisms of the vaccine.' She paused for a moment, considering the possibilities. 'However, I suppose there *is* a small chance that if one of the original team who worked with Thomas Lewis during the development phase got involved in, say, investigating some technical hitch in the production process, they just might uncover something.'

'So …' said Julian, 'unlikely, but possible.'

'Yes, I guess so.'

'OK … is there anyone there, at Saturn, who might, by any stretch, possibly be sympathetic to our cause?'

This question completely threw her; it had never occurred to her to even explore such a possibility, but just as she was about to dismiss the notion out of hand, she realised that maybe – just maybe – there *was* someone.

Chapter 29

The person that Sofía had in mind was Emily Forbes. She had obtained her PhD just over two years earlier and joined Saturn Pharmaceuticals immediately afterwards.

She was quiet – shy even – and kept herself very much to herself, but she was quite the most brilliant PhD student Sofía had ever encountered. The thing which had brought her to mind, when Julian asked his unexpected question, was the subject of her PhD thesis, which Sofía vividly remembered: 'Vaccines – Blessing or Curse?' It was an outrageous, audacious title, clearly designed to be provocative – or was it?

At the time when Sofía had originally read the thesis, she assumed that the author was playing devil's advocate – that she couldn't possibly seriously believe the premise that vaccines were anything other than one of science's greatest gifts to mankind. But, she recalled, this young woman's arguments were so cogent, and so skilfully marshalled, that she had successfully presented equally forceful cases for and against. Sofía decided to retrieve Emily's thesis and read it again.

She spent fully three evenings after work studying this young woman's work – much more carefully this time – and, at the end, still could not decide whether it represented her sincerely held views or was merely an academic exercise in the power of argument.

In favour of vaccines, she pointed out the massive reduction in human suffering which they had afforded, and the total elimination of certain diseases which had blighted mankind for decades – even centuries. Her principal case against vaccines revolved around the fact that the planet was becoming massively overpopulated, resulting in the inexorable destruction of the environment. Diseases, she argued, were one of nature's ways of controlling population and maintaining balance. Science, with the best of intentions, was interfering with the natural order of things by creating these powerful vaccines and disrupting nature's intentions.

So, on which side of the argument did Emily Forbes really sit? Sofía could still not be sure.

She decided to risk exploring the subject further.

She chose her moment carefully: a seemingly casual encounter by the drinks vending machine.

'Oh, Emily … glad I bumped into you … there's something I wanted to talk to you about.'

The other woman was of slight build, with a freckled complexion and coarse, mousy hair which seemed to be trying to escape in all directions from the numerous clips and pins struggling to restrain it. She had a slightly disconcerting trait of avoiding eye contact when involved in conversation, and this occasion was no exception.

'Oh … what was that then?' she said, casting her eyes downward.

'I've been re-reading your PhD thesis.'

'Really?' said the younger woman, her eyes suddenly coming into contact with Sofía's. 'Why would you do that?'

'As you know, the anti-vaxxer movement is rife at the moment, and the company wants me to do a couple of TV interviews to present the positive case for vaccination. Thing is, I want to make sure I'm fully prepped with all the arguments for and against before I get in front of a camera.'

'Oh, I see … well what exactly do I … I mean, what did you want to talk to me about?'

'I remembered your thesis from when you first applied to join us here, and I thought it was a fine piece of work.'

A crimson flush infused her cheeks. 'Well, thank you, but … it was just—'

'No false modesty now … It was a very well-thought-out piece.'

'Well, thank you for saying so, Doctor Méndez.'

'Look, how about joining me for a drink after work one day to explore some of your ideas?'

'I'm sure you don't need my help to—'

'Please,' interjected Sofía '… I'd really appreciate it.'

'Well, OK … I suppose.'

'Great! Are you busy this evening?'

'I … er … well, no … not really.'

'Well, shall we just walk across the road to the King's Arms then? Say about 6.30?'

'OK …'

Sofía took her coffee and left Emily standing by the vending machine. She hoped she had not said anything to spook this young woman, who was so difficult to read; in spite of her fiercely acute intellect, she always came across as slightly bemused-looking.

***

The Kings Arms was an ancient pub, with low ceilings and dark, gnarled oak beams across the ceiling. Even at 6.30 p.m. it was very busy, packed with business folk stopping for a well-earned drink after work, before heading for home. Mercifully, there was no music playing, so the ambient noise consisted only of the buzz of many conversations melding to make a sort of unintelligible white noise.

The two women glanced around, hunting for a place they could sit and have a private conversation. Fortuitously, two men in suits were just draining their glasses and preparing to leave.

'We're just leaving,' said one of them as they stood up. He gestured to the table. 'It's all yours.'

'Thanks,' said Sofía, smiling. She turned to her colleague. 'Why don't you grab the table while I get us some drinks … what would you like?'

'Er … thanks … a glass of white wine, please.'

Sofía headed for the bar, returning a few minutes later with a tray bearing a bottle of wine and two glasses. 'Hardly worth getting just two glasses and leaving a third of the bottle behind,' she laughed. She hoped that the alcohol might help the younger woman loosen up a little and perhaps speak more freely.

'Thanks,' said Emily, as her boss set down the tray and slipped into her seat, before pouring the wine.

'Cheers,' said Sofía extending her hand to clink glasses.

The other woman responded, rather hesitantly, before taking a sip of her wine. 'So what was it you wanted to discuss?'

'Well, I have to do these TV interviews … to put the positive case for vaccines and help counter the arguments of the anti-vaxxers which have spread like wildfire on social media.'

'Well, I'm not sure that I can help you much with that … after all you are an expert in the field. You know, probably better than I do, how to argue the case.'

'The positive case, yes,' replied Sofía, taking a sip of her drink and setting down her glass, but I want to be well prepared to deal with the anti-vaccine arguments which may be fired at me.'

The younger woman's eyes narrowed as she inclined her head. 'What do you mean?'

'Well, we've all heard the conspiracy theories: microchips being injected in our arms, chemicals to control our behaviour, mind-reading compounds, and so on.'

Emily gave a dismissive shrug. 'Utterly ridiculous.'

'Yes, of course, but this is just the sort of nonsense usually put forward by the anti-vaxxers. What I'm interested in is the far more credible argument which you put forward so persuasively in your thesis: the notion that our planet is overpopulated and that vaccines interfere with nature's attempts to redress the situation.'

'Ah … I see,' said Emily, taking another sip of her wine.

'So I'd like you to help me build my case to counter such an argument in case it comes up during the interviews.'

'Unlikely,' opined Emily, '…too controversial for most TV interviewers.'

'Maybe, but even so, I'd like to be ready for it.'

'OK … well here's my take on it …'

***

Two hours later, they had finished the bottle of wine and were well into a second. As they had kicked the subject around, Emily had become more and more animated. All the evasiveness and shyness which normally characterised her manner had evaporated: now she was energetic, intent, and focused. Far from presenting a counter argument to the over-population case, if anything she had reinforced it, in Sofía's view.

Then, all of a sudden there was a lull between them. It was as if both women had talked themselves to a standstill; now they were exhausted, spent.

Emily drained her glass and poured herself another before tipping the remainder of the second bottle into Sofía's glass. She took a generous swallow, before setting down the glass, pursing her lips as crinkles formed at the edges of her eyes. Sofía sensed she was struggling with whether to say something. Finally, she did.

'Doctor Méndez, can I speak freely?'

'Oh, for goodness sake ... what's with the "Doctor Méndez" thing? We're not at work now. Of course you can speak freely.'

She paused for a few moments before declaring, 'You're not a very good liar.'

Sofía felt as though her stomach had been punched by a giant, invisible fist. 'Wh-what on earth do you mean?'

'You're not doing any TV interviews are you?'

'I ... well, I've been told that I might have to—'

'Let's drop the pretence shall we? I know what you've done.'

Chapter 30

Peregrine Hartley-Briggs was on tenterhooks, as he waited for the hoped-for phone call.

The long-awaited public enquiry into the Government's handling of the pandemic had been published a couple of days earlier, and it was scathing.

The decision to introduce a national lockdown in the early days of the outbreak had, according to the report, been weeks too late. The enquiry concluded that many thousands of lives could have been saved if more decisive action had been taken.

The supply of personal protective equipment had been totally inadequate, leaving healthcare professionals and care home staff at risk, costing yet more lives.

International travel was another area which should have been clamped down on earlier to limit the import of new variants from abroad.

And the repeated opening and closing of schools was judged to have been chaotic, taking a huge toll on children's education.

The only aspect of the whole sorry saga for which some positive comment was reserved was the development and rollout of the vaccine. *Ironic*, thought Peregrine. *If only they knew what that vaccine was doing to women's fertility up and down the land, and indeed throughout the world.*

This, however, was not the aspect of the report which interested him most; no, he was focused on where blame was apportioned. The Prime Minister and the Health and Social Care Secretary had come in for the most severe kicking, while he, himself, had skilfully avoided the flak. Indeed, his 'fluent and informative' communication at the numerous TV briefings was said to have helped keep the public informed and mitigated some of the loss of confidence caused by many of the policy errors.

With the Prime Minister's position looking increasingly precarious, he did what prime ministers do in such situations: deflect the blame onto his ministers, and then try to look decisive by embarking on a Cabinet reshuffle. That reshuffle was now underway, and Peregrine sat anxiously by the phone in his Westminster office, waiting for the call which he hoped would be coming. And, finally, it did.

'Perry ...' came the familiar tones of the PM, 'it's Malcolm here.'

At last. 'Hi ... yes, Malcolm ... what can I do for you?'

'Could you pop along to number ten for a few minutes? I have something I want to discuss with you.'

'Of course ... I'll be there in ten minutes.'

***

'Thanks for coming over,' said the PM. 'Please, take a seat.'

Peregrine eyed the very firm-looking chair with trepidation. The thing was, 'Miss Belinda' had paid him another visit the previous evening, and his buttocks were still very tender from the thrashing she had administered. Still, it would have looked very odd for him to remain standing or ask for a cushion; he lowered himself as gently as possible into the chair, wincing slightly as he touched down.

'Can I get you a drink?' offered the PM. 'I have a particularly fine Islay malt here.' He gestured towards a side table bearing several bottles and a selection of glasses.

'Well, perhaps just a small one.'

It wasn't by any means a small one which the PM poured.

'Now then, you'll obviously have read the enquiry report.'

'Of course ... rather unduly harsh in my opinion.'

'Indeed, but the media have well and truly got their collective teeth into it, and that's stoking up a lot of public distrust in the Government.'

Tell me something I don't know, thought Peregrine. 'Yes ... most irresponsible reporting, if I may say so.'

'Quite. In any event, I have to take some action to restore public confidence,' – *and save your skin,* thought Peregrine – 'which is why I'm carrying out a Cabinet reshuffle.'

'Absolutely the right thing to do ... show them that you're taking decisive action.'

The PM inclined his head a little and pursed his lips, his brow wrinkling slightly. *Oh dear ... hope I haven't laid it on too thick*, thought Peregrine.

Well, if the PM *had* realised that he was being shamelessly patronised, he didn't allude to it.

'The thing is, Stuart, as Health and Social Care Secretary, has been particularly singled out for criticism in the report and, although some of the censure is a little unfair, in truth he *hasn't* handled things especially well.'

'Well,' replied Peregrine, 'it was a totally unprecedented situation; anyone would have made a few mistakes.'

'That's as maybe, but he's the one who made them, and he's the one who has to carry the can.'

Can't be much blunter than that, thought Peregrine.

'I suppose so,' he replied ... you know, I did my best to help and support him throughout; took over those tiresome TV briefings and—'

'Exactly ...' interjected the P.M., 'I was just coming to that. You did a great job on those briefings ... the public love you.'

'Well, modesty prevents me from—'

'Yes, yes ... quite. Look, let me cut to the chase: I want *you* to take over as Health and Social Care Secretary, with immediate effect.'

'Well ... Malcolm ... I don't know what to say. This is so unexpected.'

'Oh come on, Perry ... you must have known it was on the cards.'

'No ... really ... I mean ... well, of course I'd be honoured to step into the breach, as it were.' He decided it was time to show some apparent concern for the plight of his erstwhile boss. 'But what about Stuart? After all his service and dedication ...'

'Oh,' said the PM, waving his hand dismissively, 'let me worry about that. I'll find some backbench role or other for him.'

'I'm sure you will make an appointment which makes good use of his talents.'

'Yes, of course. Now I just have one or two more pieces of the jigsaw to slot into place, but I should be in a position to finalise the reshuffle this afternoon and announce all the new appointments in time for this evening's news bulletins.'

Peregrine did not want to endure that rock-hard chair for a moment longer than necessary; he placed his hands on the arms of the chair and levered himself carefully to his feet.

The PM extended his hand, which Peregrine firmly grasped, 'Welcome to the Cabinet.'

'Thank you, sir … I won't let you down.'

When he left number ten, he decided not to return immediately to his office in parliament but to head home for a lie down on a soft duvet to give his throbbing backside a chance to recover a bit, before facing the inevitable barrage of TV interviews that evening.

Chapter 31

Sofía Méndez was thrown completely off balance by the sudden and unexpected accusation from her younger colleague. Her heart was pounding furiously now.

'I … I don't know what you mean.' she protested.

'I think you do … I'm talking about the way the formulation of the vaccine in mass production is different from the version which received regulatory approval.'

Sofía was stunned; she slumped back in her chair, drained and defeated. There was no point in maintaining the pretence any longer.

'How did you know?' she sighed.

'Have you forgotten that I was the person entrusted with managing the transition from development to production?'

'Well no … of course not, but—'

'And part of that process was to verify the formulation of the initial production batches against the specification.'

'Well yes, but the specification had already been modified by that time.'

'Doctor Méndez …' – Sofía didn't bother rebutting the formal address this time – 'you know I'm a very thorough person; you have said so yourself.'

'That's true, but I still don't see how—'

'There were some aspects of the specification which didn't seem quite right to me, so I took it upon myself to test one of the original development samples.'

Understanding dawned. '…and it didn't match the specification.'

'Right … the original version didn't match the specification, but the production version did. The only conclusion I could draw is that the specification had been modified.'

'Why didn't you approach me at the time?'

'Two reasons: first, I was curious about why the change had been made, and second, I figured it was very unlikely that it could have been done without your knowledge.'

Sofía was, by now, furiously processing the options for how to deal with this desperate situation. If this girl went to the authorities, it was game over for the whole project. She had to be stopped – by any and all means necessary. The precedent had already been set with the elimination of Professor Maddocks the previous year; if necessary, Emily Forbes would have to be dealt with in the same way. And yet, if she was intending to go to the police, why hadn't she done so already? Sofía decided to ask the question.

'Look, you must have made this discovery some time ago, why have you been sitting on it all this time?'

'Oh, but I haven't. I have spent a great deal of time analysing the modification to the vaccine to try to determine its purpose.'

'And have you come to any conclusions?'

'Well, not definitively, but I would say it has something to do with disruption of a woman's reproductive system. Am I right?'

Sofía was shocked to her core. She had always known that this girl was exceptionally gifted, but to have worked all this out, single-handed? It was breathtaking.

She didn't answer the question directly. 'Look, if you have worked all this out, I still don't understand why you are keeping it all to yourself.'

'I'll take that as a "yes",' said Emily. 'So, once I had worked out the "what", I was curious as to the "why". I wasn't sure what you were trying to achieve … until today that is.'

'What do you mean?'

'All that stuff about TV interviews and so on was just an excuse to pump me about my views on overpopulation, wasn't it?'

There was no point in denying it. 'I can see I have underestimated you, Emily. So what do you intend to do with this information?'

She had hoped to have some time to consult with Julian and the rest of the group before deciding how to deal with this new threat, but it could be that the urgency of the situation would require immediate action. She didn't have any lethal weapons, and she was not skilled in unarmed combat. She did, however, carry a self-defence spray which was capable of rendering an attacker unconscious for a short while. If she could get Emily into her car she could perhaps incapacitate her with the spray and tie her up until she had a chance to deal with her permanently.

Emily's answer to her question was unexpected. 'I'm not going to do anything with it.'

'I ... I don't understand. You have spent months digging into this issue, and now you don't intend to act on what you have discovered?'

'Look, I needed to find out what you were doing, and why. Now I know. You care about the way overpopulation is destroying the planet just as much as I do. The only difference between us is how drastically we might be prepared to act to deal with the situation.'

'So you, too, would be willing to take action?'

She nodded. 'I have been concerned about this issue for years, but it was only when I was working on my PhD thesis that I began thinking about the way that medical science was exacerbating the situation by combating, and in some cases eliminating, those diseases which form part of nature's way of maintaining population balance.'

'So,' said Sofía, 'the premise in your thesis that vaccines could be considered a curse rather than a blessing wasn't just an intellectual argument?'

'No ... I believe it. The thing I wrestle with, though, is the extra suffering which would be inflicted on millions if we just let lethal diseases run their course unchecked. Reducing the birth rate would be a slower, but far more humane way of controlling, and eventually, reversing population growth.

'So you see, Doctor Méndez, we are – to use a tired old cliché – on the same page.'

This was a hell of a lot to take in. It was entirely possible that this young woman had picked up on Sofía's discomfiture and was simply telling her what she wanted to hear, to extricate herself from the current situation before going to the police. She was certainly clever enough. Yet there was something about her manner and the conviction with which she spoke which made Sofía inclined to believe her.

What to do now? If she was lying, and intended to go to the police, the consequences would be catastrophic. On the other hand, if she was telling the truth, she could be a valuable asset to the group. Sofía would be able to take up her new post in the USA, secure in the knowledge that her work at Saturn Pharmaceuticals was in safe hands. Furthermore, she could bring some of the young blood to the group as encapsulated in Julian's vision for 'Operation Next Gen'.

It was an agonising dilemma, and she needed to make a decision there and then.

Chapter 32

Doctor Matthew Turner sat opposite Professor Julian Chambers in the opulent surroundings of the study in Julian's Surrey mansion. Both men were nursing balloon-shaped crystal glasses containing a fine Cognac.

Matthew had spent around half an hour relating his various discussions with his student and how he had teased out this young man's views on the threats posed to the planet by uncontrolled population growth.

'So,' concluded Matthew, swirling the mahogany-coloured liquid in his glass, 'having spent a great deal of time with him now, I believe he sincerely shares our views and is ready to be introduced to the group.'

'And you have completed all the background checks we discussed?' asked Julian. 'You know we have to exercise extreme caution.'

'Uh huh … everything checks out OK. His name is Martin Stanton, son of Jane and Geoffrey Stanton … now both deceased. He was born and brought up in Portsmouth but now lives on his own in a rented flat in Winchester – near to the University.'

'Hmm … the fact that both parents are dead is beneficial: no-one to ask awkward questions about what he is spending his time on. How did they die?'

'The mother died of breast cancer and the father a little later, in a car accident.'

'Any long-term girlfriend … or boyfriend?'

'Not that I'm aware of.'

Julian grunted his approval. 'Very good … how old is he?'

'Twenty-four.'

'Interesting … a little older than usual to be starting on his first degree.'

'Oh, he already has a first-class honours degree in biology, but after having become keenly interested in the fate of the environment he decided to return to his studies and enrol on my Environmental Sciences course.'

'OK,' concluded Julian, 'that all sounds very good. But are you completely sure that he will be prepared to commit to our cause? Because once he knows everything, there's no turning back; you know as well as I do what we would have to do if he decided not to join us.'

'I know,' said Matthew. 'I'm as sure as I can be, but it's never going to be 100%. However, it's a risk we're going to have to take if we're to get "Operation Next Gen" up and running.'

'Indeed it is,' muttered Julian. 'Then let's do it … and while on the subject of introducing some young blood, I have some further news.'

'What's that?' enquired Matthew, intrigued.

'I've just heard from Doctor Méndez of a most unexpected development at Saturn Pharmaceuticals.'

'Go on.'

'She has been given an extremely attractive job offer at Novagen, in the USA.'

'Oh … well, perhaps not so unexpected; she's a highly respected expert in her field. We probably shouldn't be too surprised that some competitors might want to poach her. Has she decided whether to take the job?'

'Well, that's the thing: she's keen to do so, and it would be very advantageous to our cause to have someone in place in the USA. I was concerned, however, that her departure from Saturn might increase the chances of someone else who works there discovering what we have done.'

'I guess it's a possibility,' agreed Matthew.

'It's rather more than just a possibility – she's found that someone already has.'

Matthew's heart skipped a beat. 'What?' he cried, astonished that Julian appeared so calm. 'Who? How? What are we going to do?'

Julian patted the air in a calming gesture. 'Don't worry … it's not what you think. She has a bright young PhD working for her who she thought might share some of our views. She's been cautiously sounding out this girl as a possible successor as our mole in Saturn Pharmaceuticals and another candidate for "Operation Next Gen".

'It seems that this young woman has discovered the modification to the vaccine and even worked out – more or less – what its effect on a woman's reproductive system would be. She knows everything.'

'But that's a disaster,' said Matthew. 'It could wreck the whole project.'

'Apparently not … it turns out that she has known about the vaccine modification for several months, yet she has chosen not to go to the authorities.'

'But why?'

'Well, she knew the "what?", but not the "why?". She chose to keep quiet while she tried to establish the reasons for modifying the vaccine in this way. When Doctor Méndez began sounding her out, she quickly realised that the plan was one of population control in a bid to save the planet. It turns out that she herself is a fierce advocate for the very same cause.'

'Wow!' breathed Matthew. 'That's unbelievable. What incredible luck that's she's on our side.'

'Fortunate indeed,' agreed Julian.

'So what now?'

'I've asked Doctor Méndez to carry out the same background checks as you have done on this Martin Stanton. If everything checks out OK, I'll meet this young lady myself. First though, I'd like to meet your young man, Martin Stanton. When can you bring him over?'

'I'll talk to him today and get back to you.'

'Very good. Well, who knows? We may soon have *two* young advocates to add to our ranks.'

***

Martin assumed, when Matthew invited him, once again, for afternoon tea in his study, that they would just be continuing their ongoing exploration of the threat to the planet posed by overpopulation. This time, however, it soon became clear that his course leader had something else in mind.

'So,' said Matthew, as he topped up Martin's cup from the teapot on the desk, 'it's clear from our various discussions over recent weeks that you and I share similar views on the subject of overpopulation. But now I have a question for you.'

Martin was intrigued. 'And what would that be?' he enquired, inclining his head.

'How would you like to be involved in doing something about it?'

Now his interest was well and truly piqued; he set down his cup and leaned forward. 'What exactly do you mean?'

'Look, what I'm about to tell you is highly confidential. You cannot, under any circumstances, share this with anyone else … friends, family, other students … absolutely no-one.'

Martin's heart began to beat a little faster as he sensed something monumental about to unfold. 'I understand,' he said. 'You can trust me.'

'OK then … there are certain others who share our views and who would like to make a positive contribution to addressing the issue: people who believe in actions rather than just words.'

This was it: this was what all the discussions over weeks had been leading up to.

'Would you like to learn more?' continued Matthew.

'I would,' breathed Martin.

'You have to understand,' that if we take this any further there is no turning back. Now is your last chance to stop right here and turn away.'

'Why would I want to do that? If there is a chance to do something about the greatest existential threat to our planet, then I'd like to be involved.'

'In that case,' said Martin, 'there's someone I would like you to meet.'

***

Martin was excited and nervous in equal measure as he sat in the passenger seat of Matthew's car, speeding along the leafy lanes of rural Surrey. There was very little conversation passing between the two of them. Instead of the easy rapport they usually shared, now the atmosphere was tense, uneasy. However much he tried, Martin could not suppress the fluttering sensation in his stomach.

The lanes became narrower and less populated with traffic as they approached their destination. Now there were no houses or other buildings to be seen – just a dense mass of trees either side of them.

Finally, they rounded a bend and, unexpectedly, a gap in the trees came into view. They slowed to a crawl as they approached it, to reveal a pair of huge, wrought iron gates, in front of which they came to a halt. As Matthew got out of the car to speak into an intercom, Martin peered through the gates where he could just see the corner of what looked like a very large house. A gravel drive led from the gates, curving around the corner of the building and out of view.

As Matthew stepped back into the car, the gates began to swing slowly open, accompanied by a soft whirring sound. The gravel crunched beneath the tyres as they pulled forward, finally rounding the corner of the building to reveal its true scale. Martin gasped in disbelief at the huge mansion. An expansive turning circle fronted the main entrance, whose imposing oak door was elevated, approached by twin flights of stone steps.

As they drew to a halt, the door opened and out stepped a bespectacled figure, probably aged around sixty, with an abundant shock of white hair. His upright bearing spoke of a self-assured, confident character. They pulled up and stepped out of the car, Martin following Matthew up one of the flights of steps as he approached the man and shook his hand.

'Hello Matthew …' said the man, his voice soft and deep, 'nice to see you again.' He glanced past Matthew. 'And this must be Martin Stanton.'

Martin stepped forward and shook his hand. 'A pleasure to meet you, sir.'

'I've heard a great deal about you, Martin. I hope you'll like what I have to say to you today.'

'I'm sure I will, sir.'

'Please … call me Julian. You are among friends here.'

'Yes … well, thank you sir … I mean Julian.'

'Come inside,' he said beckoning for the two of them to follow him.

Martin's mouth was dry as sand as they made their way through to the study.

'Please, take a seat,' said Julian, indicating the two deep-buttoned leather chairs in front of his desk. 'Now, can I offer you each a drink?'

'Thank you ... do you have any of that excellent Cognac left?' said Matthew.

'Of course ... what about you, Martin?'

'Er, just water, please.' His throat desperately needed lubricating.

Once the three of them were settled with their drinks, Julian began ...

He went right back to the beginning: how he had been the one to develop and introduce the original coronavirus, and how he had subsequently developed the current version. He followed through the whole sequence of events leading up to the formation of the current group of like-minded people, and how they had come up with the plan to modify the vaccine to interfere with women's fertility and hence bring about a measure of population control.

Martin listened intently, stopping him occasionally to ask questions, but largely letting him just tell his story.

Finally, after some two hours, Julian concluded his account.

'So that is the current situation. It won't be a quick fix by any means, and I took some convincing by other members of the group to go the birth control route rather than let the virus do its work, but I have to concede it's a more humane way to achieve our ends. Furthermore, it enables us to piggy-back on the efforts of those scientists developing vaccines rather than fight against them.'

'It's brilliant, sir.'

'Julian,' he reminded him.

'Yes ... thank you ... Julian.'

'As you'll appreciate,' he continued, 'this plan will take many years to come to full fruition; I certainly won't be around to see it all the way through. This is why we need some young blood in the group.'

'Yes, s... I mean Julian.'

'Matthew has convinced me that you are an ideal candidate to join us. Is he right? Do you want to join our group and help drive this righteous cause forward?'

Martin was in little doubt, now, about what the consequences might be if he gave the wrong answer at this point. He took a deep breath before replying.

'I would be honoured to join your group.'

Julian stood up and came over to shake Martin's hand. 'Then you should come along to our next full group meeting and meet the other members.'

And so, Martin Stanton became the first recruit to 'Operation Next Gen.'

Except Martin Stanton wasn't his real name …

Chapter 33

Detective Constable Neil Parker had just finished briefing his boss on the progress of his very first undercover mission.

'My God, Neil,' breathed David, 'this is absolutely massive.'

'I know ... I can hardly take it all in,' replied his young assistant.

'I suspected all along,' said David, 'that Sofía Méndez was implicated in Professor Maddocks's murder, but I couldn't for the life of me figure out what the connection with Julian Chambers and these other people was. Do you realise you have helped uncover possibly the most heinous global conspiracy ever perpetrated?'

'I know ... it's horrendous ... and yet ...'

'What is it, Neil? Is the strain too much? I never intended to plunge you straight into something like this.'

Neil emitted a deep sigh. 'It's not that, sir; it's just that, awful though their tactics are, I can see they sincerely believe they are acting for the greater good.'

'What? You have to be kidding me,' said David, astonished at his younger colleague's remark.

'No, really. Look, I haven't met all of this group, but I don't see Julian Chambers or Matthew Turner as fundamentally bad people. They do actually have a valid point of view: the environment is gradually – well, not so gradually now – being destroyed by human activity. I've learned a lot from my discussions with Doctor Turner, in particular. Do you realise the consensus among experts is that global population is already something like *three times* the level which is sustainable long term? And what's more, it's still rising.'

David could not believe what he was hearing. 'Come on Neil, *nothing* can justify unleashing a deadly disease on the world or deliberately inflicting mass sterilisation on innocent people.'

'No, of course not … their actions are unforgivable. All I'm saying is that I can see where they're coming from. The cause has some validity; it's how they are going about addressing it that's all wrong.'

'Yes, *very* wrong,' reinforced David.

'Of course,' agreed Neil, appearing to shake off the shroud of doubt which had apparently descended on him. 'So … what's our next step?'

'Well, given what we now know, I'm sure we'll have no further trouble getting the super to commit whatever resources we need, but before we can start making arrests, we need to gather some evidence to back up what you have learned.'

'I can do that … like I said, they've asked me to attend the next meeting of the whole group. I could wear a wire to get the evidence we need.'

David was deeply uncomfortable about sending someone so young and inexperienced back into such a potentially hazardous situation.

'Look Neil, we need to decide whether it's safe to keep you involved. Obviously, when I first sent you in undercover, I never realised the scale of what you'd be getting into; now I do. There is no telling what lengths these people might be prepared to go to if you were found out.'

There was fierce determination in the young man's eyes when he replied. 'I can do it, sir. In any case, what alternatives do you have?'

David had to admit that was a tricky one to answer.

'You're absolutely sure that they suspected nothing?'

'As sure as I can be. I know they carried out a load of background checks on me before I was introduced to Professor Chambers, but I'm pretty sure the false history and profile you put together for me held up under scrutiny. Let me do it, sir … I'm your best chance of getting the evidence you need.'

David felt a sudden wave of emotion wash over him. During the short time the two of them had worked together he had developed an increasing attraction to this intelligent, brave, complex young man. He was unsure about Neil's sexuality, and regardless, any sort of relationship between them would have been totally inappropriate. He had tried, throughout, to suppress his feelings and hide his own sexuality, but in that moment, it suddenly became too much. He reached out and flung his arms around the young man, nuzzling the side of his neck. As he did so, he felt Neil's body stiffen and pull away.

'Sir ... what are you doing?'

Oh shit – have I got this completely wrong? 'Sorry ... I, er ... sorry. I was just ...'

'Look,' replied Neil. I don't know what you thought, but I'm not ... well, what I'm trying to say is that I have huge respect and liking for you, sir but ... well, not like that.'

David felt a crushing emptiness inside. He had never, in his entire life, made such an embarrassing blunder.

'I'm sorry,' he said, yet again. 'That was a ... mistake. Can we just pretend it never happened?'

Neil quickly recovered his composure. 'Yes ... let's. We have a job to do.'

***

They never spoke again about the embarrassing incident, but it changed the dynamic between them irreversibly; the easy familiarity between them had gone. At some point they would need to talk about it and clear the air, but for now, they were totally focused on the job in hand.

When David related what they now knew to his superintendent, the previously impossible-to-spare resources were available in abundance. David was to be allowed to lead the operation to apprehend these people. However, Willcox himself insisted on attending the operation, no doubt to ensure that most of the glory came his way.

As David had already concluded, though, they would need more evidence than the testimony of a rookie detective constable. In spite of David's trepidation, it was agreed that Neil would be allowed to attend the next meeting of the group, wearing a wire. The resources required to mount a raid would be marshalled around Julian Chambers's mansion in readiness for when Willcox determined that they had enough incriminating evidence recorded.

The main resource would be a team of forty police officers: enough to effectively surround the sprawling mansion in case anyone should try to make an escape over the perimeter wall. They would be backed up by a firearms team of eight officers; there was no reason to suppose that these people would be armed, but Willcox was taking absolutely no chances. The firearms team would, however, be kept in reserve in case needed, rather than deployed at the outset; there had been more than enough cases in recent years of unarmed suspects being shot dead by police due to misinformation or heat-of-the-moment mistakes. It was obvious to David that Willcox was not going to risk his moment of glory being tainted by any repetition of such incidents.

The final piece of the jigsaw was a police helicopter. It would be kept out of sight and out of earshot of anyone in the mansion unless and until needed, but should anyone slip through the police cordon, it would be a valuable asset to track them and facilitate their capture.

Chapter 34

Peregrine Hartley-Briggs was watching himself on the late evening news bulletin on TV. Two days after the reshuffle, the media were still picking over the bones and offering up their so-called 'analyses' of the changes.

The PM had not emerged exactly covered in glory, with some commentators likening his actions to the proverbial rearrangement of deck chairs on the Titanic, moments before it went down. Peregrine pretty much agreed with this assessment but was determined to put on a solid show of support for the PM in public.

'Congratulations, Minister, on your promotion,' said the attractive young journalist from SKY News, 'How does it feel to be part of the Cabinet?'

'Well, Samantha,' – he always made sure he used the interviewer's first name: it made him sound more 'ministerial' somehow – 'my whole reason for coming into politics was to serve my country and its people. If I can do that more effectively in my new position then that is all I can ask.' He treated her to his most engaging smile; she looked unmoved as she maintained her interviewer's game face.

'Of course,' said the girl. 'So what changes do you intend to make to the Department of Health and Social Care? I mean it's pretty clear that the Prime Minister was unhappy about the performance of your predecessor. How do you intend to turn things around?'

'Well, I'm afraid I can't agree with that assessment, Samantha. Stuart was faced with an unprecedented situation when this new, and extremely virulent coronavirus emerged. Anyone would have struggled to cope with the numerous challenges which it brought. I have to say that, under the circumstances, Stuart did an excellent job.'

She pouted her lips and knotted her forehead – an expression which somehow made her look even more fuckable. He quickly dismissed the thought: to get involved with a journalist – of all people – would be political suicide. Best to stick with girls like 'Miss Belinda'.

'Then why,' she persisted, 'was he fired?'

'Oh,' he replied, feigning an expression of disbelief, 'if I may say so, that really is a gross misrepresentation of the situation. Stuart has been appointed head of the newly created Department of Diversity and Equality: a very important step in advancing this government's manifesto commitment to a fairer society.'

In truth, he had no more idea what this department was all about – other than somewhere to park his deposed predecessor – than the hapless journalist, but he was a firm believer in the principle that any amount of bullshit would be accepted by the media if delivered with the appropriate gravitas and conviction. And so it proved on this occasion.

'R...i...ght ... well, we have limited time, so can I move on to another area?'

He smiled, indulgently, pleased to have completely sidestepped the original question regarding what changes he intended to make now that he was in charge of the Department of Health and Social Care. The time-honoured politician's technique had worked perfectly: answer a different question from that asked, and then run down the clock to ensure that there is no time to revisit the original question.

'Of course.'

'You will obviously be well aware that the government's standing in the opinion polls has slipped significantly recently. If there were to be a general election right now, it is clear that your party would no longer be able to command a majority; in fact, virtually all the polls now put the opposition ahead. You have less than eighteen months to turn this situation around before the next general election.'

'Oh,' he replied, waving a dismissive hand, 'I really don't pay too much attention to opinion polls ... the only poll which matters is that on election day.'

'Nevertheless,' she insisted, 'your government *will* be aware of the state of public opinion, and you must surely have some sort of plan to try to ensure that, come election day, things go better for your party.'

'Oh, I really don't think that—'

She cut him off, more assertive now. 'Surely that plan must include a change of leader ... and that change needs to happen sooner rather than later if the new leader is to have sufficient time to turn things around.'

OK – this was his chance to show absolute solidarity with the Prime Minister while also subtly indicating that he would be ready to serve if called upon to do so.

'No ... I simply don't accept that, Samantha. There is absolutely no prospect of a leadership challenge in the foreseeable future. Malcolm is doing an excellent job in very challenging circumstances; he is secure in his position and will be leading us into the next election.'

'But if there *were* to be a leadership election, would you throw your hat into the ring?'

'Well, there isn't going to be a leadership election, so the question doesn't arise.'

She changed tack slightly. 'Well, OK, let's say the prime minister survives until the next election, and it doesn't go well for your party. In those circumstances, your party surely *would* be looking for a new leader; would you *then* be a candidate for party leader?'

'Look ... Samantha ... we are going to win the election. As for what happens after that, well ... that's a long way in the future.'

'It is,' she persisted, 'but no-one goes on forever, so, at some point in the future, then, would you be a candidate for party leader?'

'Well, this is all very hypothetical, but I guess never say never. For now, I'm fully focused on my new job, on serving the public, and supporting the prime minister.'

'OK, thank you Minister ... well, I'm afraid we are out of time now.' Then turning to face the camera, 'That was Peregrine Hartley-Briggs: newly appointed Heath and Social Care Secretary. Samantha Collins, SKY News.'

That was the third time he had watched the interview. He was pretty satisfied with the way it had gone. Now he had to concentrate on his forthcoming leadership campaign. The journalist's assessment

179

of his party's position with the public was spot on; it was inevitable that there would have to be a leadership election within the next few months, at most, and he wanted to be sure he was ready when the time came.

Chapter 35

David and Neil had still not spoken of the incident between them, but it had clearly affected their working relationship. Whether they could continue working together long-term was a moot point, but for now, they were fully engaged in planning the forthcoming raid on Julian Chambers's mansion and, until that was over, this tricky issue would have to wait.

The planning of the operation was made more difficult by the fact that they just didn't know when the next meeting of the group would take place. Neil had been told he would be invited to join the meeting, but, so far, he had not been given a date. They were, however, fully prepared now: everything was in place and ready to go.

Finally, Neil received the WhatsApp message he had been waiting for. It was from Matthew.

Meeting this Friday 7th at 7 pm - Julian's place.

In less than forty-eight hours it would all be over. Never, thought Neil, could any rookie detective have expected to be involved in such a momentous operation so early in their fledgling career. He was excited and apprehensive in equal measure.

***

Neil's heart was hammering furiously as the various participants in the meeting took their places around Professor Chambers's expansive dining table. Whether it was fear or excitement he wasn't quite sure: probably a bit of both. He took several long, deep breaths to try to steady his nerves, pouring himself a glass of water from one of the several crystal jugs on the table. After taking a deep swallow of water, his heart rate began to settle somewhat. He glanced at Matthew, who was sitting alongside him.

'Don't be nervous,' whispered Matthew, 'you are among like-minded people here.'

Neil smiled, weakly; was his discomfort so blindingly obvious? 'Sorry,' he replied, 'it's all a little, well … overwhelming.'

'You'll be just fine.'

He nodded. There were several subdued one-on-one conversations taking place around the table; he doubted that their whispered exchange had been overheard.

The meeting had not yet started properly, so Neil used this interval to try to identify the people seated around the table. His boss's stakeout of the previous meeting had identified six people in attendance on that occasion. He and David had extensively researched each of them and studied their photographs, so he had no difficulty recognising them again.

He already knew Julian Chambers and Matthew Turner of course, and he quickly confirmed that the other four attendees at the previous meeting were also present this time. There was, however, one additional person seated opposite: a young woman – probably mid-twenties, slim, freckled complexion, and rather unruly, brown, curly hair. She was definitely not one of people whose photos he had studied so carefully.

His thoughts were interrupted by the chiming of a pen being tapped against a glass as Julian called the meeting to order. 'Right, as everyone is here now, shall we get started?'

The various individual conversations petered out and the room fell silent.

'I'm delighted to welcome two new members to our group this evening. So, let's start by getting them to introduce themselves. Emily, would you like to start?'

She cleared her throat and, when she began to speak, there was a trace of a tremor in her voice; evidently she was just as nervous as he was.

'Emily Forbes – I'm a vaccinologist working for Sofia at Saturn Pharmaceuticals. I have, for some time, been concerned about global overpopulation so when I learned about the existence of this group, I was keen to contribute.'

'But how did you find out about us?' said Joanna Prentice, a note of concern in her voice.

Julian held up his hand before Emily could answer. 'All in good time ... can I suggest we deal with the introductions first?' He turned to Neil.

'Martin?'

'Er yes ... Martin Stanton. I'm a student on Doctor Turner's Environmental Sciences course. Like Emily, I'm very concerned about the effects of overpopulation on the environment. Studying under Doctor Turner, I've become convinced that we are facing an existential crisis. I want to help address that crisis.'

He wasn't sure whether to say any more at this point for he had a tricky task to fulfil: he needed to steer the conversation, as necessary, to provide the recorded evidence which his superiors needed, but without giving any clue that he was fishing.

Julian inadvertently rescued him. 'Thank you, Martin. Now, perhaps I could ask everyone else to introduce themselves for the benefit of our two new members.'

'Hold on a moment,' cut in Joanna Prentice, evidently still edgy. 'How can we be sure that these two people are completely trustworthy? No offence,' she added, glancing at each of the newcomers.

'I can vouch for Martin,' said Matthew Turner. 'I spent a great deal of time discussing the subject with him and carried out extensive background checks before risking introducing him to the group.'

'And I also met with him before authorising his introduction to the group,' added Julian.

The worried frown was still in place across Joanna's face. 'And what about her?' she said, nodding in Emily's direction.

'I can vouch for Emily,' said Sofia. 'You asked, earlier, how she found out about us. Well, she actually discovered the modification to the formulation of the vaccine quite some time ago, long before I began tentative discussions with her on the subject of global overpopulation. She had plenty of time to go to the authorities if she wanted to, but she chose not to.'

Neil seized the opportunity presented by this remark. Maybe he could prise out a little more of the evidence he sought.

'Could I ask Emily something?' he said. 'I mean, I'm just as much at risk as the rest of you now if the secrecy of the group is breached.'

Emily glanced at Sofía, who shrugged. 'I guess.'

'Thanks.' He turned his gaze back to Emily. 'So when you discovered that the vaccine had been modified, did you know what the purpose of the modification was?'

'Not precisely, but when I analysed the compound which had been added to the vaccine, I concluded that it would be likely to have a disruptive effect on a woman's reproductive system. It was obvious that it had to be a deliberate modification, and equally obvious that it had to have been carried out by, or at least sanctioned by, Doctor Méndez.'

'So you realised, even before Doctor Méndez spoke to you on the subject of overpopulation, that she was involved in a deliberate plan to interfere with women's fertility on a worldwide scale and yet you chose not to go to the authorities. Why was that?'

'I was curious about *why* she was doing it. Once she began probing my views on overpopulation it all fell into place, and I realised we shared similar opinions. The only difference between us was that she was actually *doing* something about it.'

Joanna Prentice cut in. 'And you can corroborate all this?' she said to Sofía.

'Uh huh.'

'And have you carried out all the necessary background checks?'

'Yes, I have.'

'Then I guess we can trust her.'

'You can,' said Sofía.

'So,' said Julian, 'does anyone have any more questions for our two new members?'

There was a general shaking of heads; no-one commented further.

'Then I suggest we move on with the rest of the introductions …'

Neil was pleased to have teased out evidence of interference with the vaccine and of Sofía Méndez's direct involvement, but he knew they would need more than this. He would bide his time and wait for the next opportunity to gather more evidence.

***

Outside, DI Prendergast and DSU Damian Willcox were sitting in a black van, parked around a hundred metres away from the entrance gates to the grounds of the mansion. They were huddled around the receiving device, listening intently to everything going on in the meeting room.

'He's doing well,' said David. 'We've got enough on Sofía Méndez now to link her with the modification to the vaccine.'

'But not the murder of Professor Maddocks,' replied Willcox.

'I've warned him to be careful on that subject; if he probes too much it could raise suspicions and blow his cover. If we *do* get something on the murder it'll be a bonus.'

'Agreed … he needs to tread carefully. It's a hell of a risk, anyway, sending such a rookie undercover with people like that. We're going to have to be very careful in choosing our moment to move in.'

David felt a hollow dread in the pit of his stomach as he was reminded of the danger in which he had placed this young man. He tried not to show his concern.

'Don't worry, sir. He's a very bright guy … and has an uncanny instinct for police work for one so young.'

'I hope you're right … I hate to think what these people might do if they found out he was a cop.'

David's heart fluttered again; he had developed considerable feelings for his young assistant. It was too late for doubts now, though.

'He's doing fine, sir … let's give him more time to see what else he can get for us.'

***

Inside the mansion, each of the participants in the meeting had now introduced themselves. Neil figured that they had each said enough to incriminate themselves, but he wasn't satisfied yet. He had no sense that anyone suspected his authenticity, so he decided to push a little further.

'Wow,' he exclaimed, looking up at Julian, 'that's a formidable array of complementary skills which you've brought together, Professor Chambers. I'm really quite humbled to be invited to join your group. Er … are there any others involved? I mean other than everyone who's here in the room.'

The professor's eyes narrowed slightly, and a couple of vertical creases appeared above the bridge of his nose.

'Why would you ask that, Martin?' he enquired.

Shit! Have I blown it? Need to be careful now…

'Oh, I just wondered whether there is anyone who couldn't make it this evening … maybe someone that Emily and I need to meet separately.'

The professor's shrewd eyes remained fixed on him for several seconds. Even as Neil felt the prickle of beads of perspiration forming on his temples, he did his best to maintain an unconcerned look while matching the older man's gaze.

'There's no-one else,' said Julian, eventually. 'As you will appreciate, our work needs to be conducted in absolute secrecy; the more people involved, the greater the chance of a leak.'

His heartbeat stuttered for a moment. Was there some oblique reference there to a risk posed by inviting him – and indeed, Emily Forbes – to join the group?

'Of course,' said Neil. 'Just thought I'd ask.'

The moment of tension passed; maybe Neil had been imagining things.

'Now then,' continued Julian, we have spent quite a bit of time with the introductions and welcoming our two new members to the group, so I suggest we now move on to the rest of the agenda …'

Neil's colleagues outside would by now have assembled a considerable body of evidence but there was one more thing he really wanted to get. Should he risk it? Maybe it was the adrenaline rush he was feeling, or maybe just the heat of the moment. Who knew? He decided to go for it.

'Er, before we do that, could I just ask one question of Doctor Simmons?'

'And what would that be?' said Peter Simmons.

'Well, you've explained your role as head of the vaccine programme at Thomas Lewis College, but I remember that your predecessor – a lady professor – was mysteriously murdered a year or so back; it was all over the news at the time.'

'That's right,' replied Simmons, tipping his head to one side, enquiringly. 'So what's your question?'

'Well, I was just wondering—'

He was interrupted by a loud chiming noise.

'There's someone at the gates,' muttered Julian. He got up and walked over to the intercom and CCTV monitor in the corner of the room. 'Yes, who is it?'

The reply was clearly audible to everyone in the room. 'Professor Julian Chambers? This is Detective Inspector David Prendergast, Metropolitan Police. My colleague and I would like to have a word with you please.'

'The police? May I ask what this is concerning?' he said, sounding astonishingly composed under the circumstances.

'If you could please buzz us in and come to your front door we can explain then.'

'Of course,' he said, 'I'll be right there.'

He killed the intercom and turned around. 'I'll go down and try to get rid of them. The rest of you stay here.'

Julian left the room leaving everyone else in a stunned silence, broken eventually by Peregrine Hartley-Briggs. 'Shit! I can't be found here ... my career will be ruined.'

'To hell with your career,' growled Peter Simmons. 'We're all fucked if the police come in here. How the hell did they know about the meeting?'

'Maybe they don't,' said Matthew Turner. 'Maybe it's about something else.'

'Fat chance of that,' retorted Simmons. 'Just coincidence that he' – he pointed directly at Neil – 'was asking about Felicity's murder at the exact moment they show up? I don't think so.'

'Martin?' cried Matthew Turner, in disbelief, 'you can't be ... I mean I trusted you to—'

A loud explosion issued from the CCTV monitor, stunning everyone into a deathly silence. All heads swivelled towards the monitor, but all that could be seen was a burgeoning cloud of dense smoke.

'What the ...?' muttered Hartley-Briggs, evidently unable to finish his sentence.

After a few seconds, the smoke began to disperse and it could be seen that the gates were wide open, one of them dangling drunkenly from its hinges. A black van burst through, its tyres spinning on the loose gravel. It was swiftly followed by a whole series of marked police cars.

'They're breaking in,' cried Sofía Méndez, somewhat superfluously, as this was blindingly obvious to everyone there. 'Where the fuck is Julian?'

Chapter 36

Where, indeed, was Julian? When he'd left the room, he hadn't, as he'd suggested, gone to the front door to talk to the police. Instead, he'd headed for his study, running as fast as his not-so-young legs could carry him.

This was it: the moment he'd always hoped would never arrive, but one he'd meticulously planned for. Once he'd made it to his study, he paused for a moment to catch his breath before grabbing the rucksack that always resided on the chair near the door. He then rushed over to where his safe was located and pressed the concealed button; the wooden panel swung open, revealing the safe. With trembling fingers, he punched in the combination. A loud bleep accompanied by the illumination of a red light on the control panel indicated he'd made a mistake with the code. He took a moment to compose himself and bring his ragged breathing under control, before trying again – a little more slowly this time. A mellifluent chime and a reassuring green LED announced the successful unlocking of the safe.

He grabbed several fat bundles of banknotes and shoved them into the rucksack, followed by a large, brown envelope containing all the various documents he would need. Next, he took the loaded handgun and put that, too in the rucksack. Finally, he withdrew the submachine gun and a couple of spare ammunition clips. That was it: just what he had decided were the bare essentials if this nightmare scenario were ever to unfold.

With no time to waste now, he bolted for the door, and into the corridor outside. A short sprint took him to an external door; he burst through, onto the manicured lawn outside the building. As he began running from the building, a series of security lights illuminated his route. As far as his guests – and hopefully the police, too – knew, the only way in and out of the estate was via the huge iron gates at the front, but he knew differently ...

***

Inside the dining room, pandemonium had broken out. People were running in all directions, trying to figure out their best escape route. But Neil knew there was none: the police had every possible exit path covered. It wouldn't matter where they ran; they wouldn't be able to make it out of the estate without being apprehended. In a matter of seconds, everyone, other than Neil himself, had fled the room – except one.

'You lying little shit!' growled Peregrine Hartley-Briggs, advancing menacingly towards Neil, hands outstretched towards his throat.

Neil tensed to defend himself but, in the event it wasn't necessary.

'Police! Stop right there!' came the barked order as David Prendergast burst into the room, followed by two uniformed officers.

Hartley-Briggs froze in his tracks and, a second or two later, his arms were wrenched behind his back and clamped in handcuffs.

'You OK, Neil?' cried Prendergast, his words coming in ragged gasps.

'Uh-huh, but everyone has scattered.'

'Don't worry ... they can't escape.'

'Did you get Professor Chambers?'

'No ... where is he?'

'He was supposed to be coming to the main entrance to meet you, but when I saw you had to blow the gates, I guessed he must have done a runner.'

'Don't worry ... we'll find him. He can't get—'

'Wait ... what's that noise?' cried Neil, holding up a forefinger.

David stopped mid-sentence as they tried to home in on the sound. It was a kind of whirring, whining sound, gradually increasing in pitch and volume.

'Right, you two' – he nodded towards the two uniformed officers – 'hang on to him. Neil, come with me.'

They rushed through the door and into the corridor outside the room, stopping to ascertain where the sound was coming from. 'This way,' cried David, pointing to the right and setting off with Neil close behind.

As they rushed down the corridor, the sound became louder and louder.

'There!' yelled Neil as he caught sight of a door to the outside at the end of the corridor. 'I think it's coming from outside.'

As they burst through the door, the source of the noise became clear. Around three hundred yards away, sat a helicopter, its main rotor blades spinning up as it prepared for take-off.

'Shit!' yelled David. 'Come on – we have to stop him.'

They set off at a sprint, Neil comfortably outpacing David, who was now wheezing badly. The aircraft was evidently still not quite ready for take-off, the noise still intensifying as the blades continued to spin faster and faster. Now the familiar 'chop-chop' note began to impose itself on the insistent whirring sound.

Neil was now within a hundred yards; surely he could make it before the aircraft lifted off.

But then he caught sight of a bright flash in the cockpit, followed, a split second later, by the unmistakeable sound of a gunshot...

Chapter 37

He felt, and heard, the shock wave as the bullet sped past, just inches from his left ear. Instinctively, he dived for the ground, slamming down at just the same moment as he heard the second shot, which flew over his head.

'Stay down, Neil!' came the urgent shout from behind him. 'I'm calling for backup.'

A moment later he heard David barking orders into his radio.

'Firearms team – out on the back lawn – NOW! Armed suspect in helicopter preparing for take-off. Get the chopper over here too, for pursuit if he gets away.'

There were no further gunshots, so Neil risked lifting his head a little. The helicopter was still on the ground, but the noise had now risen to a crescendo, and the blades were spinning so fast that they were nothing more than a blur. When he saw the aircraft lift up slightly on its suspension, as the whirling blades began to take the weight, he knew they were too late. There was no way the firearms team would get there in time. Their only hope now lay with the police helicopter which he knew was already in the air and should arrive at any moment.

Finally, the aircraft lifted into the air, arcing around to face northward. With the helicopter now facing away from him, Neil judged that the danger from further gunfire had passed, and he scrambled to his feet in time to see the helicopter adopt a slightly nose-down attitude and begin accelerating away from them.

David, panting heavily, now arrived alongside him.

'You OK?' he gasped.

'Yeah, but he's getting away.'

'Where the hell is that damned chopper?' muttered David, his frustration evident in his tone.

His question was answered almost before he had framed it: the receding sound of the fleeing aircraft was suddenly subsumed by that of the police helicopter as it swept over their heads. The pilot had evidently already spotted the other helicopter as he was already up to what looked like full speed and heading directly towards it.

David's radio crackled into life. 'We have eyes on the suspect and now in pursuit. Out.'

***

They were closing fast on the other helicopter, which was not yet up to full speed. They pulled partly alongside their quarry so that they could read the registration number on the side of its fuselage, maintaining a separation of around two hundred yards. The pilot turned to his co-pilot and nodded.

The other man picked up a handset and tuned the radio to the universal distress frequency.

'Blue and white Sikorsky, registration N388KM – the aircraft alongside you is a police helicopter. You are ordered to return to your point of take-off, and touch down. I repeat: return to your point of take-off, and touch down.'

There was no response on the radio and no sign that the other aircraft was about to comply.

'Try the loud hailer,' said the pilot.

The message was repeated via the powerful external loud hailer system. Still no response or change of course.

'OK – escalate,' said the pilot.

'Blue and white Sikorsky, registration N388KM – you are ordered to comply with previous instruction. Failure to do so will result in scrambling of armed military jets to force you down.'

He repeated the message on both radio and loud hailer. Still no response.

'OK – let's do it,' said the pilot. 'Get onto the RAF.'

As his co-pilot made the call, the pilot slowed the aircraft a little and fell in behind the other helicopter at a distance of around three hundred yards, preparing to maintain station until the military aircraft arrived.

But then something changed.

'Wait! He's turning, called out the pilot

Sure enough the other helicopter was banking and turning back.

'Right … at least he's got the sense not to risk a confrontation with the RAF.'

The aircraft made a hundred-and-eighty-degree turn: on course to pass by alongside them in the opposite direction. As it drew alongside them, about a hundred yards distant, they could see that the side door of the cockpit was open, and the pilot was swivelled sideways in his seat.

Seconds too late, they realised what was happening. Before they could take evasive action, they saw the pulsating muzzle flashes accompanied by the vicious crackle of automatic weapon fire.

The torrent of bullets raked the full length of the helicopter, killing the pilot instantly and taking out the tail rotor. The co-pilot, miraculously, had not been hit. He struggled to try to bring the crippled aircraft under control, but it was hopeless: with the tail rotor smashed, the helicopter began to spin wildly, spiralling drunkenly earthwards.

'MAYDAY! MAYDAY!' he barked into the radio. 'Police helicopter registration number—'

He never completed the distress call; the aircraft smashed into the ground, exploding in a massive fireball.

Chapter 38

It was several minutes since the police helicopter had set off after Chambers, and both aircraft had long since disappeared from view. Even the pulsating note of the whirling rotor blades had receded into the distance.

David, however, continued staring in the direction the helicopters had taken, desperately searching for any sign that they were turning back. What he saw next shook him to the core: in the far distance, a sudden burst of orange light erupted into the night sky.

'What the hell was that?' cried Neil.

'I don't know ... it looks like—'

The answer to the question came several seconds after the initial flare of light: the muffled boom of a distant explosion.

The two men looked at each other in horror as the likely cause of the blast dawned on them.

David radioed the mission control centre in the black van. 'What's happening? We saw what looks like an explosion ... is it one of the choppers?'

'Looks like it, sir ... and I'm afraid it's ours. We got a mayday call just seconds before losing all contact.'

'Oh Christ! Do you have the coordinates of where the mayday call was made?'

'Yes.'

'Then get the emergency services to the site ASAP.'

'We're already on it, sir.'

'What about the other chopper?'

'Unclear ... it could be that the two aircraft collided or that just ours is down.'

'If it's just ours,' said David, 'the bastard will have escaped.' He emitted a deep sigh. 'Let me know just as soon as you have some news.'

When David signed out, Neil, who had listened in anxious silence throughout the exchange, voiced what they were obviously both thinking. 'The two guys in the helicopter … do you think they're …' His voice tailed off.

David shook his head slowly. 'The chances of anyone surviving a crash and a fireball like that are … well, minimal, at best.'

'And Chambers may have escaped.'

'We'll just have to wait and—'

His radio crackled into life. 'DSU Willcox here. We've apprehended all the suspects apart from Julian Chambers. We'll have to wait a bit to find out what's happened to him.'

'…and the two officers in the helicopter,' said David. 'But frankly, there's very little chance they'll have survived.'

His superior didn't respond to his assertion but just said, 'Come on … get back to the house … debrief with the rest of the team in the room where the meeting was held.'

'OK … we'll be there in five.' He signed out, and the two of them began to trudge back towards the house.

***

When they got back to the house, they were greeted with the news they dreaded but expected: the police helicopter was completely wrecked and the two officers piloting it were dead. And to compound this devastating news, there was no sign of the other helicopter. Police and RAF aircraft were conducting a joint search, but so far without success.

DSU Willcox did his best to raise the spirits of the dejected team by declaring the mission a success, in spite of the tragic death of two officers in the line of duty, and the failure, so far, to apprehend one of the conspirators. As he pointed out, the cracking of this criminal ring would likely save many more lives and, for innumerable couples, prevent the misery of infertility.

As far as the matter of Julian Chambers's escape was concerned, he assured them that with the resources which were now being brought to bear it could only be a matter of time before he was caught.

David could almost hear him rehearsing the line he would take with his superiors and the media. He had very much tried to position himself as the architect of this mission, which would surely enhance his career prospects. The last thing he needed now was for it to be seen as anything other than a success.

David, however, was disconsolate: while the plot had been disrupted it had been at the cost of two lives, and the ringleader had escaped.

There was also the matter of what would become of the millions of people bereaved by the loss of a loved one to the disease, and the countless couples denied the joy of children by this evil plot.

No – this was not a time for celebration.

Chapter 39

Eighteen months later

The worldwide media had been whipped into a frenzy when the news of the conspiracy had broken. And, in spite of the best efforts of the authorities to explain the misguided motivation of the shadowy group of people who had orchestrated the conspiracy, the internet was awash with alternative theories.

The most popular of these theories was that a foreign power – probably Russia or China – had devised the plot to limit population growth in Western countries to enhance their own global influence. This notion conveniently ignored the fact that these countries were hit just as hard by both the disease and the drop in birth rate as those in the West.

Another theory was that one of the big tech companies had modified the vaccine, injecting some unspecified devices into people's bodies to track their activities and spy on them, but that the plot had somehow gone wrong, and the effect on women's fertility was an accidental side effect.

The most outlandish notion of all was that aliens from another planet were behind the plot. By reducing Earth's population to a fraction of its previous scale they were preparing for an invasion which would stand a much greater chance of success against a diminished population.

And so it went on …

***

DSU Willcox's assertion that Julian Chambers would quickly be apprehended proved to be erroneous. In spite of strenuous efforts by the police, the RAF, and latterly Interpol, he had not been found.

The rest of the perpetrators were charged with various offences under terrorism legislation. Most received whole-life sentences, which was the most severe penalty available under UK law. This did not, however, stop significant sections of the public and the media calling for reinstatement of the death penalty for such heinous crimes. The campaign to have these people hanged soon ran out of steam, however, and before long the public largely lost interest in the fate of the conspirators. There were, after all, more important matters to consider …

***

While the politicians did their best to debunk all the nonsensical conspiracy theories circulating on the internet, the scientists were occupied on more serious issues: how could the deleterious effects of the vaccine be reversed?

To the horror of those entrusted with the task, it was found that all records of the original, unmodified specification of the vaccine had been lost or corrupted – even those held by the regulators who had approved it. No-one could understand or explain how this could have happened, but it left the scientists with a massive problem.

The vaccination programme was immediately halted while the vaccinologists went to work, trying to reverse-engineer the vaccine back to its original state. Unsurprisingly, the incidence of the disease began to increase as the effectiveness of previously administered vaccinations began to wane. It soon became clear that the world was, once again engaged in a race between the vaccinologists and the pandemic.

***

Sofía Méndez had been very thorough, when modifying the specification of the vaccine, to make sure that all records of the original specification were destroyed. Even those records held by the various regulators had been corrupted by some malware developed by a hacker she had paid to mount a covert cyber-attack on their systems. She knew that without the original specification, her erstwhile colleagues at Thomas Lewis College and Saturn Pharmaceuticals would struggle to recreate the unmodified vaccine, at least in the short term. This gave her the leverage she needed.

When she approached the authorities, feigning deep remorse about what she had done and offering to help, they were all ears. She convinced them, that working together with Emily Forbes, she could possibly recreate the original vaccine without access to the proper specification. But her co-operation came at a price: if they succeeded, both women were to have their prison sentences substantially reduced.

After a short negotiation, it was agreed that, pending a successful outcome, Sofía's sentence would be commuted from whole life to five years on condition that, once released, her whereabouts would be continuously monitored, and she would have to report to the authorities at six-monthly intervals for the rest of her life.

Emily Forbes's original sentence was only five years anyway, on the grounds that she had never actively participated in the plot but been guilty only of being aware of it and failing to report it: serious enough in itself but judged to be a lesser crime than the others had committed. It was agreed that her sentence could be reduced to just twelve months.

What only Sofía and Emily knew was that the original specification had not, in fact, been lost forever: Sofía had taken the precaution of saving a copy in a secret location in the Cloud. Once the deal was done, the two women were given access to their original laboratory facilities and unfettered internet access, on condition that they were guarded 24/7.

When they came up with the first samples of what they said was an exact replica of the original vaccine in just one week, their previous colleagues and the authorities alike were astonished. However, the vaccine passed all subsequent tests and evaluations, and within four months it was back in mass production.

***

Even after the vaccine was back in production and declared safe, there was massive resistance among many of the public to taking it up again. The loss of trust in vaccines, scientists, and politicians was enormous. The Conservative Government was roundly defeated at the general election and the new government was faced with a daunting task to restore public confidence. Many more lives were lost due to the delay in getting the vaccination programme back on track. Eventually, fear of the disease began to overcome fear of vaccination, and encouraged by a massive public awareness campaign, people started to come forward once again for vaccination.

As the vaccine programme was gradually re-established, infection rates were eventually brought back under control, but there was still a massive outstanding issue to resolve: what could be done for all those women who had already been rendered infertile by the modified vaccine.

Scientists the world over had laboured tirelessly for a full year to try to find a way to reverse the effects of the vaccine without success but, in the end, it was the statisticians who discovered the light at the end of the tunnel.

Painstaking analysis of birth rates comparing vaccinated and unvaccinated populations, and those vaccinated with the corrected vaccine, revealed that where science was failing to find a solution, nature was beginning to prevail. It turned out that after around twelve months, the adverse effects of the modified vaccine began to fade. Little by little, the number of healthy babies born to women who had been subjected to the modified vaccine began to increase. Before long, the statisticians were able to confidently predict that most of those who had been rendered infertile would eventually be able to conceive.

***

The deals which had been extended to Sofía Méndez and Emily Forbes were deeply unpalatable to David Prendergast, who had, after all, been instrumental in bringing the perpetrators of the crime to justice, but even he had to admit it was probably the best course of action given the urgency of the situation. Oh well – he and Neil had done their job by bringing these criminals to justice; after that, it was out of their hands.

Detective Superintendent Damian Willcox pulled off an outstandingly effective PR campaign relating to the investigation and disruption of the crime ring which had become known in the media as 'The Baby Snatchers'. Damian took every possible opportunity to be interviewed on TV, appear on TV panel discussions, and write articles for the newspapers, emphasising – subtly but unambiguously – his own role in what he explained had been a very difficult case indeed.

It worked like a dream: in spite of the tragic death of two police officers and the escape of the leader of the group, the media and most of the general public judged the operation to have been a great success, largely due to the leadership and dedication of DSU Willcox himself. His efforts were rewarded by the award of the Queen's Police Medal and, subsequently, promotion to the rank of Detective Chief Superintendent.

Detective Inspector David Prendergast and the young Detective Constable Neil Parker received barely a mention.

David was, however, reinstated to his previous position and given his old team back, with Neil also joining the team, but things just weren't the same anymore. The fact that two brave officers had lost their lives and Julian Chambers was still at large, while Willcox was engaged in blatant self-promotion, constantly preyed on David's mind. Furthermore, the way that Emily Forbes, and more particularly, Sofía Méndez had evaded justice, merely by helping undo the evil that they had themselves perpetrated, did not sit comfortably with him at all.

The relationship between David and Neil never did return to its previous state; there set in an enduring awkwardness between them, culminating in Neil requesting a transfer to another force. In spite of David's best efforts to dissuade him, and his assurances that he would never again let his feelings interfere with his professional discipline, his young assistant ended up moving far away to join the Greater Manchester Police.

David never saw Neil again.

In the end, he became so disillusioned by the politics and futility of it all that he approached his new boss – for Damian Willcox had now moved on to higher things – to discuss, once again the possibility of early retirement. The financial offer was not as generous as that previously offered, but such was his disenchantment with his situation that he accepted.

And so, David Prendergast returned to a life of tending the plants in his conservatory, and posterity never recorded that he had

had any part in the cracking of the infamous 'Baby Snatchers' crime ring.

Chapter 40

Tessa Blackmore gazed in disbelief at the device she held in her hand. It was barely two minutes since she had taken the test and already there were two distinct blue lines. Could it be true? Was she really pregnant?

Luriana – they had decided to stick with her birth name, which they both loved – was a toddler now: beautiful, joyful, funny, adorable. With the addition of this lovely little girl, their family was complete; they never expected to be able to conceive naturally again. But now, against the odds, Luriana was to have a little brother or sister: unbelievable.

She placed the pregnancy test on the windowsill, before pulling up her underwear and jeans. She took another look at the device on the windowsill, irrationally fearful that the second blue line would have somehow disappeared. No – it was still there, even stronger now.

She washed her hands and picked up the test strip before making her way through to the living room, where James was seated on the couch.

'Well?' he said.

She withdrew her hand from behind her back, showing him the pregnancy test result. 'We're going to have another baby.'

James jumped to his feet, flinging his arms around her. 'Oh Tessa, that's wonderful!'

'I know … we thought it would never happen, but … oh, I don't know what to say.'

She disentangled herself from his embrace. 'Where are we going to put him?'

'What do you mean … "him"?' he laughed. 'You don't know if it's a boy or a girl.'

'Oh, I don't know … it's just that I always dreamed of a girl and a boy.'

'Well I don't care whether it's a boy or a girl. It's just … wonderful.'

'But we don't have the space … where will the baby sleep?'

'Look,' he said, 'we always knew that spending the money we needed to get Luriana would set back our house plans, but wasn't she worth every penny?'

'Yes, of course but …'

'We'll find a way … the car we were going to replace can soldier on for a couple more years, and we can take a bigger mortgage … we'll get by. The important thing is … we'll have the family we always wanted.'

She flung her arms around his neck. 'I love you, James Blackmore.'

***

Sue Hancock had been utterly devastated by the untimely death of her husband, and her two girls were completely uncomprehending. How could their Daddy, fit and healthy one day, be taken from them just a few days later?

Somehow, all three of them had managed to avoid catching the deadly disease which had snatched Ron away from them, in the prime of his life, but they derived little comfort from that; the pain was raw, visceral.

But once the funeral was over, and the searing edge of grief had begun to ease a little, there were practical considerations to confront. Sue was now a widow, with two young children to support and steadily increasing bills to pay. She had no income other than what she could glean from her telephone market research work, supplemented by the widow's pension from Ron's employment and meagre state benefits.

It was barely enough.

During those dark months, the one person who had been able to lift her spirits was Adrian, a lovely man whom she had met at the gym she regularly attended. He, too, had lost his partner, to the devastating motor neurone disease. He and Sue had become great friends, but it was never anything more than that; everything was too raw for both of them.

They had fallen into a routine of meeting at the gym every Thursday evening, while Sue's neighbour, Alice, kindly looked after her two girls. This particular Thursday, they had finished their respective workouts and were chatting over a coffee in the cafeteria.

After a little of the usual chit-chat, Sue needed to tell him what was on her mind. 'I'm afraid this will be our last Thursday evening chat here, Adrian.'

'Why ... what's wrong?'

'Well, my subscription's about to expire and I really don't think I can afford to renew it.'

'But will I still be able to see you?'

'Well yes, of course, but just not here.'

He fell silent for a few moments, looking distinctly nervous and uncomfortable.

'Adrian? What is it?'

He looked up at her. 'Look, I've been trying to pluck up courage to raise this for weeks ... I guess this is as good a time as ever.'

She was puzzled. 'Go on.'

'Over the months we've known each other I've become, well ... very fond of you. I'd like us to have more of a relationship than a weekly coffee here at the gym.'

She had sensed, for some time, that he was looking for something more than mere friendship and, truth be told, she was now ready, too. Something though, had until now, inhibited both of them from voicing their feelings. Maybe it was just the comfortable routine they had slipped into; maybe they were scared to spoil things between them. Whatever, her disclosure that she was about to upset their cosy weekly routine, had proved the trigger for unspoken feelings to be revealed. Now that he had opened up, she was ready to do so, too.

She placed her hand on his. 'I feel the same.'

Evidently encouraged by the way she had reciprocated, he continued, 'Look, you're struggling to maintain an apartment which you can no longer afford, while I'm rattling around in a house which is too big for just me. Why don't you rent the apartment out and then you and the girls move in with me?'

She was stunned. 'I ... I don't know what to say.'

Now the words came tumbling out. 'I mean ... it might not work, but ... well, we could give it a try, couldn't we? But if you don't want to, well … I'd understand of course. And don't think that I … well, I have enough bedrooms. You wouldn't have to—'

She silenced him by putting a forefinger gently to his lips.

'I'd love to.'

'You would? That's fantastic. And you wouldn't be burning any boats … if you keep your apartment on you could go back at any time if …well …' His words petered out.

'I said yes,' she laughed. 'Now shut up before I change my mind.'

Chapter 41

Peregrine Hartley-Briggs lay on his upper-level bunk in the gloomy surroundings of his cell in Springfield Park High Security Prison, hands interlaced behind his head, gazing up at the ceiling. His cellmate, Sidney 'Buster' Brown, was, judging by the snoring from the bunk below, fast asleep.

For about an hour now, Peregrine had been observing the labours of a spider in the far corner of the ceiling. There was something strangely fascinating about watching the little creature going about weaving its web. It had made remarkable progress in such a short time. From a standing start, it had now fashioned a circular structure some twelve inches or so in diameter, artfully anchored in around eight or nine places to the two adjacent walls and the ceiling. It was almost perfectly symmetrical, and really rather beautiful.

Evidently now satisfied with the result of its efforts, the spider took up residence in the epicentre of the web, two of its legs outstretched on the silken threads, ready to detect the vibrations which would signal that some unsuspecting insect had strayed into its deadly trap.

At least, thought Peregrine, he – or was it she? – had some purpose in life, some reason to labour so industriously ... even if it was nothing more than creating the means to secure its next meal. This was more than could be said for his own situation. His life was now utterly pointless. A promising career in politics had come crashing to earth, his lucrative baby-smuggling business was ruined, and he was now condemned to the crushing boredom of hours spent in this cell with the Neanderthal currently snoring and spluttering below him. This mind-numbing existence was interrupted only by regular breaks for the ghastly prison food and time spent 'paying something back to society' – in his case, operating a bloody sewing machine, of all things, to make pillowcases. There was also an hour each day allocated for exercise outdoors followed by a shower in a communal washroom.

These communal sessions were even worse than the hours spent in the company of the oaf with whom he shared a cell; at least Buster Brown largely left him alone. Many of the other inmates just could not resist the opportunity to bully and torment a former government minister: a representative of a system and a class they utterly despised. Even now, his back passage was still throbbing from the unwelcome attentions of a muscular, tattooed, shaven-headed gorilla of a man in the showers the previous day, and his wrists raw from where two laughing accomplices had held him down while his tormentor did his worst.

He just could not face the prospect of a similar ordeal today, and in any case, he had other plans for the exercise hour which was due very shortly.

He waited patiently until, bang on time, a strident bell announced the commencement of the exercise hour and, seconds later, a whirring sound and a loud click signalled that the cell door had unlocked itself. The regular snoring from the bunk below morphed into a kind of irregular spluttering for a few seconds but then the sound settled back to its previous rhythm. God, that man could sleep through a hurricane.

His cellmate's attempt to resume his slumbers were, however rudely interrupted by the arrival of a prison officer who raked his truncheon across the bars of the cell, creating a harsh, metallic rattle, somewhat akin to a large truck traversing a cattle grid.

'Come on you lazy bastards … exercise time,' he yelled, banging his truncheon loudly against the bars once again, for emphasis.

The snores and snorts from below finally petered out as Buster dragged himself, wearily, to his feet. Peregrine, however, had other intentions.

'Sorry Boss' – he absolutely hated referring to these little Hitlers, who strutted about in their stupid uniforms, as 'Boss', but that was what they expected, and it was easier to go with the flow than be awkward – 'but I'm not at all well … I need to give exercise a miss today.'

'Don't give me that crap, HB ... get your fat arse out of that bunk.'

'No, really Boss ... I've got a bad case of the shits. You don't want to have to clear up after me if it all erupts down there in the exercise yard, do you?'

The man's nose wrinkled in disgust. 'Alright, stay there then ... but you'd better not shit in that bunk either. Got it?'

'Got it, Boss.'

The officer shook his head, exhaling loudly, before moving onward.

'Hope you feel better soon,' said Buster, before heading off for his daily exercise.

Maybe his cellmate wasn't such a bad person after all.

Once everyone had gone and silence asserted itself, Peregrine reached down to the foot of the mattress and located the small split in the seam. Rummaging inside the mattress, he found the mobile phone which was concealed there. Phones were strictly forbidden for inmates but Peregrine, for all his fall from grace, still had contacts on the outside and a not-insubstantial amount of money stashed away. It hadn't been too difficult for him to acquire a phone, and keep it concealed from the prison authorities.

He hoisted himself off the bunk and slithered down to the floor, moving over to the open door of the cell and casting furtive glances to left and right. The only person to be seen was a solitary prison officer standing right at the far end of the corridor, around a hundred yards distant. This was as good an opportunity as he was likely to get.

He tapped out a number on his phone, and the cryptic response came on the second ring. 'You ready?'

'Yes ... send it up right now,' he whispered.

He didn't hang up but kept the call open while he moved over to the window, opening the glass section and peering through the bars outside. It was barely a minute before he detected a faint humming sound. Turning to look in the direction of the sound, he saw it: a drone with a small parcel dangling beneath it. He couldn't locate the person operating the drone but evidently they could see him, for the craft sped unerringly towards him before slowing to a standstill just a couple of yards from the window.

He thrust his arm through the bars and beckoned the drone towards him, as though it were a sentient entity which could interpret such a gesture. Obviously it couldn't, but wherever the pilot was, he clearly could, for the machine began edging towards the window, inch by inch. The noise of the motor and whirling rotor blades was worryingly loud now; he just hoped it was inaudible to the prison officer at the end of the corridor. He willed it to move faster, but this was a delicate operation and he had to trust in the skill of the pilot; if one of the spinning blades were to clash with the bars outside the window the whole plan would be ruined.

As the drone approached almost within reach of his outstretched hand, it moved a little higher, bringing the parcel suspended below level with his fingers. With one final stretch of his arm, he managed to grab the string from which the parcel hung, sliding his hand upward to locate the hook which attached it to the underside of the drone. He lifted the hook a fraction, feeling the heft of the surprisingly weighty package; the drone immediately moved upward an inch or two picking up the weight again, as though it were reluctant to relinquish its load. Peregrine was sweating profusely now; it was clear he would have to be swift and decisive when it came to unhooking the package, but if he screwed up the manoeuvre, all would be lost. He took a deep breath, tensed his fingers, and made his move.

As he unhooked the package, the drone once again rose up a few inches but swiftly settled back to its original position as the pilot reasserted control of the now much lighter craft. More importantly, Peregrine maintained a firm grasp of the hook and string, the package swinging a few inches below. He pulled it closer to the window and thrust his other arm through so as to grasp the package itself, shifting his grip to grab it firmly with both hands. His heart was pounding as he paused for a few seconds to allow his ragged breathing to stabilise. Now there was just one more hurdle to navigate: threading the bulky package through one of the gaps in the bars.

He had previously managed to obtain a ruler from the prison's rudimentary library and measured the gaps between the bars. They varied slightly with the largest being around half an inch greater than the smallest. For safety's sake the measurement he had given his accomplice was that of the smallest gap. However, when he attempted to slide the package through one of the gaps it jammed solid. *Damn!*

OK – this was no time to panic. He knew the largest gap was the one on the far left. He adjusted his grip so as to grasp the package by one hand only and withdrew the other, before thrusting it back through a different gap in the bars. Awkwardly, but very carefully, he passed the package from one hand to the other and then offered it up to what he knew was the largest gap. No luck: it jammed again. *Shit!*

But this time it only just jammed; it was tantalisingly close to passing through. He withdrew his free hand from the bars and grabbed that part of the package which now projected through the bars. So now he had one hand on the package pushing from the outside, and one pulling from the inside. He wriggled it back and forth, perspiration now stinging his eyes until, with a ripping sound as the brown paper wrapping was shaved off by the rusty bars, it burst through.

He staggered backwards, clutching the package to his chest, panting heavily, blood oozing from his skinned knuckles. *Thank God!*

He swiftly stowed the package under the bedcover on the top bunk and rushed over to take a look through the open cell door. All was well; the guard was still right at the end of the corridor, blissfully unaware of what had transpired. Peregrine grabbed his phone. The call was still live.

'OK, I've got it … no thanks to you. That fucking package almost wouldn't fit through the bars.'

The tone of the reply was notably unconcerned. 'No need to get all abusive like … you've got your package … I've got my money. What's to stress about?'

'I'll tell you what's to—'

The other man had hung up.

Peregrine exhaled heavily, pressing his grazed knuckles against his prison tunic to staunch the trickle of blood, before sitting down on the single chair in the cell with the package on his knees. He began carefully removing the brown paper and the layer of cloth beneath. Finally, his prize was revealed.

***

Jonathon Whitehouse, age twenty-seven, had been a prison officer for just six months, but already he was beginning to regret his career choice.

Following completion of his first degree in politics, his Master's in Social Sciences, and his prison officer training course, he had been eager to put all his training to good use. He thought he could contribute in some way to helping turn around the lives of some of those who had lost their way and embarked on a life of crime.

It hadn't taken him long to realise this was a lost cause: the soulless environment of the prison and the crushingly tedious routine of prison life seemed to serve only to harden the attitudes of the inmates. He was shocked to learn that over 70% of them go on to reoffend after release from prison. What on earth was the point of it all?

The system clearly needed radical overhaul, but most of his colleagues simply accepted that was the way things were, and that meaningful change was next to impossible. Jonathon didn't agree, but he quickly dismissed the idea of trying to single-handedly bring about such change; the task was just too daunting. Instead, he had begun thinking about alternative careers: ones in which he could perhaps make a difference. Right now, though, there was no time to dwell further on his options; he needed to prepare for the raucous and chaotic return of the prisoners from their exercise session. He glanced at his watch; the bedlam was due to commence in just seven minutes.

His introspective musing was suddenly curtailed as the silence was shattered by the ear-splitting sound of an explosion. The sound reverberated back and forth in the echoey corridor taking several seconds to die away.

He was, for the moment, stunned into complete inaction, but as the silence reasserted itself, he shook himself free of the trance which had enveloped him and set off, at a jog, down the corridor in the direction from which the sound had come. Glancing briefly into each cell he passed, he could detect nothing unusual, until three-quarters of the way down the corridor, his nostrils flared as he picked up the acrid tang of an unfamiliar odour in the air. He slowed to walking pace checking each cell more carefully now.

And then he found it: in the third cell he checked after first detecting the odour of what he now realised was gun smoke, was the body of Peregrine Hartley-Briggs, slumped in the chair, a handgun hanging loosely from his hand, which dangled at his side. On his right temple, there was a small, neat hole from which a small trickle of blood oozed. The other side of his head, where the bullet had emerged, however, was a ruined, bloody mess; the wall alongside him was splattered with a nauseating mixture of blood and whitish-grey brain matter.

Jonathon Whitehouse dropped to his knees, fighting for breath as a dark curtain began to descend and, finally, his consciousness deserted him.

Epilogue

One year later - Brazil

The building looked ordinary enough: a blocky, grey, concrete structure rubbing shoulders with many others of similar ilk in a rather run-down industrial estate. Inside, though, it was a different story. The laboratory concealed behind the drab exterior was a spotless, shining array of stainless-steel cabinets and gleaming white bench tops. The state-of-the-art scientific equipment on display would not have been out of place in a top European or North American research establishment.

The man seated in a wheelchair manipulating the controls of the scanning electron microscope was none other than Professor Julian Chambers. He printed off an image of the virus he had been studying and sat back gazing at it with a satisfied sigh.

Julian had prepared well for the day when the authorities back in England might discover his activities; it was always a strong possibility that they would do so at some point. The cash, weapons, documents, and other essentials stowed in his safe were ready to be grabbed at a moment's notice and the helicopter was maintained in a state of constant readiness should a quick getaway be required. But these preparations would only take care of his short-term needs. His long-term requirements needed a more fundamental approach: one which he had prepared well in advance.

Some months before that fateful day when he had made his escape, he had sold his sprawling mansion to a Russian oligarch for the sum of thirty-five million pounds, on condition that he could rent it back from its new owner for as long as he needed to. That money was deposited in a Swiss bank account ready for the day when it might be needed to set up a new research facility. The cost of setting up such a facility and fully equipping it had been eye-watering, consuming more than half of the fortune he had stashed away. But it was worth it, for they were getting very close now. However, whether his health would hold out long enough for him to see his ambition realised was another matter.

He had, for some weeks before his flight from England, been experiencing some difficulty walking – or especially running – for any significant distance, a nagging pain and weakness in his legs hampering his progress. During the months after his escape that he had spent finding suitable premises for his new laboratory and equipping it for his needs, the condition had become much worse. In spite of this, however, he was so preoccupied with the project in hand that he delayed seeing a specialist until the laboratory was complete. By this time, he could only walk with the aid of two walking sticks.

The diagnosis, when he finally received it, was devastating: an inoperable brain tumour. The prognosis was that he had only a year or two left to live. Thankfully, the malignant tumour which had ruined the motor function in his legs had not impaired his mental faculties and, according to the doctors probably never would. He was, nevertheless, now on borrowed time.

His thoughts were interrupted by a female voice.

'Julian … I have some great news.'

He swung his wheelchair around to face Doctor Emily Forbes. Emily had served just twelve months in prison due to her co-operation with the authorities; as soon as she was released, Julian had contacted her to sound her out on her situation. It turned out she still believed fiercely in the cause and jumped at the opportunity to come and work with Julian in his quest to develop a virus which would defeat the efforts of the vaccinologists.

'Go on,' said Julian.

'The results of the latest lab trial are in, and they show our current variant to have an extremely aggressive attachment to human cells and 99% evasion of all existing vaccines. If these results are confirmed by clinical trials, it's very unlikely that anyone will be able to develop an effective vaccine … at least in the foreseeable future.'

'That's tremendous news, Emily. It seems we are close to the point of organising clinical trials, which will, of course, need to be of a covert nature as we will be deliberately infecting unsuspecting subjects with the virus.'

She smiled. 'We're almost there.'

'Indeed we are, but I fear that time may be running out for me.'

'Oh, don't say that, Julian,' she said, placing a hand on his shoulder.

'Just being realistic. Look, I need to talk to you both about something important. Where's Neil?'

'He's in the kitchen I think, grabbing a coffee and a snack. You want me to go and get him?'

'Please.'

Emily left the lab, returning a few minutes later accompanied by Neil Parker.

***

After Neil had transferred to the Greater Manchester Police he never really settled. He became increasingly conflicted about the pivotal role he had played in infiltrating, and eventually destroying, Julian Chambers's group. For although their methods were highly illegal – some would even say evil – the truth was their objective was actually laudable. Human activity was gradually destroying the planet, and unless something was done to halt, and eventually reverse, the inexorable growth in global population, mankind would eventually destroy itself.

No, these people were not evil; in fact, if one considered the big picture they were, actually, dedicated professionals sincerely trying to save mankind from itself. The only one in the group who Neil sensed did not share this objective was the slimy Peregrine Hartley-Briggs; he seemed to be in it for himself. When Neil heard the news of Hartley-Briggs's suicide, he shed no tears. He was, however, surprised; it was probably the only courageous thing that the self-serving bastard had ever done in his life.

As Neil gradually came around to embracing the views of Julian and his group, he realised he could not, in all conscience, continue to work for the police. He resigned and took a temporary job as a delivery driver while he tried to decide what he would do with the rest of his life.

When Emily Forbes was released from prison, he made contact with her, saying he wanted to talk, to build bridges, to try to make amends for what he had done. She was reluctant, but eventually agreed to meet him. When she did, Neil poured it all out: how he had come around to supporting the aims of the group, how he now bitterly regretted what he had done. Her reaction was initially guarded, but she did agree to keep in touch and, to his surprise, called him a few days later saying she wanted to meet him again.

When Emily told him she was in contact with Julian Chambers and intended to join him in searching for a new means of curbing global population, he was astounded. She would not reveal Julian's whereabouts or what, precisely, he was working on, but she did say Julian was willing to talk to him.

Sure enough, the following day Julian called him. To Neil's intense surprise, there was no acrimony, no recrimination, but instead the professor seemed only to want to ascertain the sincerity of Neil's radical change of view. Nothing was decided during that first phone call, but it left Neil wondering ... was this a possible path to redemption?

When they spoke again, the following day, Neil said he would be honoured if Julian would include him in his project. He would be willing to work anywhere in the world and would need no remuneration beyond what was needed for basic subsistence. He was not an expert in virology like the professor but, in common with the fictitious Martin Stanton, he did have a degree in biology. He was keen to learn and felt sure he could be of some value to the project.

And so, after several further telephone conversations, Neil Parker found himself on a plane bound for Brazil, sitting alongside Emily Forbes. Both young people were ready to dedicate themselves fully to the cause.

***

'Ah, come here and sit down, both of you,' said Julian, indicating the lab stools alongside his wheelchair. 'I want to talk to you about the future of our project.'

They sat down as requested, and he began.

'Emily has just told me of the final results of the lab trials on the latest variant, which are extremely encouraging. I believe we are ready to start clinical trials, so our next task will be to design those trials. But even assuming positive results of the trials, it will be several months before we are ready to deploy the virus. I fear, however, that I may not have enough time to complete the journey.'

Emily interrupted him. 'Oh, Julian ... don't start that again.'

'Emily, I'm a scientist ... and so are you. I'm simply stating the facts. My condition is rapidly deteriorating, and the symptoms now extend far beyond my legs. I may only have months, or even weeks, left.'

'I suppose so, but ...' her voice tailed off.

Julian continued. 'If I don't make it through to the fruition of our work, I will be relying on you two to see it through.'

'We won't let you down,' replied Neil.

The professor smiled. 'I know ... now listen. I have made certain provisions to ensure you are able to pick up the reins, so to speak.'

'OK,' said Neil, 'can you explain what they are?'

'Of course. As you know, we spent a considerable amount of money setting up this laboratory ... but there is still around fourteen million pounds left in the bank. I have made a will leaving the remaining money to be split equally between the two of you. I am trusting you to use the money wisely. The success of the project takes precedence over everything else ... agreed?'

'Yes ... of course,' sniffed Emily, her eyes moist.

'Absolutely,' agreed Neil.

'Good. Now, we must also consider the possibility that before I die, I may become incapacitated. In that case you two will need to take over. I am therefore giving you both power of attorney to sign for anything on my behalf.'

Neil interjected. 'Is that really necessary at this stage? I mean ... well, I know you have lost the use of your legs, but your mind is still sharp.'

'Not as sharp as it was, I'm afraid. In the last few weeks I have, on several occasions, found myself struggling to recall a word which should be second nature.'

Emily gave a small gasp. 'I've noticed it,' she murmured, a hitch in her voice. 'I've seen you stop for a moment mid-sentence as though searching for a word. That's it, isn't it?'

The professor gave a wry smile. 'It is ... I didn't think anyone had noticed. It may be unconnected to my condition ... perhaps just my age, but I can't afford to risk the project if it gets worse.'

'I didn't know,' muttered Neil.

'So,' said Julian, 'I have made an appointment for the three of us to see a lawyer this afternoon to attend to the necessary paperwork for the power of attorney. From that point onwards you will both be able to make decisions on my behalf as and when you judge it to be necessary.'

'This is all so sad,' whispered Emily.

'Not sad at all,' declared Julian. 'We are on the brink of a breakthrough. This,' he continued, picking up the SEM image he had just printed and holding it aloft, 'is the key to saving the planet. It is the variant to surpass all the variants which have gone before. We will call it "The Ultima Variant".'

THE END

About the Author

Ray Green is married with two daughters and lives in West Sussex, England. He graduated from Southampton University with a BSc in Physics and then went on to a career spanning some 30 years in the electronics manufacturing industry. For much of that time he was operating at Director or Managing Director level in several different companies, so he is well qualified to give an insight into the world of business and corporate politics and intrigue.

His business career culminated in his participation in a management buyout of his last company. It was an incredibly tortuous process, and the experience that provided the inspiration for his first novel

'Buyout' in which the principal protagonist, Roy Groves, battles similar issues in a fictionalised management buyout. The sequel 'Payback' tells what happens when the human desire for revenge takes hold. Ray's third novel 'Chinese Whispers' explores the shocking consequences when legitimate business is infiltrated by organised crime. The fourth book, which completes the 'Roy Groves Thriller' series, is a comedy-thriller charting Roy's fortunes after he decides to quit the corporate rat race and retire to an upmarket expat community on Spain's Costa del Sol.

'Lost Identity', the first book in the 'Identity Thrillers' series, is a tense psychological thriller set in the criminal world of drug trafficking and murder. And the second, 'Identity Found' is the thrilling sequel. The third, 'New Identity' is the thrilling, shocking finale to the trilogy.

His latest novel 'The Ultima Variant' is … Oh, I guess you've just read it!

The Ultima Variant
Author's Notes

The Ultima Variant is a novel – it's fiction. So to all those conspiracy theorists out there, please don't take this story as any sort of endorsement for the various wild theories which abound regarding the Covid 19 pandemic.

The next thing to make clear is that although I am a scientist (a physicist), I am not a virologist or vaccinologist and have no expert knowledge about how viruses transmit or how vaccines work. So to any of my readers who do have some knowledge of these matters, I apologise for my ignorance and for the various implausible, or even impossible things which I have, in all likelihood, inadvertently included in this book. As I said, it's fiction – a story. It's not the first book to contain such factual errors, and it certainly won't be the last!

Many of the locations mentioned in the book are fictitious. Since there are many nefarious deeds which take place in the story, I had no wish to besmirch the reputations of genuine respected universities, pharmaceutical companies, or other institutions. The following, then, are all products of my imagination.

Thomas Lewis College, University of London
University of Hampshire
Saturn Pharmaceuticals
Fenmore Sciences
Novagen
Schwartz Pharmacueticals
Springfield Park High Security Prison

I should also point out that I have no knowledge whatsoever of the 'dark web', other than what I could glean from trawling the 'normal' web. So for any of you who *do* frequent the dark web – sorry if I've got the details wrong. I'm guessing, though, that the majority of my readers probably don't go there.

It's tough being an author – you often have to write about things that you actually know little or nothing about!

Anyway, I hope you enjoyed the book.

Ray Green

www.ingramcontent.com/pod-product-compliance
Lightning Source LLC
Chambersburg PA
CBHW020106180626
46812CB00006B/2495